What Reviewers Say About BOLD STROKES Authors

❧

KIM BALDWIN

"*A riveting novel of suspense* seems to be a very overworked phrase. However, it is extremely apt when discussing Kim Baldwin's [*Hunter's Pursuit*]. An exciting page turner [features] Katarzyna Demetrious, a bounty hunter...with a million dollar price on her head. Look for this excellent novel of suspense..." – **R. Lynne Watson**, *MegaScene*

"*Force of Nature* is an exciting and substantial reading experience which will long remain with the reader. Likeable characters with plausible problems and concerns, imaginative settings, engrossing events, and a well-tailored writing style all contribute to an exceptional novel. Baldwin's characterization is acutely and meticulously circumscribed and expansive. It is indeed gratifying to see a new author attempt and succeed in expanding her literary technique and writing style. Kim Baldwin is an author who has achieved both." – **Arlene Germain**, reviewer for the *Lambda Book Report* and the *Midwest Book Review*

❧

ROSE BEECHAM

"...her characters seem fully capable of walking away from the particulars of whodunit and engaging the reader in other aspects of their lives." – *Lambda Book Report*

"When Jennifer Fulton writes mysteries, she writes them as Rose Beecham. And since Jennifer Fulton is a very fine writer, you might expect that Rose Beecham is a fine writer too. You're right...On the way to a remarkable, and thoroughly convincing climax, Beecham creates believable characters in compelling situations, with enough humor to provide effective counterpoint to the work of detecting." – *Bay Area Reporter*

≈

RONICA BLACK

"Black juggles the assorted elements of her first book with assured pacing and estimable panache…[including]…the relative depth—for genre fiction—of the central characters: Erin, the married-but-separated detective who comes to her lesbian senses; loner Patricia, the policewoman-mentor who finds herself falling for Erin; and sultry club owner Elizabeth, the sexually predatory suspect who discards women like Kleenex…until she meets Erin." – **Richard Labonte**, Book Marks, Q Syndicate, 2005

"Black's characterization is skillful, and the sexual chemistry surrounding the three major characters is palpable and definitely hot-hot-hot. If you're looking for a more traditional murder mystery, *In Too Deep* might not be entirely your cup of Earl. On the other hand, if you're looking for a solid read with ample amounts of eroticism and a red herring or two, you're sure to find *In Too Deep* a satisfying read." –**Lynne Jamneck**, L-Word.com Literature

≈

GUN BROOKE

"*Course of Action* is a romance…populated with a host of captivating and amiable characters. The glimpses into the lifestyles of the rich and beautiful people are rather like guilty pleasures.…[A] most satisfying and entertaining reading experience." – **Arlene Germain**, reviewer for the *Lambda Book Report* and the *Midwest Book Review*

"*Protector of the Realm* has it all; sabotage, corruption, erotic love and exhilarating space fights. Gun Brooke's second novel is forceful with a winning combination of solid characters and a brilliant plot." – **Kathi Isserman**, *JustAboutWrite*

≈

JANE FLETCHER

"*The Walls of Westernfort* is not only a highly engaging and fast-paced adventure novel, it provides the reader with an interesting framework for examining the same questions of loyalty, faith, family and love that [the characters] must face." – **M. J. Lowe**, *Midwest Book Review*

LEE LYNCH

"There's a heady sense of '60s back-to-the-land communal idealism and '70s woman-power feminism (with hints of lesbian separatism) to this spirited novel—even though it's set in contemporary rural Oregon. Partners Donny (she's black and blue-collar) and Chick (she's plus-sized and motherly) are both in their 50s, owners of the dyke-centric Natural Woman Foods store, a homey nexus for *Sweet Creek*'s expansive cast of characters....Lynch, with a dozen novels to her credit dating back to the early days of Naiad Press, has earned her stripes as a writerly elder; she was contributing stories to the lesbian magazine *The Ladder* four decades ago. But this latest is sublimely in tune with the times." – **Richard Labonte**, Book Marks, Q Syndicate, 2005

RADCLY*f*FE

"…well-honed storytelling skills…solid prose and sure-handedness of the narrative…" – **Elizabeth Flynn**, *Lambda Book Report*

"…well-plotted…lovely romance...I couldn't turn the pages fast enough!" – **Ann Bannon**, author of *The Beebo Brinker Chronicles*

ALI VALI

"Rich in character portrayal, *The Devil Inside* by Ali Vali is an unusual, unpredictable, and thought-provoking love story that will have the reader questioning the definition of right and wrong long after she finishes the book....*The Devil Inside*'s strength is that it is unlike most romance novels. Nothing about the story and its characters is conventional. We do not know what the future holds for Emma and Cain, but Vali tempts us with every word so we want to find out. I am very much looking forward to the sequel *The Devil Unleashed*." – **Kathi Isserman**, JustAboutWrite

Visit us at www.boldstrokesbooks.com

FRESH TRACKS

by

Georgia Beers

2006

FRESH TRACKS

ISBN 1-933110-63-5

This Trade Paperback Original Is Published By
Bold Strokes Books, Inc.,
New York, USA

First Printing: November 2006

CREDITS
EDITORS: JENNIFER KNIGHT AND STACIA SEAMAN
PRODUCTION DESIGN: STACIA SEAMAN
COVER DESIGN BY SHERI (GRAPHICARTIST2020@HOTMAIL.COM)

Acknowledgments

My posse came through for me yet again. Most sincere thanks to Stacy Harp, Steff Obkirchner, and Jackie Ciresi. Their sharp eyes, warm hearts, and honesty made this a much better book.

Once again, thank you to Jennifer Knight, my editor and Guru of All Things Writing. I couldn't ask for a better teacher and hope she's always up for helping me with the next lesson. She sees things I miss, she suggests things I never thought of, and just when I'm ready to throw in the towel and give up on writing altogether, she comes through with a compliment or a pat on the back and I'm her willing student once again. Anything Jennifer misses (and there isn't much, believe me), Stacia Seaman picks up with her Eagle Eyes of the English Language. Because of these two amazing editors, my story is so much more than it was when I started and I owe them both a world of thanks.

As always, unending appreciation to Radclyffe and the entire staff of Bold Strokes Books. Every day, I realize how lucky I am to be part of such an incredible publishing company. Connie, Lori, Sheri, Lee, Paula, and the whole gang that works behind the scenes: thank you for taking such good care of us authors. You are all inspirational.

Forever and always, my eternal, loving gratitude to my partner and wife, Bonnie Mowry. I don't know how she's put up with me and my idiosyncrasies for all these years, but I'm so glad she has. She's not the luckiest girl in the world. I am. I love you, baby.

Dedication

To Bonnie
I don't know how,
but it just keeps getting better...

Monday, December 26

PREPARATIONS

"The weather looks like it's going to be beautiful for the whole week, babe." Jo Cooper sipped her coffee as she read the paper. She was a beacon of calm in the otherwise hurricane-like whirlwind of her wife. Whenever they had to ready the house for guests, Jo affectionately referred to Amy as The Cleaning Machine. The rules were simple: stay alert and stay out of the way or you'd be sucked up and disposed of with the rest of the grime.

"Any snow?" Amy whipped a cloth over the small dining table as she asked the question.

Jo raised the paper and her cup without missing a beat, her eyes never leaving the column she was reading. After fifteen years with Amy Forrester, she knew the maneuvers well. "Probably around Wednesday and then a little more toward the end of the week. No big storms in the area, though. Should be perfect."

"Thank God." The last thing Amy wanted was for her friends to either be snowed in and regret ever coming, or to not be able to get there at all. The cabin wasn't terribly far from the city—a little over an hour—but the snow could be a very deterring factor when it came to driving any farther than a few minutes, even for those born and raised in upstate New York and used to the winters. Driving in a snowstorm was nothing to fool with, and their location was fairly remote. Better safe than sorry. "I'm going to need you to get the extra table leaf—maybe two of them—from the basement for me," she said as she regarded the small table. "And the chairs."

"Whatever you want." Jo finished reading and folded the paper neatly, holding her lukewarm cup between her hands while she watched her wife with a smile.

Amy's wavy red hair was pulled back into a haphazard ponytail, wisps of it escaping and dangling around her ears. Her face was devoid of any makeup, the peaches-and-cream complexion dotted all over with faded freckles. Nobody would ever peg her for a day over thirty-five, but in reality, Amy was forty-two and just as sexy and beautiful as the first time Jo had ever laid eyes on her. Dressed in what she called her "cleaning sweats," she flitted around the house, dusting tabletops and straightening knick-knacks. She'd pulled the sleeves of her long-sleeved black T-shirt up to her elbows and the old, ratty gray sweatpants clung to her hips like a small child to its mother. Jo felt a familiar tingle low in her body as Amy bent to pick up a dust bunny from the floor. When she made her way past the table, Jo hooked a finger into the waistband of the sweats and pulled back until Amy plopped into her lap.

"Honey, I'm cleaning," Amy whined in protest.

"I see that." Jo buried her face in the crook of her neck and nuzzled.

"Stop it. I'm gross."

"You're never gross. You're gorgeous."

"Oh, please."

"I love the way you smell." Jo inhaled deeply to prove her point.

"Like Pledge and Windex?"

"Exactly. It's intoxicating."

Amy slapped playfully at her. "I've got work to do, you brute. Let go."

Jo nipped at the side of Amy's neck as her long fingers ventured under the hem of the T-shirt, gently teasing over the bare skin. "Nobody will be here until later."

Amy squirmed and her voice was suddenly hoarse as she felt Jo's hand sliding up her torso. "Joanna." Trying for sternness and failing miserably.

"There's plenty of time."

Amy closed her eyes. She was used to her inability to resist Jo's touch, but her brain surprised her by taking control away from her untrustworthy libido. She caught Jo's hand through the fabric and stopped its progress just before it could close over her bare breast. She pecked Jo on the cheek and hopped off her lap. Jo blinked in surprise and then narrowed her eyes, smiling with playful wolfishness.

"Later." Amy held her hands up in a placating gesture. "I promise."

"Don't think I'm not going to collect on that."

"I'm counting on the fact that you will." Amy's eyes twinkled.

"It's really not fair that you wear your cleaning sweats with no bra or underwear. You know that, right?"

Amy winked and dragged the vacuum cleaner from a nearby closet. "Hey, I have to keep the upper hand somehow."

"You always have and always will have the upper hand. And you know it."

Amy clicked on the machine, the smug expression of satisfaction on her face saying she knew Jo was exactly right about that.

"And you use it to your advantage every chance you get," Jo shouted over the humming. Amy grinned, but didn't look up from the floor.

Jo got to her feet and headed for the back hallway, reluctantly moving her thoughts to the tasks she needed to complete outdoors. The cold air would do her good, help to cool her heated blood. Her sexual attraction to her partner had never let up, not once in all the years they'd been together. They seemed to have the healthiest sex life of any of their friends, a fact of which she was absurdly proud. She knew how common it was for the sex drives of women to taper off as they aged, but hers had stayed strong through her forties. Turning fifty last year hadn't changed a thing—she still felt the urge to chase Amy around the bedroom, and did just that.

Smiling at the thought, she stepped into her boots, donned her coat, and tromped through the snow in the back yard of the cabin to the giant pile of split wood stacked neatly near the edge of the trees. Although she loved their house in the city—there was something wonderful about the hustle and bustle, being five minutes from everything, knowing your neighbors—the peacefulness she felt at the cabin was incomparable. She could literally feel herself breathe a sigh of relief whenever she pulled into the driveway, every muscle in her body relaxing and every worry on her mind flying right out of her head to be dealt with at another time. She needed this respite from everyday life and tried to get out to the cabin as often as possible.

Jo stopped walking and stood completely still. The sky was a brilliant blue, the fresh snow blanketing the ground in a blinding white, glistening as though there were tiny pieces of cut glass sprinkled across the surface. She inhaled the cold, crisp air, letting it freeze her lungs and awaken her senses. The gentle quiet filled her ears, broken only by the chattering sound of the winter birds feasting at the feeders Amy had scattered around the property. In the distance, she could hear something else, another inhabitant of the woods working diligently. A squirrel, perhaps? A small deer? She let the peace of nature wash over her and felt...home.

The cabin had belonged to Amy's family for more than a century. It started out as nothing more than a shack and gradually, additions were built, walls and foundations were reinforced, the garage was added, more land was cleared.

The Forrester family owned a total of seventy-five acres around it, so the peacefulness was guaranteed. Nobody would be building next door. Ever, if Jo had any say. Amy's mother had died when Amy was just a teenager and ownership of the cabin was passed down to Amy, her brother, and her sister in equal shares after their father died five years ago. It soon became clear to everybody that Amy's siblings had neither the time nor the desire to visit the cabin, and it made perfect sense for Amy to buy them out. She had done so happily and over the past three years, she and Jo had spent as many weekends and vacations as possible fixing, repairing, and remodeling the place.

Sometimes Amy was too busy with the restaurant she owned and Jo came up alone, whiling away her spare time by lovingly transforming the house into what they wanted. It could hardly be called a cabin at this point. It was nicer than most people's homes. The giant master suite in the back on the first floor was Jo's pride and joy. She had surprised her wife with a sunken Jacuzzi tub surrounded by windows and skylights. Soaking in the tub encircled by candles was Amy's favorite way to relax after a long and stressful day; Jo would never forget the look on her face and the grateful tears glimmering in her eyes when she saw the newly remodeled master bath for the first time. It made her thank all the gods above that she'd decided on a career as a contractor.

The second floor held two more bedrooms and a full bath tucked between them. A large stone fireplace and hearth was the centerpiece of the living room, perfect for creating ambiance at this time of year. There was a furnace, but Jo preferred to heat with wood whenever possible. The beige and deep hunter green kitchen was state-of-the-art, with nothing but the best Corian countertops, ceramic tile floor, and the most modern appliances for Amy, who was the most fantastic cook Jo had ever known.

I am a lucky woman. The thought crossed her mind as she loaded up an armful of logs. Life had been good to her. She didn't like to dwell on the fact, for fear she might jinx things, so when the phrase did go zipping through her brain, she'd often freeze and then glance around in paranoia as though expecting a bus to come speeding out of nowhere and run her down or a plane to plummet from the sky and squish her into a pancake.

Back in the cabin, Amy was still cleaning feverishly, a fine sheen of sweat covering her forehead. Jo dumped the logs into their cast iron holder near the fireplace.

"Do you want me to start the fire now, Your Highness?"

Amy quirked a brow at the title. "Why yes, lowly servant. That would be lovely."

Jo shed her winter outerwear and went to work with newspaper and kindling. "Who's coming first?"

"Molly and Kristin should be here this afternoon." Amy ticked the guests off on her fingers. "Sophie will be here tonight. Laura can't make it until Wednesday morning."

"Well, the place looks terrific."

Amy looked around. "I hate to say it, but I think I'm done."

Jo grinned as she struck a long match against its flint. "Honey, you've been cleaning nonstop since six o'clock this morning. The place isn't that big." She set flame to paper. "And frankly, it wasn't that dirty."

"All the sheets are clean. All the rooms are vacuumed. Everybody's got fresh towels. I've got enough food."

"More than enough food."

"We've got enough alcohol."

"More than enough alcohol."

"More than enough alcohol." As if pulled magnetically, Amy dropped her butt onto the plaid couch and finally let out a *whew*.

"Nice work, baby."

"Right back atcha, love."

"I didn't do much. Watching you clean is hardly work."

"Snow-blowing the driveway is tough. Don't sell yourself short. Plus, the way you build a fire is practically an art form." Amy watched her wife's hands as they expertly placed small logs, coaxing the fire to consume more. Could it be considered an art form? Fire building? It should have been, as far as Amy was concerned.

She studied Jo as she crouched in front of the fireplace. Jo's curly, chestnut brown hair just brushed along the nape of her neck and had begun to show just the slightest sprinkling of gray over the past couple years. Her skin was smooth and her brown eyes were soft and kind. Amy allowed her eyes to linger on Jo's strong back before traveling along the deceptively powerful body. Jo was nearly six feet tall and very lean. But lean wasn't the same as skinny, and her wife often shocked onlookers with her strength and vigor. It was a good trait to have up her sleeve working in the male-dominated field of contracting and construction. Jo always pulled more than her weight, much more, and Amy admired her like no other. She had fallen head over heels in love with Jo fifteen years ago and that hadn't changed, not even a little.

When the flames were steady and a pleasant crackling emanated from the fire, Jo set the black screen in place and stood, brushing her hands along her jean-clad thighs. She surveyed her handiwork for several minutes before giving one quick nod of satisfaction. She stepped back and sat next to Amy, automatically lifting an arm so Amy could tuck herself against the body she knew and loved so well.

"How's that for a fire?"

"It's perfect, as usual." They sat quietly, mesmerized by the hypnotic blue and orange of the flames licking sensuously along the wood. "I feel like we've been running nonstop for days."

Jo smiled against Amy's hair. "That's because we have." From two days before Christmas until the previous night when they'd arrived at the cabin, their schedule had been jam-packed. "You want me to call everybody and tell them not to come? That we're too old for this shit and the week in the woods has been cancelled?"

She felt more than heard Amy chuckle. "After all my work today? Have you lost your mind? What good is my spotlessly clean house if nobody sees it but you?"

"That's what I thought you'd say."

"It'll be fun. I'm looking forward to having an uninterrupted week with our friends."

Jo nodded. "Me, too."

After a few beats of silence, Amy said, "I hope they like each other."

"It's not like they've never met."

"I know, but a fleeting introduction at a couple of parties isn't quite the same as spending a week holed up with one another."

Sensing her wife careening down a new path of worry, Jo headed her off at the pass. "It'll be fine, baby. Don't worry. Our friends are all good people. Good people like one another. It'll be fine. Okay?"

Amy inhaled deeply and let her breath out a little at a time until she felt relaxed. She burrowed farther into Jo's embrace. "Okay, boss."

MOLLY

The day was gorgeous and went a long way toward helping Molly DiPrima take a deep breath and relax as she drove along the country roads that would lead her to Amy and Jo's cabin in the woods. The sky was so blue it almost seemed artificial, and she'd been pleasantly surprised to have to don her sunglasses as she settled into the driver's seat. Gray was the common color for this time of year in upstate New York, and an appearance by the sun did much to lighten moods. The farther away from the city she got, the more relaxed she felt. Actually, the farther away from her *life* she got, the more relaxed she felt, and that made her sad.

Christmas had been chaotic. She'd been ecstatic to be done with work. She loved her job, but the closer the holiday got, the more out of control her kindergarten students became. Sending the last one home on the twenty-third had wrung a relieved breath from her lungs so large, it had collapsed her into her chair where she simply sat and stared off into space for the better part of a half hour.

Spending the night before Christmas Eve in the mall had been a treat, she thought sarcastically. She rolled her eyes as she recalled that most stressful of trips. She'd fallen behind on her shopping and Kristin had been no help, saying she had a proposal for one of the firm's biggest clients due by the end of the day on Friday—*The day before Christmas Eve? Seriously?*—and wouldn't be able to get to the store. She handed a short list to Molly on her way out the door Friday morning and asked if she'd mind grabbing gifts for these few people, not really waiting for an answer. Molly hated shopping. Despised it, especially in a crowd of people, and Kristin knew it. She was amazed she got in and out of the mall without actually beating somebody to death with her bare hands.

Then, of course, there was Christmas with the family: always fun, but at the same time, always loud. Being Italian definitely had its disadvantages. Molly loved her clan, but when her mother and her mother's brothers and sisters all got talking at the same time, the volume increasing exponentially, none of them listening to anybody but themselves, it was all she could do to keep from screaming at the top of her lungs, "*Shut up!*" More often than not, she left her mother's house with a headache and the burning need for several hours of silence as a remedy.

Easing to a halt at a stop sign, she noted with amusement that there wasn't another car in sight. She stared past the empty seat on the passenger side, then immediately berated herself for inviting her mind to slide toward the topic she wanted to ignore. *You made a pact, Mol,* she told herself. *No wallowing. You're here to relax, be with your friends, and have fun.* The fact that she was alone in the car was a glaring issue, one she'd been trying to avoid, and it wasn't like Amy and Jo wouldn't notice. But so be it. Kristin had other priorities and there was absolutely nothing Molly could do to change that reality.

"I just need to get this contract ironed out, baby," Kristin had told her that morning. "I promise I'll do it as quickly as possible."

Molly was packing for both of them, and Kristin's sudden change in plans had taken her completely off guard. She held a T-shirt in mid-fold. "What?"

Kristin had smiled that smile, the skin around her crystal blue eyes crinkling. "I promise. Trust me." When she grinned like that, there was almost nothing Molly wouldn't give her, despite how angry, hurt, or disappointed she was. This time, though, Kristin was pushing it.

"But we planned this months ago," Molly said, nearly wincing at the whining tone of her own voice. "You requested this vacation time in September."

Kristin rested her hands on Molly's shoulders. She was taller and stronger and her hands felt large, holding Molly in place as if she were a doll. Molly resisted the urge to shrug them off, her irritation beginning to build.

"I know. But Reeves is counting on me to be his right hand here. This could mean big things for the firm, and you know how close he is to retiring. If I can show him I can handle whatever he throws at me…" Kristin let the sentence dangle in the air, knowing Molly was well aware of what remained unsaid.

Kristin was in line to take over. It wasn't the largest advertising firm in the city, but it was sizable, growing by leaps and bounds, and had a sterling reputation. Once Jack Reeves retired, the title of president would most likely fall to Kristin. She was constantly reminding Molly what that would mean for them financially.

Molly had sighed, knowing she wasn't going to win this one, as usual. There was no way to change Kristin's mind, and she was suddenly just too exhausted to fight about it. "When will you be able to make it?" she asked, feeling small and defeated and knowing she sounded that way, too.

"I'll be there by Tuesday night, okay? You'll only have to be there for one night without me. One night. I promise."

"We're going to have two cars there now." Grasping at straws.

Kristin shrugged. "That's all right. It won't kill us. No big deal." They stood in silence. "Okay?" Kristin prodded. Molly's reluctant nod earned her a bear hug from her wife of seven years. When Kristin set her down, she took Molly's face in her hands and kissed her forehead. "You're the best, Mol."

Surprised by the nearly overwhelming urge to cry that suddenly seeped in on her like warm water, Molly went back to her packing and barely registered Kristin's departing ritual—the briefcase, the quick kiss dropped on her mouth,

"I'll see you tomorrow, sweetheart. Be careful driving." Kristin tapped the Blackberry in its holder clipped to her waist. It was her lifeline—a cell phone, mini computer, and PDA all in one—and Molly hated it. "Call me if you need me." As she left the room, she tossed over her shoulder, "I love you."

"Love you, too," Molly muttered.

Standing alone in their bedroom, she felt like a child who'd been left behind. She glanced at the bed and tried to remember the last time they'd made love. It had been months, she was sure—she couldn't recall the last time Kristin had even *looked* at her with any inkling of sexual interest. The tears came then and she'd been powerless to stop them. She sat down on the bed, dropped her face into her hands, and wept openly, letting all the pain and frustration overcome her.

Now, an hour away from her home and partner, she sat in her Honda Accord and felt annoyed that she *hadn't* put up a fight. She was beginning to feel as if Kristin's order of priorities went something like this: Reeves & Associates, their personal finances, and then Molly. She was sure if she added it all up, she actually got much less of Kristin's time than any of her clients or coworkers. And when had Kristin become so focused on money? Had she been like that seven years ago when they'd first begun dating?

Molly pressed a hand to her forehead, trying to stave off the gnawing beginnings of a headache. It was a pain that had recently become familiar and didn't seem like it was leaving any time soon. Gritting her teeth, she punched the power button on the CD player and let Gretchen Wilson sing to her about being a redneck. Tears pooled in her eyes but she refused to let them spill, angry with herself for allowing her brain to take her down this well-known, over-traveled path yet again. She was sick of crying all the time. She was going to have fun this week, damn it. She was going to have fun if it killed her.

Forcing herself to concentrate on the beauty of nature that surrounded her, Molly was able to calm down ever so slightly. Upstate New York had everything, she reflected as she drove; it was one of the amazing benefits of this part of the United States. You could live and work in the heart of the city, as she and Kristin did, but within an hour of driving, you could find yourself in the middle of the countryside. Cow-filled pastures, sprawling farms, even vineyards were scattered across the northern parts of the state, easily accessible to anybody willing to sit in the car for a bit.

Civilization was beginning to spread out, away from downtown, even beyond the suburbs, as people realized they could live in the "country" and still commute to the city each day. Yes, it was a longer drive each morning and night, but for some, the ability to leave work, drive home, and sit in the open back yard listening to crickets and watching fireflies was much more appealing than the sounds of traffic or the wailing of the occasional police siren. And there were people like Amy and Jo, who loved both lifestyles and were hard-pressed to choose between them so they didn't choose at all. They kept a place in the city, worked during the week, and spent weekends and vacations far away from the hustle and bustle of downtown. Amy often said their cabin in the woods felt a million miles away from her everyday life. If you could afford it, it was the best of both worlds.

The rolling hills on either side of Molly's car were gorgeous no matter what time of year. Right now, they were covered with snow, the trees bare, branches poking upward like dark, bony fingers in sharp contrast to the color of the sky. White to brown to brilliant blue, the distinction was clear cut and precise, as if the landscape had been cut with scissors out of construction paper and pasted together, a project created by one of Molly's young students to be hung on the refrigerator at home.

In the summer, the difference was less defined, the white of the snow replaced by dozens of varying shades of green with sporadic splashes of color…grass, leaves, wildflowers, apple trees. It constantly amazed her how the different seasons could bring about such completely opposite color schemes. Molly said often that she really wanted to retire to someplace warmer, someplace with no winter at all, but she knew deep down that in the very soul of her being, she'd miss the change of seasons. They were in her blood. They were a part of her childhood and a part of her now and she wasn't entirely sure she could survive being stuck in an eternal summer, no matter how much she despised being cold.

She slowed the car slightly, going from memory now, even though it had been a long while since she'd visited Amy's cabin, and she'd ridden with Amy, so hadn't really paid much attention to the directions. Recognizing the split-wood fence marking the property, she made a right and turned into the impeccably clear driveway, smiling at the fact that Jo had been hard at work that morning to clear the snow for her friends.

Molly could already taste the cleanliness of the country air that had worked its way through the car vents during the ride. As she turned off the ignition and got out of the car, she inhaled gradually and let the breath out bit by bit, trying hard to erase the worry and stress from her mind. She knew instinctively that a warm fire and a glass of wine were waiting for her inside. A smile touched her lips as the front door of the cabin flew open and Amy appeared in all her red-haired glory, arms outstretched, shouting her pet name for Molly as if it had been years rather than a month since they'd seen each other last.

"Primo!"

Molly was promptly enveloped in Amy's arms and she clung tightly, feeling such relief to be held by her friend that she almost wept, her emotions were sitting so close to the surface. She managed to pull herself together before Amy let her go and held her at arms' length, a whirlwind, as always.

"God, you are so fucking gorgeous." Amy sounded as if she was scolding Molly, but her face shone with pride. "How is it that you always look this fucking gorgeous when the rest of us are simply getting old? Your hair looks fantastic. And you've been working out, haven't you? You've lost weight."

Molly let the compliments settle over her like a warm, thick, and cozy blanket, cushioning her from the current jagged rockiness of her life. She made no attempt at explaining that she seemed to have misplaced her appetite lately, thus the weight loss. Instead she allowed herself to be coddled, to be nurtured by her closest friend in the world, leaning into her shoulder, mentally letting Amy hold her up.

"Hi there, beautiful." Jo appeared and opened her arms to Molly. She was a good six or seven inches taller and Molly always felt indescribably safe around her. Locking her arms around Jo's neck, she hoped her solid grip didn't feel too much like desperation. It was just so good to feel loved, and Jo had always seemed like a guardian angel, the one who could be counted on to chase the boogeyman away.

"Doesn't she look amazing?" Amy said.

"She always does," was Jo's answer, as she gave Molly's cheek a quick stroke of her thumb before moving to the back of the car.

"You should talk, Ames," Molly said, pushing playfully at her. "I don't know why you're complaining about getting old. You still look thirty."

It was true. Whether dressed to the nines or slumming it in ratty old sweats, Amy had always been a head-turner, looking classy, elegant, and approachable. It was a rare combination and one that made men and women alike stop in mid-sentence to watch her walk through her restaurant; Molly had seen it happen over and over again.

Jo knocked on the trunk and Molly obediently popped it open. Slinging a bag over her shoulder and hauling out a second one, Jo asked the question Molly had been waiting for.

"Where's Kristin?"

"Something came up at work." Molly leaned into the front seat to grab her shoulder bag and school her expression. She didn't have to look to know Amy and Jo were exchanging a knowing glance over the roof of the car. "She'll be here tomorrow." Standing up straight, she jerked her chin toward the house and asked, "Is there wine in there?"

"You know it." Amy hooked an arm through Molly's and led her indoors.

"Holy shit." Molly's jaw dropped open as she took in an interior she didn't recognize.

Pride flushed Amy's cheeks. "You like it?"

"Like it? *Like* it? My God, Ames." Molly turned to Jo, whose arms were still full of baggage. "Did you do all this?"

Amy answered for her. "Damn right she did."

"Holy shit," Molly said again as she shed her white, down-filled coat. "The last time I was here was…when?"

"Two years ago?" Amy clarified.

"At least. Too long. God, it looked like…a *cabin* then. Nice, but bare and…" Her voice trailed off as she searched for the right words. "Like a cabin. This is nicer than my house. Hell, this is nicer than most houses. Unbelievable."

Amy took her coat and Molly stepped out of her hikers before following Jo and her bags up the stairs that were tucked off in a corner to the right of the living room. The walls were regular drywall, painted a soothing khaki color, but the artwork and accessories scattered about kept the overall atmosphere one of nature and the woods. Molly glanced at a painting on the wall of the stairway. It was a Native American piece showing an adult and a small child watching the sun set over a lake in autumn. The oranges, reds, and browns gave off a surprisingly soothing aura and Molly had to resist the urge to stop and stare.

Jo made a right at the top of the stairs and Molly followed her into what would be her bedroom for the week. The floor was hardwood, the visible knots lending it a rustic look. The bed was queen-sized, centered on a braided rug and made neatly with a quilt and throw pillows in the same reds, oranges, and browns of the painting with a few greens tossed in for good measure, giving the whole room a sense of earthiness and comfort.

"Jo," she said, her voice hushed with awe as if she was afraid of disturbing the calm. "This is beautiful."

"Thanks, Molly-girl." Jo's cheeks flushed with pride. "I'm glad you like it. I hope you can kick back and relax this week."

"I'm sure as hell going to try." Molly crossed the room to the window, which looked out the back of the house onto the yard and the woods beyond. *If I can't relax in this place, I'm doomed.* "Thank you so much for inviting us. We can really use the get-away."

The statement was a loaded one and Jo's expression showed she understood. "The bathroom's right here." She indicated the room at the top of the stairs. "You'll be sharing with two of our friends. You'll remember Sophie, but I'm not sure you've ever met Laura. They'll be in the room across the hall."

Molly peeked into the other room. It was very much like hers but contained two twin beds instead of a queen.

"Even the youngest nieces and nephews are getting too old to share a bed," Jo said with a wink.

Molly agreed. "I remember my teenage years, and the last thing in the world I wanted to do was share anything with my sister."

They returned to the living room and Molly warmed her hands by the fire, amazed by how much her body and mind were already beginning to feel at ease.

Amy promptly handed her a glass of deep ruby red wine and toasted, "To the new year."

Molly clinked her glass against Amy's, adding, "It can only be better than the last."

They sipped, the sound of crystal on crystal still ringing sweetly through the room.

"Oh, this is good," Molly said as a delicious warmth spread across her palate and seemed to fill her soul as well.

"One of the biggest benefits of owning a restaurant…you get to taste all the best wines." Amy gestured to the couch. "Sit with me. Tell me what's been happening in your life."

"I've missed you, Ames." Molly said two and a half hours later.

She and Amy were still chattering on like birds in springtime. Feet were curled up under legs on the couch as they faced one another, taking turns filling in the space of the last month, unable to believe they'd gone four weeks without more than a quick hello on the telephone.

"I've missed you, too, Primo. Any time you need to talk, call the cell phone."

Molly grimaced and shook her head. "I don't like to interrupt your work day. I know how busy you get."

Amy held up a hand, forestalling any further comment. "The sale of the restaurant is almost final. I have much more free time than I used to. Besides, I wouldn't tell you to call the cell if I was worried about you interrupting me. You're never an interruption. Understand?" She reached over and stroked a hand affectionately down Molly's arm.

Molly studied the empty glass in her hand, turning it slowly in her fingers and watching the tiny burgundy-colored remnant of liquid coat the bottom. "Okay."

Before they could pick up their conversation again, the front door opened and Jo appeared from the garage where she'd been puttering, allowing the two friends time to catch up. "Look what I found wandering around outside."

A tall, striking figure stepped through the door behind Jo, and Amy jumped up from the couch. "Sophie! You made it."

"What a gorgeous drive it was today," Sophie said as Amy helped her off with her coat and Jo took hold of the duffel bag at her feet. "I don't know that I've ever paid as much attention before."

Molly studied the newcomer, trying to remember where she'd met her before. Sophie was of average height, which put her a few inches shorter than Jo and a few inches taller than Molly. Her black hair fell in corkscrew curls and just skimmed her shoulders, the ends tipped with blond highlighting in a very hip style. Her eyes were such a light brown, Molly suspected they changed color slightly depending on her outfit. Her skin was the rich and creamy brown of coffee with just a touch of milk and her figure was lean, but curvaceously feminine, with broad shoulders and rounded hips.

"Molly?" Amy held her arm out and Molly stood. "You remember our friend, Sophie Wilson?"

Sophie held out her hand. "The Memorial Day party, maybe?"

As Molly took her hand, recognition clicked. Amy and Jo had thrown a party at their home in the city the previous May. "That's it.

You're the graphic designer, right? I knew we'd met before. Molly DiPrima."

"And you're a teacher?"

Molly nodded, pleased.

"Big kids or small?" Sophie asked.

"Kindergarten."

"Yikes. So, *really* small. And how excited were they at the approaching vacation?"

"Almost as excited as their teacher," Molly said with a smirk.

Sophie laughed warmly. "I'll bet. Well, it's good to see you again."

"Same here."As Jo led Sophie away upstairs, Molly commented quietly to Amy, "She seems nice."

"Sophie's great." Lowering her voice, Amy added, "She's had a recent breakup, about five or six months ago."

Molly grimaced. "Oh, that's too bad. Were they together long?"

"At least a few years, but I'm not sure exactly. I don't really know a lot about their relationship. Kelly didn't seem to go many places with Sophie. They each kind of did their own thing." Amy wrinkled her nose. "I'll never understand couples who live that way."

"I had a boss whose marriage was like that," Molly said. "He and his wife always took separate vacations. She'd go with her friends to the Bahamas or something. He'd take a week in Myrtle Beach and play golf with his buddies. I don't even think they shared a bed half the time. They had separate bathrooms. Call me old-fashioned, but I just think that's weird. Why bother being married at all?"

"People have their reasons, I guess." Keeping an eye on the stairs, Amy lowered her voice to the barest of whispers. "Sophie almost always showed up at parties and get-togethers alone. I think Jo and I have met Kelly all of three times. I'm not even sure I could pick her out of a line-up, now that I think about it. How sad is that?"

"It says a lot about their relationship, don't you think? Not that I know a thing about them, but still… Maybe it's better that they broke up."

"I suppose." Amy looked dubious. "This was Sophie's first holiday alone, so we thought it would be good for her to be around some new people. Plus, our friend Laura, who's coming on Wednesday, is also alone after several years."

Molly grinned and poked her friend playfully. "Are you playing matchmaker?"

"No! Absolutely not."

"Because Jo told you that you weren't allowed?"

Amy smirked. "There is that." They both laughed. "Seriously, though, I'm simply trying to help out a couple of friends. I just thought that this way, neither of them will be the only singles on New Year's Eve. We all know how much fun that is."

"Ugh. Been there, done that. It sucks."

"Sure does."

AMY

Steam was filling the master bath with a thick, warm fog that smelled of vanilla and brown sugar. Amy slipped her fingers under the faucet, testing the temperature. She made a minor adjustment to the cold and then searched the drawer under the sink for a box of matches. The simple ritual of lighting each of the eight fat, scented candles that surrounded the oversized tub comforted her.

Soaking in a hot bath was Amy's idea of bliss. She didn't get to do it nearly often enough, but there were nights that Jo insisted, going so far as to fill the tub for her, light the candles, and deliver a soothing glass of red wine or brandy. "It's good for your body and it's good for your head," she would say, and Amy tended to agree.

Jo had remodeled the master bath just for her, and done it as a surprise, making sure the tub was large and deep, with whirlpool jets and a skylight above. It was a haven for Amy and she adored it.

She twisted her auburn red hair back into a knot and clipped it at the base of her neck, doing one last mental check to make sure her guests had everything they needed. They'd had a terrific dinner and were enjoying some pleasant conversation, but when three of the four of them yawned simultaneously around ten o'clock, Jo had taken the bull by the horns and suggested they call it a night. Everybody had laughed, and comments about age were tossed about, but nobody had argued. The day had been busy and all four of them were still coming down from the chaos of the Christmas holiday.

Amy had double-checked the upstairs bathroom for towels, made sure the guest bedrooms were warm enough, and was asking about extra pillows when Sophie had threatened to toss her bodily down the stairs if she didn't leave them alone and get herself some rest.

"God, you're beautiful."

Amy looked up, startled, and caught Jo's admiring glance in the mirror. Leaning against the door frame in her panties and a Buffalo Bills T-shirt, arms folded over her chest, Jo let her rich brown eyes travel slowly down Amy's body, causing goose bumps to break out despite the silken warmth of her ivory-colored robe. Her expression was so full of affection that Amy felt her eyes well.

"Care to join me?" she asked, cocking her head toward the tub.

"Don't mind if I do."

They disrobed together, neither taking their eyes off the other. Amy admired the lean, firm body of her partner. She knew it so well, every inch, every dimple, every curve and plane and dip, and yet it always felt new. The long limbs, the high, small breasts, the surprisingly shapely legs. Each time Jo's naked body was revealed, Amy felt as though she was watching for the first time, and she knew how lucky that made her.

She took Jo's hand for support as she stepped into the tub and sank slowly into the scented liquid heat. Jo stepped in behind her carefully and hissed as she lowered herself gingerly into the bath.

"God *damn*, you like your water hot." She always spoke the same line in the same circumstance.

"Sitting in a tub of cold water doesn't help me relax, love." Amy gave her stock answer.

They settled down together, tandem sighs of relief escaping their mouths and causing them both to chuckle. Jo leaned back and tugged Amy against her chest, wrapping her arms around her midsection.

"Today went well," Jo stated, her lips close to Amy's ear.

Amy nodded against Jo's shoulder, loving the feeling of being surrounded by Jo's body.

"Sophie looks good," Jo continued. "She seems to be doing okay."

"I imagine Christmas was really hard for her," Amy said. "She told me she's always spent it with Kelly's family and though I'm sure her brother and his wife did their best to keep her entertained, it probably wasn't the same for her."

"She laughed a lot tonight. That was good."

"That's because you're a witty woman."

"That's very true." Jo smirked. "But I mean she didn't look like she was about to burst into tears at any given moment like she did a few months ago."

"Time heals all wounds, or so they tell me." Amy picked up one of Jo's hands and examined it, touching and feeling each individual finger, watching the water run down the palm and across the wrist. She loved Jo's hands. Feminine but strong, they could caress skin gently or wield a power tool with vicious precision.

Jo placed a soft kiss on her temple. "The first two guests seemed to get along very well."

"They did, didn't they?"

"And you were worried."

"Not about those two," Amy said. "Not really. I mean, how do you not immediately fall in love with Molly?"

"It's impossible."

Amy pressed her lips together as her thoughts turned to her dear friend. "I don't think things are good for her right now."

Jo inhaled deeply and Amy could feel her nodding. "I know. I feel the same way."

"Maybe when Kristin gets here, you could take her out behind the garage and rough her up a little bit? Beat some sense into her?"

Jo grinned. "Think that'll help?"

"I don't know. It might."

"Kristin's not a bad person, honey. You and I both know that. A *blind* person, maybe…"

Amy snorted. "Do you think she has any idea what she has in Molly? How many women would give their right arm to be with her?"

Amy had known Molly for nearly thirty years and there was barely a moment that she hadn't adored her. When they were young, their parents were friends and twelve-year-old Amy had often babysat four-year-old Molly. Despite the odds their age difference stacked against them, they remained friends, drifting apart for a few formative years during high school and college, but getting back in touch when Molly was coming to terms with her sexuality.

"I'll say it again. Kristin's not a bad person. I like her very much. So do you."

"I don't like what she's doing to Molly."

Jo pressed her nose into Amy's hair. "Don't take this the wrong way, okay? But it takes two to tango."

Amy ran her hand along Jo's thigh, accepting the statement for what it was: the truth. "I know. I wish I knew how to help."

"Maybe you can't. Couples go through stuff, baby," Jo said, her voice gentle as a light breeze. "It happens."

"It's never happened to us." Amy felt Jo's arms tighten around her and squeeze, tender fingertips skimming across her stomach in lazy, circular patterns.

"We're lucky."

"I'm still worried about Molly."

"I know you are."

"I think *she's* worried and I don't know how to help her. She loves Kristin so much and I think she has this dread setting in. Like she knows something has to be done, but she has no idea what. And she's afraid. I hate that she's afraid."

"You are such a sweet woman. You know that?"

Amy turned so she could look into Jo's eyes. "Tell me I'll never have to worry about us falling apart."

Jo's gaze never wavered. "You will *never* have to worry about us falling apart. Ever."

"Promise?"

"I promise."

"I love you, Joanna." Amy's voice was just above a whisper and she barely got the words out before Jo's mouth covered hers.

They kissed slowly, deeply, with little urgency but with a complete, comfortable knowledge of one another's bodies. Amy was always amazed by how well they knew each other. Their lovemaking could be primal and raw, but more often than not, it seemed almost an extension or continuation of a hug, a conversation, a simple touch. It was common for an intimate exchange of dialogue to blend into foreplay, then blend into lovemaking without any clear lines between the three. It was a by-product of their years together, their knowledge of one another, and Amy loved it. Like now.

She couldn't pinpoint the exact moment when Jo's fingers had moved between her thighs, but then…there they were, pressing, softly exploring, creating a wetness that was thicker and hotter than the bathwater, spreading it over and around Amy's suddenly swollen flesh.

Amy opened her legs willingly, as much as she could in the large tub. The feeling of safety she had when Jo was behind her, surrounding her, was palpable. Nobody could ever love her like this. She reached back and hooked her hand behind Jo's neck, breaking their kiss to arch into Jo's shoulder as she felt her alarmingly sensitive nipples caressed.

She was unaware of her own groaning until Jo smiled against her ear and teased, "We have houseguests, baby. You might want to keep it down."

Amy clenched her teeth and growled, frustration and arousal battling with one another as Jo's fingers continued to work her body mercilessly. She would never refer to herself as a screamer, but she wasn't silent in bed either and Jo knew it. She tangled her fingers into the curls at the back of Jo's neck and tugged firmly.

"You're evil," she hissed, then gasped as a spasm took her by surprise.

"You owe me, remember?" Desire colored Jo's voice. "If you'd have let me have my way this morning, you could have been as loud as you wanted. Now, I'm afraid you have to pay the price."

Amy jerked in her lover's arms again. Jo's voice in her ear, possessive and dominating, was all she ever really needed. Their relationship was one based on mutual love and equality, but in the bedroom, Amy was more than pleased to let Jo have the upper hand, something that seemed to make her wife inordinately happy. Amy's legs began to tense and she tightened her grip on Jo's hair once more. She was so close…

Jo groaned softly as her fingers slipped into Amy's core. "God, I've wanted to fuck you all day long," she said in a hoarse whisper.

That was it. *Why does the F word always send me into oblivion?* Amy wondered absently, just as she plunged over the edge, and her flesh clamped down on Jo's hand, holding it in place. She turned her face into Jo's neck in the hopes of muffling her own cries, grinding her teeth with the effort to remain quiet and riding out the orgasm cradled in the arms of the woman she loved most in the world. There was no other position, physically or emotionally, that she'd rather be in than the one she occupied at that moment.

She was unsure how much time passed before her heart rate slowed down to a speed that was near normal. "Wow."

"You always say that," Jo teased.

"I always mean it."

"Good." There was a beat of silence before Jo stated simply, "I'm pruning."

Amy laughed. "Is that your not-so-subtle way of saying you want to get out?"

"Yes." Jo kissed her temple.

Amy sat up with a groan, but her eyes twinkled. "Fine. Get the hell out of my bath. I don't appreciate you coming in here and interrupting me like that."

Jo grabbed a nearby towel and grinned. "Oh, yes you do."

Amy was still smiling helplessly as Jo left the room. She sat back and allowed herself to relax in the still-warm water for a bit longer, waiting for the feeling to return to her legs, the pleasant afterglow of lovemaking enveloping her like a fine mist. Her thoughts turned again to how lucky she was to have the partner she did. It wasn't like there had never been rough patches. It wasn't like her relationship with Jo was perfect, but they were good communicators and that was key as far as Amy was concerned. As long as she felt like she could talk to Jo about anything, they'd be fine.

She glanced at the ceiling, thinking of Molly upstairs alone in the big bed, and her heart ached. *Speak up, my friend. It's the only way. You have to open your mouth.* It was an easy piece of advice to give, but what seemed like a simple thing to do was very difficult for somebody like Molly. Being raised by a very dominant father and a sweet, kind mother with low self-esteem wasn't terribly conducive to teaching a young woman to speak her mind when she should. More likely, Molly would allow somebody to walk all over her like she was some cheap throw rug, and would probably smile politely while it was happening. Amy had seen it occur more than once and it was painful to watch, especially as a friend who cared.

Taking a deep breath, she shook the thoughts from her head. She could ponder the situation all night long; she had done so in the past. Molly was like a little sister to her and she wanted nothing more than to help her. Jo's words of wisdom from a few months ago echoed in Amy's head. *Molly's a big girl. She's going to have to stand on her own two feet sooner or later.* It was true and Amy knew it. Still...

She got out of the bath, dried herself quickly, and smoothed on some lotion, all the while intensely aware that she had a naked woman waiting for her in bed. As she clicked off the light, the sight before her stopped her in her tracks. Jo was curled up on her side under the comforter sound asleep, facing the bathroom. Moonlight shone through the open curtains and across her smooth face, relaxed in repose, her tousled curls dark against the white of the pillowcase. Amy just stared, her heart swelling with love. Dropping the towel, she scooted under the covers naked and backed gently against Jo's front. Jo's arm immediately draped across her waist and she was drawn closer. Without ever waking fully, Jo buried her face in Amy's hair, her breathing barely changing.

Amy breathed in deeply, contentedly, and then let it out. Thoughts of her dear friend gradually left her alone as she relaxed completely, reveling in the warmth that was her life and finally surrendering to sleep spooned tightly in Jo's arms.

Tuesday, December 27

DARBY

I t's very simple, Julie. As far as you're concerned, you haven't seen me. That's it. End of discussion. Okay? Just...tell her I usually go away to my family's cabin over break and you're not sure when I'll be back. She's got to head back down to Pennsylvania next week to go back to work anyway. I just have to disappear until then."

Darby Cooper eased her ten-year-old Toyota to a halt at a four-way stop and looked both ways, rolling her eyes as her best friend scolded her from the other end of the cell phone illegally pressed to her ear. "I know. I know," she said when Julie paused for breath. "But by then her classes will be starting up again at Penn State and she'll forget all about me." Lowering her voice to the barest of whispers, she added, "I hope."

"God, you're acting like a guy," Julie admonished. "No, you're worse. Worse than a guy. You're being a pig."

"I know. You're absolutely right. But I couldn't help myself. Did you see her, Jules? Did you *look* at her at all? Those eyes? That *ass*? Come on. You can't blame me."

"What, you're trying to tell me you have zero control over your hormones? Take some responsibility. You're twenty-five, not fifteen."

"Okay. Fine. You're right. I'm like a guy. I'm *worse* than a guy. I'm a pig. Happy now?" Darby listened to some more stern and sensible Julie-isms, telling herself she deserved the lecture, after all, and the least she could do was take it like a dyke. As her friend wound down, she inquired, "Feel better?"

"A little." Julie's voice softened. She always came around in the end.

"Good." Darby finally got through the intersection. "I'll have the cell with me, but I'm going to go dark for a few days, just in case. Leave a voicemail if you need me, okay?"

"Stay out of trouble," Julie said by way of a good-bye.

With a grin, Darby flipped the phone shut and tossed it onto the passenger seat where it became lost in a sea of loose CDs. She turned the volume up on the Gwen Stefani song that was playing and slapped out a beat on the steering wheel, singing along with Gwen in a surprisingly on-key voice as she chugged down the country road.

She thought of the object of her avoidance. Rebecca. Aqua blue eyes, aerobics instructor body, firm, tight ass, and talent in the sack that Darby had never seen before. It was the whole propensity-to-cling issue that had become a problem. An immediate problem. Darby had seen her—and had mind-blowing sex with her—for five nights in a row before she realized that Rebecca viewed their pairing as a "relationship" as opposed to the "fun and amazing fuck" that Darby preferred to call it. Christmas was coming and Rebecca wanted to take Darby home to meet her parents.

Red flags shot up all over the place, accompanied by the clanging of alarm bells in Darby's head. The next thing she knew, she was avoiding Rebecca like the plague and Rebecca had become some sort of video game vixen. Queen Rebecca: Lesbian Hunter of the Dark. She'd begun popping up at Darby's friends' homes looking for her. She called Darby's cell phone every hour on the hour. She even waited for Darby in the parking lot of the Blockbuster where she worked. Darby had stayed locked in the manager's office until three o'clock in the morning to avoid her, wondering if there would ever be an escape.

That's when she decided hiding out at Aunt Jo's place was the perfect solution. Rebecca had no idea where it was or that it even existed. Darby would hang there until early next week and once Rebecca went back to college, she'd be home free. It wasn't the bravest of plans—which would be to actually talk to the girl and tell her the truth about not wanting a relationship. But face-to-face honesty wasn't something Darby was experienced at, nor was she any good at it. For now, any plan was better than none and better than taking her chances on Rebecca acting rational all of a sudden.

Aunt Jo and Aunt Amy would be surprised to see her. She hadn't initially planned on spending any time at their cabin, but they'd always told her she was welcome any time—she was family and didn't need an invitation. Aunt Jo was the best. They'd been close since Darby was a baby and having a lesbian in the family had made things a whole lot easier when Darby was coming to terms with her own sexuality. During her teen years, she'd spent many a weekend at Aunt Jo's, sometimes talking in depth, sometimes not talking at all, just hanging out and enjoying the company while Aunt Amy cooked the most amazing meals. How Aunt Jo didn't weigh three hundred pounds by now, Darby had no idea.

She refocused on the road in plenty of time to see the large deer standing on the shoulder with the intent of crossing, no matter what size vehicle might be barreling toward him. Darby hit the brakes, coasting to a stop and lowering the volume on the radio as she watched the large, majestic animal wander gracefully across the snow-covered pavement as if he owned it. His head boasted solid-looking antlers and Darby could hear her father's excited voice in her head. *An eight-pointer. Nice!*

Though she completely understood the need for hunting season in this area of the country, she couldn't imagine killing something as regal and impressive as the buck before her. She remembered being eleven years old when her father took her out into the garage where his pride and joy hung from its beautiful head. It was a very large buck, solid and strong with a twelve-point set of antlers. His torso was hollow, his dead eyes glassy. The garage smelled of copper and iron.

Darby remembered the effort it had taken for her not to cry in the presence of what was once a proud and gorgeous living creature. Though still very young, she was tough in almost every aspect, a classic tomboy, and she knew her father hoped she'd warm to the tradition of deer hunting, which he'd practiced faithfully every November since he was a boy. He'd painstakingly explained to Darby the dangers of the overpopulation of deer in their area, the threat of death by starvation, and therefore, the necessity of hunting season. He told her it was very regulated and the rules strictly enforced. Knowing she was particularly fond of the spring fawns, all white-spotted and innocent, he promised her that no respectable hunter would ever dream of harming a young deer.

They had talked for the whole afternoon, Darby eyeing the dead buck warily. She asked many questions and listened intently to her father's answers. When they finished, she had to admit that she did understand the theory behind hunting season, even began to reluctantly accept it. But join in? No way. It would never happen. She just couldn't be the reason such a magnificent animal would no longer roam the woods. Her father had been disappointed, but to his credit, he'd never pushed her on it.

"Hello, you beautiful thing," she whispered as he made visual contact with her through the windshield, his round brown eyes looking like smooth, giant marbles.

The sight of the deer made her almost giddy and Darby sighed wistfully when he looked away after a long pregnant moment and meandered into the trees as if he knew he had nothing to fear from her.

Turning the music back up, she continued on her way, her old tires fighting for a grip as they slid on the snowy pavement. She was glad the sky was clear. She'd meant to get some snow tires, but money had been tight and frankly, she'd forgotten about them until the first big snowfall came a week before Christmas. Driving had been a heart-pounding adventure ever since.

Fifteen minutes later, she was turning into the meticulously cleared driveway of Aunt Jo's cabin, hesitating only for a split second when noticing an unfamiliar Honda parked in front of the unfamiliar Jeep. It had never occurred to her that her aunts might have company.

She parked behind Aunt Jo's king cab pick-up, killed her own engine, and got out, inhaling deeply. Darby was a city girl at heart, but there was something about the crisp, clean smell and feel of the country air that made her want to slow down just a tad. She retrieved a beat-up duffel bag from the backseat just as she heard her aunt's voice call to her from behind the garage.

"Darby? Is that you?" Aunt Jo approached, smiling. "What are you doing here?"

"I thought you might need some help carrying wood into the house," Darby answered with a smirk.

"Well, then, you're just in time." Aunt Jo palmed the back of Darby's head, a sign of affection she'd always used; Darby considered it their version of a hug. "This is new," she commented, flicking the small silver hoop piercing Darby's eyebrow.

"So's this," Darby said with a grin and stuck out her tongue to show the stud piercing through it. "I got them both last month as a birthday present to myself."

"Mmm." Aunt Jo tried unsuccessfully to hide her wince.

Darby grinned at her aunt's attempt to be nonjudgmental.

Aunt Jo took Darby's bag off her shoulder and slung it over her own. "Come on. Let's fill up those young arms."

Inside, Aunt Amy and two other women sat around the dining room table, mugs in their hands and smiles on their faces.

"I found this apparently homeless person wandering around our driveway," Aunt Jo said as they entered the front door.

"Darby!" Aunt Amy jumped up from the table and Darby dropped her armload of wood onto the brick hearth just in time to catch her aunt as she threw her arms around Darby's neck. Darby laughed, surprised but loving it. Aunt Amy always gave real hugs, warm, firm, and filled with emotion.

Darby mock-groaned as she was squeezed. "Hey, Aunt Ame. Merry Christmas."

"What are you doing here? We missed you at your parents' house on Christmas Eve."

"I think I got there about twenty minutes after you left."

"It figures." Aunt Amy began unzipping Darby's coat as if she were still ten years old. "Take this off. Come in. Sit down. Have some coffee. Do you know our friends?"

Darby glanced toward the two very attractive women at the table. "I don't think so…" Her eyes rested on the smaller of the two, the one with the arresting green eyes. Her heart began to pound. "Wait…we've met, haven't we?"

"Probably more than once," Aunt Jo said as she took Darby's coat and hung it on a hook with her own. "This is Molly DiPrima. She's one of Aunt Amy's oldest and dearest friends. And this is Sophie Wilson, another very good friend. This is my niece, Darby."

Darby shook hands with Sophie first, smiling, then took Molly's warm, smaller hand, momentarily captivated to watch it disappear in her own.

The green in Molly's eyes sparkled. "I think I helped your aunt baby-sit you long, long ago."

"Oh, my God, that's right," Aunt Amy said, "You were about twelve and Jo and I hadn't been together very long…maybe a year or two. You stayed with us for the weekend and Molly came over for dinner. You had *such* a crush on her." She pushed at Darby playfully.

Darby could feel her cheeks flame as she remembered. The statement was absolutely true; she'd had it bad for Molly and she'd had no idea why. Molly had been her very first crush. *And damn if I didn't have great taste in women even back then.*

"I think I followed her all over the place that evening."

"You sure did," Aunt Jo said. "I knew right then you would be playing for my team."

"How could I not?" Darby gestured at her two aunts. "Look at my role models."

"Well, you're certainly all grown up now," Molly commented. "How old are you?"

"I turned twenty-five in November."

"Holy crap." Molly threw a panicked look in Aunt Amy's direction. "We're so old."

"Some of us are older than others," Aunt Jo added. "But you're only as old as you feel."

"Then I must be pushing eighty," Molly said, grimacing.

"Hottest damn elderly woman I've ever seen," Darby said, feeling a perverse sense of pleasure at seeing Molly's cheeks turning red this time as she grinned and glanced down at her steaming mug.

Aunt Jo whacked her upside the head. "Stop flirting with my friends, you little punk," she scolded with affection.

Aunt Amy ushered her to the table. "Sit. I'll get you some coffee."

Darby sat and looked back and forth at Sophie and Molly.

"Are you staying for the week?" Sophie asked, sipping from her own mug. She wore an ivory-colored turtleneck sweater that looked as though it was woven just for her. Her light brown eyes were the color of the cocoa powder Aunt Amy used for baking cookies.

"Actually, I've sort of come by unannounced and I didn't realize my aunts had guests. I don't want to be in the way."

"Nonsense," Aunt Amy said, returning to the table with a mug of coffee for Darby. "As long as you don't mind the couch, you can stay as long as you like. You know that."

"I don't want to crash your little party."

"You're always welcome, Darby. Our friends don't mind."

Darby glanced at the friends in question, her eyes resting on Molly. "You're sure?"

Molly grinned. "As long as you don't mind our kind of parties."

Darby furrowed her brow and waited with an expectant smile for Molly to elaborate.

"You know, old lady parties. We'll be playing canasta..."

"And bridge," Sophie added. "I brought my dominoes, too."

"We'll be falling asleep during the six o'clock news," Aunt Jo tossed in.

"And then we'll go to bed by nine," Aunt Amy said.

Darby laughed heartily. "Who do you think you're kidding? You're obviously unaware of how well I know my aunts. You'll probably drink me under the table. There are probably strippers coming tonight."

"Who told you?" Aunt Jo asked, feigning horror.

The Proper Décor

Amy hung up the phone, a pleased smile on her face. "Laura's coming tonight instead of tomorrow. She's on her way."

Jo nodded. "Good. The more the merrier."

They were all relaxing in the living room by the fire, stretched out on the floor and on furniture in various states of repose. It was still early in the week and would be several more days before this type of lounging made them feel like lazy sacks of uselessness.

"Laura...blonde?" Darby asked from her spot on the floor, to which she'd been relegated as the youngest and therefore the one who'd have the least trouble getting back up. "The one who used to work in your restaurant, Aunt Ame?"

"Good memory. That's the one."

"I've met her a couple times, too, right?" Molly asked, feeling slightly appalled at the number of people her best friend knew that she didn't. She hadn't been spending nearly enough time with Amy, especially over the past year, and she was starting to feel guilty about it.

"I think so. She started as a chef for me about three years ago. We hit it off right away and were immediate friends. However, it soon became obvious that our styles of running the kitchen were very, very different. And you know me..." Amy let the sentence dangle, looking chagrined.

"You couldn't let her run things her way," Molly supplied with a knowing smirk.

"Exactly." Amy shook her head at her age-old inability to understand her own reactions to certain situations. "So, we had to decide which was more important, Laura running my kitchen or us being friends. As luck would have it, Shadow Oaks had a scout looking for a kitchen manager-slash-head chef. Laura jumped at it."

"Smart girl," Sophie commented, stretching out in the leather club chair, her socked feet crossed at the ankle on the matching ottoman. "That place is the retirement community of some of the richest people in western New York. Tons of money there."

"They *love* her. It was a great move for her. And she and I are still very good friends," Amy said.

"Everything happens for a reason," Molly said. "Or so I've been told."

"Okay," Darby piped in. "If that's true, then give me a reason for this: why is there no Christmas tree in this joint?" Darby looked around, her blue eyes scanning the downstairs just to be sure she hadn't missed one someplace. "Are you slipping, Aunt Ame?"

Molly smiled. "You know, I almost asked the same question."

"Me, too," Sophie said. "You're the queen of interior décor, it's only two days after Christmas, and you're having a party. Where the hell's the tree?" The good-natured tone of her voice took any sting out of her words, letting Amy know she was razzing her.

Jo tugged at a lock of Amy's hair. "Told you."

Amy held up her hands in surrender. "I didn't get to it. We had such a ridiculously chaotic holiday, we only just got here Sunday night, and I completely forgot."

"Then I say we get to it now." Darby stood up, tugging her low-rise jeans a bit higher on her hips. "There are seventy-five acres out there and I *know* my Aunt Jo has a saw. Let's go find a little tree." She glanced expectantly around the room for support from the others.

Amy seemed a little panicked. "I don't have any decorations for it here."

"I saw popcorn in the cupboard," Molly offered. "We could string some of that. Some pinecones would work, too. Cranberries?"

Amy looked uncertain, no doubt seeing her neat and organized living room in unplanned-for disarray.

"We'll figure it out, baby," Jo reassured her often anal-retentive wife. "The fresh air will do us all good. Let's show off our land. Wanna?"

❖

The sky was once again a crystal blue, the sun shining so brightly some of the women had to shield their eyes and scramble to their cars for their sunglasses. Jo and Amy led the way along a path that wound through the woods which Jo had worked on for almost two years. Sophie jogged up beside them, leaving Molly and Darby to follow.

"I really despise winter," Molly said as Darby fell into step beside her, "but I have to admit there are times when the snow is just gorgeous. I'm almost hesitant to say that if I lived in a warmer climate, I think I'd miss it just the teeniest bit."

"I'm right there with you," Darby agreed as her old, beat-up boots crunched through the whiteness. "I hate being cold, but this…" She made a large sweep of her arm to encompass their surroundings, being sure to include Molly. "This is breathtaking."

Molly smiled and looked off into the woods, pushing her sunglasses up onto her head as the trees filtered out the sun. "So. Darby. What do you do? You've graduated, I take it. Weren't you majoring in computer science or something brainy like that?"

"Yep." Darby nodded, inordinately pleased that Molly remembered her course of study and trying hard not to stare at her. The white down ski jacket looked adorable on her and the sunglasses that now held her dark hair off her face added a sexiness that caused a wave of desire Darby had to swallow down. Molly's hair fell in waves around the back of her head and when she turned her eyes in Darby's direction…Darby cleared her throat and tried to focus on the conversation. "I got a degree in computer science and I actually had a job at Langford for a while."

"Wow. Impressive." Langford was a well-known, up-and-coming software technology firm in the area. Landing a job there straight out of college was quite a feat. "What happened?"

Darby shrugged. "I didn't like Corporate America, you know?"

Molly nodded.

"It was all designer suits and ass kissing and…I didn't feel like I could be me, like there would ever be a chance of me fitting in. I thought a software company would be more hip, more open-minded, but it felt like high school all over again. The cliques and the hierarchy. I couldn't stand it. I stayed for three weeks before I bailed."

"Well, I admire you. It takes guts to stand up for what you believe in."

"Now I manage a Blockbuster."

"Oh. That's…a change."

Darby laughed. "It's okay. You can be horrified. Everybody else is. But it's a good company to work for. I get great benefits, I can watch whatever I want for free, and I like it there. I'm happy."

"Happy counts for a lot," Molly said, her voice wistful. "Happy counts for just about everything." She stepped slightly off the path and her boot sank into the snow up to her calf. "Damn." She reached out and balanced herself on Darby's shoulder, feeling Darby's surprisingly strong arm slip around her waist to keep her upright.

She tried to ignore the zing of pleasure that shot through her and dug the snow out of her boot, taking longer than necessary. She was having trouble reconciling Darby the kid who was stored in her memory and Darby the woman—the very sexy, attentive woman—who was holding her steady now. Clearing her throat, she smiled up at her and felt a quick jolt of surprise at the blueness of Darby's eyes, so completely different from the deep brown of her aunt's.

"Thanks," she said.

"Sure." Darby kept her arm around Molly until she let go of her shoulder, not wanting to release her. They continued to follow the three up ahead, but Darby narrowed the space between herself and Molly just a little bit, walking as close to the other woman as she could without bumping into her. She could smell Molly's perfume and she tried to be subtle about the deep, greedy breaths she took.

"Tell me more," Molly requested. "About you. Where do you live? Are you seeing someone? What do you do for fun?"

"So many questions. Well…I have a little apartment in the city that I love. I could use a little more space, but mine is such a great place that I'm hesitant to give it up. I really want a dog, but my hours are kind of funky, so I've settled for a cat. His name's Chuck and he's very cool. Am I seeing someone?" She shrugged. "I see a lot of someones."

Molly laughed and Darby felt her heart warm at the sound, feminine and musical.

"For fun? I don't know. I go out with my friends. I play softball in the summer. I read. I watch a lot of movies." The threesome in front had moved quite far ahead of them and Darby had the sudden sense that she was on a stroll through the woods with just Molly. She didn't dislike the feeling and she fought off the urge to simply push her against a tree and kiss her senseless. "What about you?"

"What about me?"

"Where do you live? Are you seeing someone? What do you do for fun? Come on. Eye for an eye."

Molly looked up at the blue sky and watched a chickadee zip by. "We've got a house by the canal. It's a little too big, but it's very pretty and it's in a nice neighborhood. I miss the city, though. We used to have a place on the East Side."

A house on the Erie Canal didn't come cheap, Darby noted. "And then suburbia?"

"And then suburbia. We thought that's what we were supposed to do, the next logical step."

"And 'we' is?"

"'We' is me and Kristin. We've been together for a little over seven years."

"Wow. Congratulations." Darby forced cheerfulness into her voice. Of course somebody like Molly had a partner. Why wouldn't she? That didn't really mean anything anyway, did it?

"Thanks."

Molly's voice contained slightly less pride than Darby expected, but she left it alone for the time being. "Is she coming this week?"

"She had some work stuff to take care of. She should be here today."

"Oh. Cool." Darby didn't like the far-off quality that suddenly encompassed Molly. Wanting to get her talking about happier subjects, she prompted, "Keep going."

"Going where?"

"Fun, smart-ass. What do you do for fun?"

"Ah." Molly nodded and Darby could feel her returning to their conversation. "Let's see. I garden in the summer. Flowers and vegetables. And I have a lot of houseplants, so that helps to keep me busy in the winter. I love to walk. That's a huge advantage of living on the canal."

"I bet. I like to take my bike there and just ride and ride."

"I've got a bike, too." The corner of Molly's mouth turned up slightly. "You should come get me some time. We can ride together."

"I'd like that."

Before they could continue, they heard a shout from around the bend ahead of them. As they rounded it, the others came into view, off the path and into the woods about twenty yards.

"What do you think of this one?" Jo asked, squatting down next to a small evergreen. It stood about five feet tall, its branches surprisingly thick and lush.

Molly had completely forgotten the hunt for a tree and realized she'd never even glanced at one as they walked. "I think it's perfect," she said.

Darby nodded and stepped forward to help her aunt as she sawed.

"We'll have to remember to come out here and plant another one in the spring," Amy commented.

"We're in the middle of a forest, Aunt Ame. Who's going to see one little bare spot?"

Amy shot a stern look at Darby. "We always replace what we take, unless it's fallen all on its own."

Darby made the face of a child who'd been scolded. "Okay, then."

Twenty minutes later, they were nearly back to the house, Darby and Jo dragging the small tree behind them. Sophie was describing the design she was working on for a client when a shrill beeping cut through the air, causing many of the women to jump.

"Jesus." Amy laughed, pressing a hand to her chest.

"Sorry," Molly said sheepishly. "It's me. I forgot it was in my coat." She pulled a cell phone from her coat pocket and glanced at the screen. "It's Kristin. She's probably on her way. I'll catch up with you." She walked backward, putting distance between herself and the group.

Darby watched over her shoulder, barely able to register Molly's voice as she moved farther away. She turned face forward just in time to catch a low-slung branch on the forehead.

"Ow." She rubbed the spot.

Aunt Jo studied her with a cocked eyebrow. "Watch where you're walking," she suggested mildly.

"Now you tell me."

"Found it." Amy came up from the basement carrying an old metal tree stand and handed it to Jo. "I have no idea why it's here since we've got no decorations, but…"

"I brought it up last fall after we got a new stand at home, remember?" Jo had moved a knee-high table in front of the living room window and she and Darby balanced the tree on top. The extra height centered it perfectly. "What do you think?"

Amy suppressed a grin.

"You're warming to it," Jo said, waving a finger at her beloved. "I can tell."

"It looks terrific," Amy conceded. "Good call, Darby."

Darby looked pleased with herself as she took the stand from Amy and helped Aunt Jo position the tree's trunk correctly.

Sophie came out of the kitchen with a bowl of microwave popcorn. "Got a needle and some thread?"

"I'm sure I do." Amy glanced toward the door. "Where's Primo? Is she still out there?"

"Why do you call her that?" Darby asked, holding the tree straight in the stand while Jo tightened the screws against the trunk.

Jo chuckled in anticipation of the adorable story.

Amy rummaged through a drawer as she spoke, found a small sewing kit, and handed it to Sophie. "I used to baby-sit Molly way, way back. She was four, I think, the first time I met her. I was twelve."

"Wow," Darby said. "You *have* known her a long time."

"Longer than you've been alive, honey. Anyway, when Molly was little, she had trouble with her Rs and she couldn't quite pronounce DiPrima correctly. She was 'Mauwy Pweemo.' I started calling her Primo and it just sort of stuck."

Sophie and Darby looked at one another and then gave tandem *awwww*s at the idea of tiny little Molly trying to pronounce her own name.

As if on cue, the front door opened and Molly came in, stomping the snow off her feet. Her sunglasses covered her eyes and she made no immediate attempt at removing them.

"Everything okay?" Jo asked innocently.

"Oh, yeah. Fine. Kristin's going to be stuck longer than she thought, so she won't be here until tomorrow." The group was silent and Molly continued on. "Hey, the tree looks fantastic. Very nice." She took off her boots and lined them up neatly on the mat, then shed her coat and hung it up on the rack. Clearing her throat, she excused herself to the bathroom upstairs, her sunglasses still shading her eyes.

Amy and Jo exchanged glances and Amy waited a couple minutes before following her friend up the stairs.

The sun spilled through the window of the guest room, making the dust motes floating in the air visible like tiny snowflakes and bathing the quilt-covered bed in warm, inviting light. Despite the ambience, Molly felt cold. She sat on the edge of the bed, her hands tucked between her knees, and gazed out onto the snowy landscape. The sunglasses were tossed onto the nightstand.

Amy sat gently next to her. "You okay?" Her quiet voice still seemed a loud disturbance in the stillness of the room.

"Do you think she's having an affair?" Molly didn't turn to look at her friend.

Amy inhaled and slowly let out her breath. She tucked a lock of Molly's dark hair behind her ear. "Do you?"

"I don't know. I want to say no. I want to say I know her better than that, that she'd never do such a thing, but the truth is, how would I know? I never see her. We hardly ever talk any more. I can't even remember the last time we made love. She spends so much time working, it seems like all she thinks about is more money. I feel like I hardly know her anymore. And she certainly doesn't know me."

"What do you mean?"

Molly stood and crossed the room to her bag. Rifling through it, she came out with a square blue box and sat back down next to Amy. She handed Amy the box. "This is what she gave me for Christmas."

Amy opened the hinged box and sucked in a breath. Nestled in the navy blue velvet interior was a watch. It was gold and dainty, exceptionally fancy and encrusted with diamonds. "God, it's beautiful," she whispered.

"Isn't it?"

Amy looked up and met Molly's green eyes, tinged red around the edges. She'd known Molly for thirty years and though she cleaned up tremendously well and was an extremely beautiful woman, she was also what Amy liked to call "earthy." She wore denim skirts and cotton blouses and hammered silver jewelry. She preferred a ratty sweatshirt to silk, she preferred leather to gold. She wore a single silver band on her left hand, not interested in a diamond version at all. The watch Amy held was as far from Molly's personality as one could get. Shouldn't her partner know that?

Molly watched the pieces fall into place on Amy's freckled face.

"You'd never wear this," Amy stated.

"No. I'd be afraid to."

"I bet it was expensive."

"Hugely. Ridiculously."

"Does she know how you feel?"

Molly snorted. "Of course not. I oohed and aahed over it like a good little wife."

"Jesus, Molly."

"I know." Molly closed her eyes. "I know."

"You have *got* to talk to her. I don't like that she's spending so much time away from you either, but in her defense, the girl's not a mind reader."

"I know," Molly said again.

She was well aware of her propensity toward passive-aggressiveness. It came from her mother, from years of watching a good, kind-hearted woman think too little of herself and allow others to make all her decisions, run her life, and trod all over her like an old doormat in the process. You do that long enough and you don't know how to live any other way, and Molly had followed obediently in her mother's footsteps.

Now, she found herself breaking out in a cold sweat, dread seeping into her bloodstream like poison at so much as the thought of a confrontation that might end unpleasantly. Better to go on miserable but conflict-free, right? She'd had this conversation in her head so many times, it was practically scripted. She was starting to understand, though. The reality of what was happening was becoming searingly, painfully clear. If she didn't do something—and do it soon—her relationship of more than seven years was doomed. That thought made her stomach churn and bile rise in her throat.

"I love her so much, Ames," she choked out, tears welling in her eyes. "And I miss her. God, I miss her."

"Oh, I know you do, sweetheart." Amy wrapped an arm around Molly's shoulders. Molly leaned into her, a quiet sob escaping from her lips.

"I'm so unhappy." Her voice was no more than a whisper and it broke Amy's heart. She kissed the top of Molly's head and tightened her hold on her dear friend, hoping to convey her love and support through her arms as she rocked her gently back and forth on the bed.

❖

It was a good half hour before Amy had Molly calm enough and cleaned up enough to head back downstairs to the others in the group. When they reached the bottom of the stairs and rounded the corner, they stopped in their tracks. Amy began to laugh and Molly actually smiled.

Darby saw them first. She swept her arm over the tree like one of the models from *The Price is Right* showing a prize. "What do you think?"

"What in the world is that?" Amy asked.

"It's a lesbian Christmas tree," Jo said, an unspoken *duh* in her voice.

Amy glanced around, seeing the tossed-aside pair of scissors and the scattered remnants of half a dozen magazines including *Curve*, *The Advocate*, and *People*. The tree held more than twenty pictures of various women, hanging from branches with bent paperclips. A string of popcorn circled the entire thing. Amy and Molly moved closer, studying the "decorations" with big grins on their faces. Angelina Jolie, k.d. lang, Jennifer Beals, Maya Angelou, Mariska Hargitay, Melissa Etheridge, and Ellen DeGeneres all hung dutifully. Amy's eyes trailed up the tree to the top where Jodie Foster was perched like a queen looking down at her subjects.

"Jodie was Aunt Jo's addition," Darby informed her.

"I'm not surprised," Amy replied, knowing her wife's age-old love for the actress. She glanced sideways at Molly and almost sighed aloud with relief. Her face was lit up, and the pain had left her green eyes.

"This is awesome," Molly said and vowed anew to enjoy herself this week, with or without Kristin standing by her side.

Darby inched up next to her. "You okay?" she asked softly as the others were talking.

Molly shot her a look of gratitude. "Yeah. I will be. Thanks."

"Sure." Darby quickly touched Molly's cheek in an affectionate way, not quite a pinch, but more than a stroke. It reminded Molly of the way her grandfather used to touch her face, with such fondness, and she swallowed down an unexpected lump.

"Hey, Molly." Sophie held out a needle with a long strand of thread and a bowl of raw cranberries. "I saved these in case you wanted to do them. If not, I can."

"No, no, that's great." Molly took the offered items, knowing some busywork to keep her hands moving would help calm her roiling, churning thoughts. "Thanks."

Sophie nodded, trying not to look too sympathetic. She remembered when her own relationship was beginning to crumble, how helpless she'd felt and how much she *didn't* want people looking at her like they felt sorry for her. "Here." She offered the club chair she'd been occupying. Molly took a seat gratefully and set to work on her string of cranberries.

Amy stood with her arms around Jo's waist, admiring the tree. "You're very creative, I must admit. I've never seen anything quite like…this."

"Only the best for my woman," Jo said, squeezing her. "I think we should have a lesbian tree every year."

"Let's not get carried away."

SOPHIE

Sophie Wilson was doing okay. She was doing better than she'd expected, certainly. *Only five more days,* she'd been telling herself. *Only five more days and I'll be home free.* She had expected the holidays to be hard. It was true that Kelly had been gone for close to six months, but being alone for the holidays brought everything back in a rush and she felt like Kelly had only left her last week. She just had to get through New Year's Eve—which she suspected was going to be the hardest of the cluster of days focused on togetherness and love—and she'd be ready to move forward with her life.

She tended to oscillate between bitter and angry, and hurt and heartbroken. Neither side was preferable. Bitter and angry at least kept her from crying constantly, but it was exhausting to hate everybody and everything all the time. And it wasn't her; she wasn't like that. Bitter and angry didn't become her. Hurt and heartbroken was harder. She didn't like feeling vulnerable or allowing her emotions that close to the surface. She didn't like that people could take one quick glance her way and know she'd been destroyed by somebody she loved and trusted. Hurt and heartbroken sucked. Mostly, she'd thrown herself into her work. It had been the only thing that kept her sane. Ironically, she was getting more freelance graphic business now than she'd gotten in the five years she'd been offering her services. Life was so weird.

Leaning against the front door and surveying the group around her, she recognized the expression on Molly's face, knew it too well from seeing it in the mirror every morning for three months before Kelly finally dropped her bomb. It was the expression of confusion, of loss of control, of *I'm worried my life is about to fall apart and there isn't a damn thing I can do to stop it.*

Part of her wanted to help, wanted to take Molly aside and fill her in on the dark and dirty details of what might come. But she didn't know Molly, and she didn't know anything about her relationship with her partner. She could be totally off base. And the truth was, Sophie didn't want to rehash her own experience, not this soon. She was afraid doing so might send her into a tailspin, a backward slide. She'd worked too hard to claw her way up from the depths of destruction and depression. You couldn't pay her enough to skid back down even a few feet. The very thought terrified her.

Only five more days…

A knock on the door startled her, vibrating through her shoulder, and she jerked away. Amy looked up from the counter in the kitchen where she was filling wineglasses with the deep red selection from the shelves Jo had built in the basement. "That's Laura. Would you let her in, Soph?"

Nodding, Sophie opened the front door to a smiling blonde with the dimples of a six-year-old.

"Hi," the new guest said in a voice not at all childish, but surprisingly robust. "I'm Laura Baker."

Sophie stepped aside and let the shorter woman in. "I'm Sophie." She waited for Laura to set down her bag, then shook hands with her. Laura's was cool and soft. "Sophie Wilson."

"We've met, haven't we?" Laura asked.

"Probably at one of their parties."

Laura studied her, not releasing her hand. "Or maybe at Amy's restaurant?"

Sophie surprised herself by not pulling away. These days she flinched at the touch of others, wishing she had a force field to guard her personal space. Laura's grip wasn't at all threatening, though. Not even a little uncomfortable. It was steady, sure. "That could be…"

"The day you came in with the ideas for the new logo," Amy offered as she approached, flipping a dish towel over her shoulder. Sophie noticed that she glanced quickly at their still-linked hands, then up at Laura's face. "Hi, sweetie." She reached out for a hug. Laura did let go of Sophie then.

"That's right," Sophie said, snapping her fingers as recognition dawned. "You were looking for a specific kind of wine behind the bar the day I was there." She recalled sitting at the bar early in the day with

Amy, showing her a few designs for the new logo she was suggesting. Laura had slipped behind the bar and began reading each and every label of every bottle of white wine in the cooler until she found what she wanted for the evening's special. Sophie remembered the blond hair pulled back in a smooth twist, the pristine white chef's jacket, and the sparkling distraction in the blue eyes when Amy called her over and introduced her to Sophie. And she remembered those dimples.

"For my Artichokes French. You're right."

"Well." Sophie shifted her weight from one foot to the other. "It's good to see you again."

Laura's smile seemed very genuine as she replied, "It's good to see you, too, Sophie."

Sophie watched as introductions were made to Molly and Darby and Laura was enveloped in a huge hug from Jo, who commented on not seeing enough of her. Sophie's mind gave her a jolt of surprise when it tossed her the idea that she'd like to see more of Laura, too. It had been such a long time since she'd had any thoughts even remotely sexual, she often wondered if her vibrator had collected so much dust by now that it wouldn't run ever again. But there was something about Laura.

Sophie studied her as she was stripped of her coat by her hostess and chatted with Darby about her Toyota. She wasn't conventionally pretty; she was actually rather plain, but in a wholesome, girl-next-door kind of way. Her dark blond hair was pin-straight, some of it fastened with a black clip at the back of her head. She was of average height, maybe an inch shorter than Sophie, and her build was pleasing…round in the right places, curved where it should be. Sophie forced her eyes away from Laura's backside before anybody could catch her staring. *I couldn't help it; girl knows how to fill out a pair of jeans!* Her face was round and her complexion as smooth and soft as the skin of a peach. The pink sweater she wore highlighted the rosy tint of her cheeks, the only color on skin so pale, Sophie was sure the slightest amount of sun would burn her as red as a cherry Life Saver.

Laura followed Jo and her bag upstairs, and Sophie had the happy realization that Laura would be occupying the other twin bed in the room where she was staying. She suppressed a grin as Amy handed her a glass of wine.

❖

Two hours later, the six women sat around the dining room table, pleasantly full from the enormous pot of chili Amy had made. They sipped coffee and tea and picked from a variety of sweets scattered about the table.

"That was delicious, as always, Amy," Sophie said, leaning back in her chair and patting her belly. "I think this week is going to be bad for the scale."

"Like you couldn't stand to gain a few pounds, Soph," Jo commented.

"I know. But a breakup will do that to you." She eyed the chocolate cheesecake in the middle of the table.

"It's definitely the only surefire way I've found to lose weight," Laura said. "I dropped almost twenty pounds when I got a divorce."

"You were married?" Darby asked. "Like, to a guy?"

"Sadly, not every woman is a lesbian," Sophie responded, gently chiding Darby and hoping to hide her own disappointment.

"Oh, I'm a lesbian," Laura said. "Thus the divorcing of my husband."

Sophie was curious and wanted to hear more. "Do tell."

Laura shrugged. "It's not really anything earth-shattering. I was married to Stephen for eleven years. Two years ago, I met Amanda, the wife of one of his work buddies. She was classy, gorgeous, and very accomplished in the art of seduction." She grimaced in a self-deprecating way. "I fell head over heels in love with her, and for the first time in my life I felt comfortable with who I was. And I was certain we would be together forever." She sipped her coffee.

"What happened?" Molly asked, sitting forward, her elbows on the table.

Sophie watched Laura shrug, recognizing the movement as a way to make something appear not as hurtful as it actually was. She'd used that same gesture herself many times when talking about Kelly.

"My husband found out. He was livid, of course."

"Wait. You and this Amanda were together while you were still married to him?" Nausea churned in Sophie's stomach. "You were cheating on him with her?"

Laura nodded. "Yes. I'm not proud of it, but I couldn't help myself. I just wanted to be with her." She sipped from her mug again, out of self-consciousness, Sophie suspected. "Apparently, Amanda had no such intentions. She was never going to leave her husband. In fact, I was simply a fling to her. She'd had several with other women. I had no idea."

The table was quiet aside from the gentle murmurs of pity. Sophie watched Laura's face seeing the hurt that hid just beneath the surface, but at the same time feeling that she deserved it. "Your poor husband," she said quietly.

Laura's blue eyes turned to her, a split second of icy defiance visible in them before it melted into guilt. "Yeah."

"Right, but what was she supposed to do?" Darby asked. "She's realizing she might be gay."

"How about talking to her husband?" Sophie tried not to make the suggestion through clenched teeth. "Telling him the truth? Giving him a chance?"

"A chance to what?" Darby countered. "It's good in theory, but doesn't really hold any water. There's nothing he can do to make her not gay, right?"

Laura's head cranked back and forth between the two as they spoke, as if she was watching a tennis match.

"They still could have talked," Sophie said, her anger building.

"It wouldn't have mattered," Darby insisted.

"It might have."

"How? Was she just supposed to stay in a relationship where she wasn't happy?"

"*Yes!*"

Darby flinched as though Sophie had slapped her and fell silent, the pieces of the puzzle falling into place. The entire table had grown quiet, the atmosphere suddenly filled with discomfort as people focused on their drinks or their food, afraid to look up.

"Kelly cheated on me." Sophie said it matter-of-factly, as if remarking on the weather. She felt the stares of Amy and Jo, knowing this was news to them.

"What?" Jo said, surprise clear in her voice.

"Kelly was having an affair. With that…*woman* from the gym." She spat the word "woman" with the same inflection she'd have given if she'd said "mucus" or "vomit." "That's who she's living with now. Evidently, they're very happy."

"Oh, Sophie." Amy reached over and placed her hand over Sophie's. "Why didn't you tell us?"

Sophie half-shrugged. "It's not really something that's fun to share. It makes you feel worthless, like all your years together were a lie, like your partner has been settling for second best the whole time." She glanced pointedly at Laura, who pressed her lips together and studied the contents of her mug.

"Well, obviously Kelly was a moron," Molly piped up, looking slightly ill herself.

Sophie chuckled, grateful for the comment of solidarity. "Thanks, Molly."

There was an awkward silence, the sounds of silverware on plates and the sipping of coffee filling the room.

Jo cleared her throat. "So. How 'bout those Buffalo Bills?"

Sophie felt a small smile make an attempt to appear on her face, acknowledging gratitude to Jo for at least trying to lighten the moment.

Jo continued, her strong voice cutting through the quiet. "Amy. Tell the story." At Amy's quizzical expression, she clarified, "About the woods."

"Oh, no," Darby grumbled good-naturedly. "Not the Magic Acre story."

"Shut up, Darby," Amy scolded with a grin. Looking around the table, she asked her dearest friends, "I've never told you this story? Molly? Surely you must have heard it."

"Magic Acre? I don't think so." Molly raised her eyebrows in uncertainty. "Maybe. Refresh my memory."

Sophie loved to listen to Amy's voice. She had a decidedly feminine lilt with a little bit of hoarseness underneath that put her on Sophie's list of Women Who Can Read the Phone Book to Me. She sat back in her chair and listened to her friend speak.

Amy had tied her hair back into a ponytail when she began cooking dinner. It now hung over the front of her left shoulder, the end curling in a corkscrew. She wound it around her finger and pursed her lips, finding the right place to start. "When I was a kid—a little kid, like four or five—my grandmother used to tell me the woods around here were enchanted. She said that a hundred or so years ago, there was a structure back farther on the property." She jerked a thumb over her shoulder to indicate the back yard. "Apparently, a witch lived there."

Sophie chuckled, as did Laura. Darby hid her smile in her cup.

Molly gave them each a mock-scolding look and elbowed Darby. "Go on, Amy."

Amy inclined her head in thanks and continued. "She was a good witch, gentle, and looked out for those around her who also lived in this area. Nothing huge or what you'd consider traditional witchcraft. She didn't cast scary spells. There was no fire and brimstone. Grandma said she made 'magic nudges' to help teach people lessons or understand things they already knew but had trouble accepting."

"So, she was, like, a witch psychiatrist?" Sophie asked with a giggle.

Amy allowed herself to be teased. "Yeah, I guess you could say that."

"So," Darby continued, "Amy's grandma liked to call this spot in the woods the Magic Acre. Even though there are seventy-five of them."

"Are all the acres magic or is there one specific one?" Laura asked, biting her bottom lip to keep from cracking up.

"Hey, you guys can make fun all you want. *I* believe it to be true," Amy said firmly, the remnants of a grin tugging at the corners of her mouth.

Sophie helped herself to a cookie off a plate in the center of the table. "And Jo? What do you think?"

Jo's brown eyes glittered. "I think whatever Amy says is the absolute truth."

"A good, wifely answer," Molly commented. "Smart if you don't want to get cut off in the bedroom."

"Hey," Jo grinned. "My mother drowned all the dumb kids."

The laughter continued and the tension previously filling the room seemed to dissipate. Sophie still felt the prick of disappointment in Laura, but managed to keep it in check. Laura's revelation would most likely keep them from becoming friends, and Sophie almost felt it was something over which she had no control. She could use all the new friends she could get at this point in her life, but Laura? Her still-aching soul and forever-shattered heart wouldn't allow it. How could she possibly like somebody who'd done the same, horrible thing to her spouse that Kelly had done to her? She shook her head very slightly from side to side, a movement she hoped was indiscernible to the rest of the crew at the table. *Impossible*, she thought.

Much later, she exited the bathroom upstairs with her teeth brushed, her face washed, and her pajamas on. Laura was sitting on the edge of her own bed in their room. Sophie felt the blue eyes zip over her body and an expression she couldn't quite figure out crossed Laura's face. She looked like she wanted to say something as she got to her feet, and the two of them stood in the room for what felt like several long minutes, looking at each other but saying nothing.

Finally, Laura pressed her lips together in a small semblance of a smile and left to take her turn in the bathroom. Sophie watched her go, feeling guilt, anger, disappointment, hurt, attraction, and curiosity. She dropped down onto her own bed, suddenly exhausted, and wondered how she could possibly feel so many feelings all at once and not simply have her head explode.

Wednesday, December 28

LAURA

As had become her habit since living on her own, Laura Baker was awake at the crack of dawn. "Oh Dark Thirty," Amanda would have called it; she hated getting up early. Amanda's idea of a perfect Saturday was to sleep until eleven and then wander around in her pajamas until dinnertime. Laura had always hoped there would come a time when she and Amanda shared a house and they could spend a Saturday in just that way. Now, it would never happen.

As usual when she thought of Amanda and what would never be, her stomach cramped, her body's very physical way of warning her off the subject. She shook the dark-haired, smiling temptress out of her head and sat up in the twin bed. She felt rested, surprisingly so given such a small sleeping space. But it was comfortable, the mattress firm. Stretching her arms over her head, she glanced across the nightstand at Sophie's sleeping figure in the next bed.

Sophie was definitely attractive, her dark skin smooth and unblemished. Her curly hair was tousled and spread out all over the pillow, and Laura smiled when she thought about the mess it would most likely be when she sat up. The smile slid away, though, when she recalled the conversation over coffee the previous night and Sophie's obvious revulsion. She understood Sophie's pain, she really did, but Laura had enough of her own guilt. She didn't need somebody she'd just met heaping more on top of her. Stephen had made his hurt very, very clear; she could see it on his face any time they were in the same room, and the responsibility she felt for it made her head ache and her stomach churn. That, combined with Amanda's betrayal, had made her wonder how she hadn't just curled up into the fetal position in a corner and withered away to nothing.

She lifted some clean clothes from her bag and tiptoed quietly to the bathroom, hoping neither Sophie nor Molly across the hall was awakened by the squeaky hinges on the bedroom door.

As she brushed her teeth, she thought about the last year of her life. She hadn't withered away because she'd surprised herself with her own strength. That didn't mean she didn't feel horribly guilty about the devastation she'd caused Stephen. It didn't mean she didn't feel annihilated by her misjudgment and loss of Amanda. What it *did* mean was that she was a much stronger person than she'd given herself credit for. And that made her proud…lonely, but proud.

After dressing in jeans and a turtleneck, she padded quietly down the stairs, past what she assumed was the sleeping form of Darby on the couch—it looked like nothing more than a large pile of blankets—and was startled to find Jo at the dining room table, sipping a mug of coffee and reading the paper. A new fire was crackling to life in the fireplace.

"Morning," Jo whispered. "Did you sleep okay?"

Laura nodded. "I slept great."

"Coffee?"

"Not yet. I think I'd like to take a walk first. Is that okay?"

"Sure." Jo pointed toward the back of the house. "There's a path that starts about here and cuts through the woods. Stay on that and it loops around." Her arm made a semicircle, her finger ending up indicating the garage. "You'll come out over here. It's about a half hour. You could do it twice if you wanted to be out longer."

"Once should be enough. I like to get the blood flowing first thing in the morning. Helps me wake up."

"You got boots? Gloves and hat? It's not snowing now, but we got a little overnight and we'll probably get more today."

Laura smiled at Jo's motherly concern. "Yep. I brought it all. I'm good."

"Okay. Enjoy." Jo went back to her paper.

Laura was surprised that a paper got delivered out here, but then had to remind herself that they weren't exactly in the middle of nowhere and there were certainly other people who lived in this area. As she headed out the front door, she noticed a single set of footprints that led to the end of the driveway and back: Jo retrieving the paper from the mailbox by the road.

The air was brisk; it wasn't supposed to get above twenty-five degrees today. She trudged around the house through the snow, which was a little more than ankle deep. It hadn't occurred to her to bring her cross-country skis; what a perfect opportunity to glide silently through some beautiful scenery. She made a mental note to ask if Amy had a pair she could borrow. Laura loved her job at Shadow Oaks, but it was hectic and time-consuming and she needed to grab on to every opportunity for relaxation that she could.

The sun hadn't quite risen, but the sky was smoothly fading from deep gray to light silver and the snow allowed for more than enough visibility for her to trek along as the morning broke fully. She could hear the winter birds chirping in the distance as though discussing breakfast and their plans for the day. She'd also noticed a handful of bird feeders dotting the property, courtesy of Amy, most likely. The woman was a serious nature lover. Laura suspected that if she looked hard enough, she'd probably also find peanuts scattered about for the squirrels and chipmunks and a salt lick or two for the deer.

Ten minutes into her walk, she stood completely still, breathing in the clean, crisp air, listening to the sounds of nature around her. Laura was a country girl at heart. She'd spent much of her childhood at her grandparents' in a house very much like Amy's. She'd built forts in the woods, caught toads from the nearby creek, and eaten wild raspberries on lazy Sunday afternoons. This was home to her. She'd discovered recently, for the first time in her life, that she was okay being alone with herself from time to time. Since moving out of her house with Stephen and renting half a duplex, she'd begun to enjoy her own quiet time. That didn't mean she didn't like going out, hanging with her friends or attending the occasional party. It just meant that she was no longer cast into a blind panic when she had plans with nobody but herself. Strange as it sounded, she felt that at forty years old she was finally beginning to understand herself.

There was still the loneliness, but she was managing.

By her calculations, she was a little over halfway through her walk on the woodsy path. She could feel the rosiness in her cheeks from the brisk air, the blood coursing through her veins, and then she heard a small whimper. She stopped in her tracks and cocked her head to listen, furrowing her brow and wondering if she'd imagined the sound.

It came again, sort of a combination whine and snort. She followed it, the direction taking her off the path several yards, until she came upon a small dog. He was a terrier mix of some kind, curled in a ball and shivering at the base of a tree. His brown wiry hair was matted and his big brown eyes were sad and wary. He saw Laura and shivered some more, obviously too cold and lost to jump up and run away from her.

"Oh," she breathed, approaching him slowly. "Hey there, little guy." She removed her glove and held her hand out to the dog's nose, keeping her voice soft and steady. "What are you doing out here? You must be freezing."

The dog gave Laura's fingertips a halfhearted sniff and then his pink tongue darted out and swiped them gently, once. She moved her hand to his chin and scratched gently underneath it, taking her time and letting him get used to her.

"We need to warm you up, little guy, and we need to do it soon. Have you been out here all night?"

She scanned the area, noting with bewilderment that there were no fresh tracks aside from her own. Could the poor dog have possibly spent the entire night in that one spot? The thought broke her heart. She removed her other glove and gently worked her hands beneath his furry body, noting with a small bit of relief that his underbelly was still warm, although that fact made it seem even more impossible that he could have been there for longer than an hour or two. Maybe the snow had fallen more recently than she'd suspected. She made a mental note to ask Jo if she knew.

She scooped the little dog up in her arms. He couldn't weigh more than fifteen or twenty pounds. She unzipped her ski jacket, tucked him into the front of it, and zipped it back up part way, hoping her body heat would warm him up sufficiently. To her surprise, he didn't struggle at all. In fact, he seemed relieved and gave her chin a small lick of thanks. Laura smiled, scratching his furry head.

"You're welcome, little guy," she said as she put her gloves back on and began walking back to the path. She took her time, not wanting to jostle him too much, talking to him like he actually understood what she was saying. "You don't have a collar on, buddy. Did you run away or did some mean person leave you out here?"

The thought of somebody dumping a poor, helpless animal in the middle of nowhere made her blood boil and she knew Amy would feel the same way. She hoped they didn't mind if she brought the dog into the house. There was something about him...she couldn't put her finger on it, but she felt drawn to the pooch, connected to him like they had something in common. She snuggled him closer to her body, pleased to note that his shivers had eased somewhat.

"We'll get you back to the cabin, get you all warmed up, and make you some breakfast, okay, little guy? How do you feel about rice? I'm sure Amy has some. Maybe some eggs? You should take it easy at first; you're pretty skinny. You don't want to gorge yourself and then get sick. A little at a time, okay?"

The dog breathed in deeply and sighed, very much like he was relieved. Laura dropped a kiss onto his head and kept walking, feeling needed for the first time in ages.

THE STRAY

Amy was in the kitchen gathering the makings for a big country breakfast when Molly came downstairs. The smell of bacon was mouthwatering and Molly followed her nose through the living room, then stopped and did a double take at the pile of blankets on the couch. Grinning mischievously at Jo, she backpedaled and plopped down onto the couch, delighted at the grunt that issued from beneath her.

"Oh, man." Darby's voice was muffled. "I think a giant boulder just fell on me."

Molly slapped at her and got up. "Funny."

Darby peeked out from under the blankets, taking in Molly's attire of striped cotton pajama pants and a deep green, long-sleeve Adidas T-shirt. Her bare feet were tipped by toes polished a deep burgundy and the shirt brought out the green of her eyes. Darby swallowed hard at the sight, internally shaking her head at herself.

"I forgot extra socks," Molly said to Amy as she located a mug and poured herself a cup of coffee. She tugged on Amy's auburn ponytail. "Can I borrow a pair?"

"Absolutely," Amy replied, cracking eggs into a large stainless steel bowl. "Jo-Jo, would you be a dear and get this lovely lady a pair of socks for her icy toes?"

"It would be my pleasure." Jo kissed the top of Molly's head as she passed by and disappeared into the master bedroom.

"How'd you sleep?" Amy asked. "Were you warm enough?"

"Oh, God yes. That quilt is wonderful. Where'd you find it?"

"My grandmother made that one. Isn't it beautiful?" Amy smiled wistfully. "I had the two for the twin beds in the other room made to match so they'd all be the same. I love the homey, outdoorsy feel it gives to the place."

"I've got to say," Darby said, her voice scratchy as she shuffled in with a fleece blanket wrapped around her shoulders. "That couch I slept on? Homey *and* outdoorsy. Very, very nice."

Amy reached out and tousled Darby's sleep-mussed dark hair affectionately, then went back to her eggs.

"What the hell time is it, anyway?" Darby asked. "It was barely light out when Laura went for a walk. What's the matter with you people? After forty you don't have to sleep any more?"

"Hey," Molly scolded, playfully pushing at her. "Some of us have a ways to go before we hit that milestone. Besides, that's all your generation ever does. Sleep."

"You're a lazy bunch, that's for sure," Jo added, handing Molly a pair of white socks upon her return. "Sleep till noon. Live with Mom and Dad until you're thirty…"

"I have my own place, thank you very much." Darby felt slightly insulted at the assumptions.

"If you want to go back to sleep, you can take my bed," Molly offered.

Darby took several seconds to actually think about it before deciding it was better to decline. "Thank you, Molly, but I'm fine being up at the crack of dawn." She stuck her tongue out at her aunt. "I do it all the time."

Jo snorted but made no further comment as she handed her niece a cup of coffee.

"I love you all, but get the hell out of my kitchen," Amy said. "You're crowding me."

"The artist needs her space," Jo said, herding them a few feet away to the dining room table.

The open design of the house allowed for Amy to participate in conversations while keeping guests out of her immediate way. It was the only way Jo would have it; their home in the city was designed the same way. If Amy was going to spend so much time in the kitchen, Jo wanted to be able to see her and chat with her while she worked.

"Sophie still sleeping?" Jo directed her question to Molly.

"I think so. The door was closed when I got up." Turning to Darby,

Molly asked, "Did you say Laura went out for a walk already?" When both Darby and Jo nodded, Molly raised her eyebrows in surprised admiration. "Wow. That's ambitious."

As if on cue, the front door opened and Laura stepped in, stomping the snow from her boots. Her cheeks had a healthy pink flush to them and her clear blue eyes were glittering. A small canine head peeked out from the top of the zipper of her ski jacket.

Molly squinted. "What the—?"

"I'm afraid I found a little something in the woods." Laura directed her gaze toward Jo. "I hope you don't mind, but the little guy was frozen stiff." She unzipped her jacket to reveal the rest of the dog.

He was brown, his fur wiry and in need of a cleaning. His legs were short and stubby and he had a sweet and gentle face. His ears were mismatched, one pointed straight up and one folded in half and flopping down, giving him a slightly comical appearance. Laura shed her jacket and stepped out of her boots, holding the dog to her chest the whole time. Moving toward the fireplace, she sat down on the wide brick hearth, letting the dog absorb the warmth as the other women approached cautiously.

"Well would you look at that," Jo said softly, holding a hand out to the animal. "Hi there, buddy boy." The dog sniffed the offered fingertips. "You found him?"

"Yeah, it was kind of weird. He was whimpering at the base of a tree about halfway along the path. I have no idea how he got there. When did it snow, do you know?"

"I got up around two to go to the bathroom and it was snowing pretty good then." Amy brought small containers with cream and sugar to the table and set them down, along with a handful of spoons.

Laura shook her head, not believing the poor dog could have stayed in that one spot for more than four hours, but having no other explanation. "Weird," she said under her breath.

Darby squatted down and put her face near the dog's. "Hey, furry butt. What were you doing out there all alone?" The dog swiped his pink tongue over her nose. Darby smiled up at Laura. "No collar, huh?"

"Nothing on him or around him."

"Looks like you might have yourself a new pal," Jo grinned.

"Would it be okay if I kept him here until I figure out the next course of action?"

"I don't see why not," Jo said. "We can't very well have him out in the woods all alone. Either somebody's looking for him or somebody dumped him."

"He's so sweet," Laura said, unable to believe somebody could just leave a helpless animal to fend for itself alone in the snowy woods. "Why would somebody do that?"

"People are assholes, that's why." Darby made the statement and there were nods all around.

"Amy? Do you think we can scramble him up some eggs or make him some rice or something? He's awfully skinny."

"Consider it done." After scratching the top of the dog's head, Amy left them to take care of the task.

Laura saw Sophie standing behind the others, her approach unnoticed, looking as if she hadn't slept more than two or three hours all night. She smiled at her temporary roommate. "Morning, Sophie."

Sophie inclined her head in a nod of greeting.

"Want to pet him?"

"Sure." Sophie squatted in front of the animal, who was a mess and in need of a bath. "You stink, pal," she said, but the affection in her voice betrayed the indifference she was trying for.

Laura smiled. "He does, doesn't he? I want to give him a bath, but I think I'd better make sure he's warmed up first. I'm afraid of shocking his system."

Sophie stood. "Is there coffee?" she asked nobody in particular, effectively ending any attempt at conversation. Jo pointed to the table and Sophie went to help herself. Laura frowned slightly as she met Jo's eyes. Jo gave her a don't-worry-about-it smile of reassurance.

Darby bent down to the dog's level once again. "Do you have any idea how lucky you are to have ended up in a house full of lesbians? You hit the mother lode, buddy. Nice work."

Forty-five minutes later, they were all seated at the dining room table enjoying a hearty breakfast of eggs, bacon, and pancakes. The dog was on the floor at Laura's feet after refusing to stay by the fire alone. He picked daintily from a paper plate of plain scrambled eggs Amy had fixed for him and glanced up every so often as if checking to make sure Laura hadn't disappeared into thin air. She reached down periodically to caress him.

"This is delicious, Amy," Sophie commented, working on her

second helping of eggs. "I don't know what you do to these damn things, but I've never had scrambled eggs this good."

"Secret ingredients," Darby said. "Aunt Jo doesn't even know what goes into them."

"True story," Jo agreed.

"If I told you, I'd have to kill you," Amy said with a shrug, then held up a hand forestalling Laura as she opened her mouth to speak. "One chef is not allowed to tell another's secrets."

Laura smiled. "Fair enough. I'm shutting up."

"Thank you. And thank you, Sophie. I'm glad you like them."

"You know, I was going to try to guess what's in them," Sophie said with a grin. "But now that there's the whole possibility of murder, I think I'll just eat and enjoy."

"Smart move," Darby said.

"So," Jo began, setting down her fork. "I know this is vacation for most of us and I certainly don't intend to put you on a schedule, but I do want to let you know what some of your options are while you spend the week in our fine establishment." She smiled at Amy's grin. "There are two pairs of cross-country skis in the garage, along with snowshoes and toboggans. We have a satellite dish, so watching television is a possibility, even out here in the boondocks. There is also a DVD player and a PlayStation. We've got some board games in one of the closets upstairs and there are several decks of cards."

"There's also lots of wine and beer in the basement," Amy said. "Please help yourselves to all the food and drink you want. *Mi casa es su casa*."

"And, of course, there's always the sit-on-your-ass option, which many of us choose on vacation," Jo finished up.

There were nods and murmurs all around the table. Darby began wiggling her thumbs in midair. "I don't know about you guys, but I think I'm feeling a game of Resident Evil coming on. Anybody want to help me shoot some zombies?"

"I'll take you up on that," Sophie responded.

"Can I play after I go snowshoeing?" Molly asked. "One of you will have to teach me."

"You got it." Darby smiled at her.

"What time will Kristin be here?" Jo asked.

"She said she was going to head out sometime this morning,"

Molly said, leaving out the part about how she'd turned her cell phone completely off last night and left it upstairs on the nightstand next to the bed she'd occupied alone. *Because ignoring the problem will make it go away*, she thought with disdain, knowing she'd run upstairs and check the voicemail at some point during the day. Sometimes the worst part of being passive-aggressive is actually *knowing* that you are.

KRISTIN

*H*i, this is Molly and you've reached my voicemail. Please leave me your name, number, and a brief message and I'll get back to you as soon as I can. Thanks."

"God damn it."

Kristin Collins was exhausted. She pushed the end button and tossed the Blackberry into the passenger seat with great annoyance, yanking the earpiece from her ear and sending it in the same direction.

As it was, she had to drive with the stereo blasting and the back windows cracked enough to let an uncomfortable amount of cold air blast through the interior of the Lexus SUV. It was the only way to keep herself from drifting off at the wheel. She honestly didn't know how much longer she could keep up this pace before she'd simply keel over from fatigue, irritation, stress, or all three combined.

She wished she could drive faster, but the snow had been falling steadily all afternoon and apparently, this particular road wasn't high on the list of priorities for the snowplow drivers. She forced herself to drive smartly, even though she wanted to blink her eyes like in *I Dream of Jeannie* and be at the cabin. She should have been there about six hours ago, but damn Jack Reeves had happily heaped more work on her and she'd been stuck in the office. It never seemed to be the right opportunity to mention to Jack that she was actually supposed to be on her third day of vacation. She was sure he knew. She was also suddenly sure that he didn't care.

She let her mind drift fully to the subject of her boss. Jack Reeves had been her mentor, her one-time role model. He was a large and handsome African American man with graying temples and a deep, booming voice that commanded attention. When she joined his team many years ago, she'd come in at the bottom rung, and on the ground floor. His company was small, but he was a smart man with a hell of a business sense and Kristin knew he was going nowhere but up. She'd listened to everything he said with rapt fascination, taken notes, asked questions, followed him around like a puppy. A puppy who wanted to learn.

It didn't take long for him to notice. He began tossing small responsibilities her way—making her part of the brainstorming team for one project, putting her in charge of gathering quotes for another, and finally letting her deal face-to-face with a client. That had been her crowning moment. The client loved Kristin because Kristin had actually listened. She had the uncanny ability not only to understand what her customers wanted, but more importantly, what they didn't. Reeves saw that right away and it wasn't long before clients were *requesting* Kristin. She became his most sought-after and successful account executive in a matter of months. She was a VP by the time she was thirty-five.

She'd never forget that promotion. Molly was so proud of her. They'd gone out to a very fancy dinner and had checked into a five-star hotel for the weekend, ordering room service and making love for two days straight. She could still see the glittering delight in Molly's green eyes, shining on her, making her feel like she was capable of anything just because Molly believed in her.

It had gone steadily downhill from there.

She glanced at her own eyes in the rearview mirror, noting the dark circles and the appearance of some fairly new crow's feet. She'd always gotten compliments on her looks and she'd learned to use them. During her career, her All-American, blond-haired, blue-eyed appearance, she had to admit, had gotten her through more than one door that was otherwise shut tightly. Now, she hardly recognized the tired, haggard-looking woman gazing back at her.

I'm aging way too fast, she thought, depressed. *I look ten years older than I am*.

Shaking her head, she mentally replayed her telephone conversation with Molly the day before, when she'd called to tell her she was going to arrive later than she'd thought.

"You *promised*," Molly had said, the low volume and tone

conveying two crystal-clear facts to Kristin: she was trying to keep her voice down so the others didn't hear her, and she was *pissed*. "You promised you'd be here today."

"I know, baby. I know. I'm really sorry. I can get there tomorrow morning."

Molly's silence might as well have been her shrieking in anger; it meant the same thing.

"Look, Mol, I know you're upset. I don't blame you. There just isn't a lot I can do about it, so I need to accept the fact that I've got to stay one more day and finish this stuff that Jack needs done. It's a huge project and it's going to bring in a bunch of money and five new accounts for us. And I'll get a bonus for my time. We'll go someplace fun with it, okay? Maybe take a long weekend in New York? See a show? What do you say?"

"I say, why don't you take Jack to a show?"

The line had gone dead after that and Molly had either turned the phone off altogether or just wasn't answering. Kristin had called ten times since then and had connected only with Molly's voicemail.

Now, not only had she not been able to get a hold of her partner, but she was also half a day later than she was supposed to be. If Molly was pissed already, things were only going to get worse.

"Like that's anything new," she muttered aloud. It seemed like Molly was mad at her more often than not these days. Suddenly annoyed at the harsh volume of the stereo, she hit the off button. Silence closed around her.

She pumped the brakes of the Lexus gently, coasting to a stop at a stop sign. Visibility was getting worse as the sunlight faded into dusk. God, she hated winter. Dark at four thirty, gray, sunless days. She should have been born in Arizona or New Mexico or Southern California. Someplace warm and sunny. She wanted to retire to the Southwest, but pulling Molly away from her family would be a Herculean feat, one she wasn't sure she had the energy for anymore. Pushing smoothly on the gas pedal, she urged the vehicle forward again, clicking on her high beams. They only made her attempts to see worse. She'd just have to take it slow and hope no deer decided to leap out in front of her car. That was the last thing she needed.

She peered at the directions she'd scrawled on the back of a takeout menu and tried to come up with a good opening line for when she saw

Molly. For about the seventeenth time in the last couple of hours, she reached across for the Blackberry and looked at the screen, hoping the little telephone icon that indicated voicemail was just late in showing up. She was stung that Molly hadn't even called her to make sure she hadn't driven into a ditch somewhere. Of course, if Molly had been checking her voicemail, she would have gotten Kristin's pathetically cheerful message letting her know that she'd lost track of time, but was heading out and would be there before Molly knew it.

Kristin rolled her eyes at herself. That was dumb. She shouldn't have been cheerful, she should have been angry. Pissed off that Jack had held her up yet again. Molly might have related to that a little better.

What the hell happened to us?

She pressed a hand to her forehead as she felt tears spring into her eyes. "God damn it," she said to the quiet inside the car. This had been happening more and more often lately. She wanted to blame it on PMS, on her emotions being too close to the surface because of her period, but it was happening at all times of the month. She'd get to thinking about Molly and her home and her life and the issues and frustrations would close in on her until she felt like she was going to have yet another panic attack.

And then she'd cry.

She missed Molly.

It was a vicious cycle that had begun about a year ago and had proceeded to rotate ever more quickly as time went on. She'd become stressed at work, she'd get home late—again—and try to be cheerful about how well work was going. Molly would get quiet, Kristin would feel guilty and throw herself further into her work, come home later and more cheerful, buy Molly something expensive. Molly would get quieter. Kristin could see the cycle very clearly, like it was painted as a giant mural in the sky for her, but she had no idea how to slow it down, let alone how to stop it.

"A little more support from my wife wouldn't be a bad thing," she said aloud, wishing somebody—anybody—was listening and at least attempting to understand. "Is that so much to ask? I'm working my ass off here. Why is it so hard for her to understand that I'm doing all of this for us? So we can have a better life? A worry-free retirement? Why can't she try, just once, to see things from my side? Why is that so difficult for her?"

The Blackberry buzzed from its place on the seat and Kristin jumped at the sound, snatching it up before it stopped vibrating, hoping it was a message from Molly. She frowned when she looked at the screen and saw there was an e-mail from the client she'd just sent a project outline to before she left.

"Jesus Christ, can't you people leave me alone for five seconds?" she muttered at the apparatus through clenched teeth. She punched a couple of buttons and read, her eyes ping-ponging from the electronic device to the windshield and back.

Hi, Kristin—

> *Just a couple of small inquiries regarding the proposed outline. Jack said you're away from the office, but you'd have your Blackberry and would call ASAP. I'll wait to hear.*
>
> *Thanks so much!*
> *Howard*

"Great. Thanks a lot, Jack, you prick." Damn him. Sometimes she really thought he was useless. He dumped so much stuff in her lap, she might as well be running the joint. No, she *was* running the joint. Just without the fancy title and the larger paycheck. The entire firm would fall apart if it weren't for her holding it together.

She flung the Blackberry back to its nest on the passenger seat once again and heaved a huge sigh.

She was just so goddamn tired.

Twenty minutes later, she made the right-hand turn that took her down the slightly snow-covered driveway of Amy and Jo's place. The flakes were beginning to thicken, falling steadily, and Kristin was grateful she had arrived in one piece, happy to stop driving for the time being. Throwing her Blackberry and its attachments into her soft-sided leather briefcase, she hauled it and the Pullman suitcase Molly had packed for her out of the SUV and tromped up the driveway toward the cabin. She could smell the fire burning in the air, and the light spilling out of the front windows gave off a warm, inviting glow. Knowing Molly was inside both excited her and terrified her—a combination of feelings she was almost used to at this point.

Her breath was visible in the chilly evening air, mingling with the falling snow, leaving no doubt that she was in the Northeast. A part of her smiled inside, feeling at home in this weather she always claimed to despise, knowing it was in her blood regardless of how much she loved the sun.

Her leather boots protected the bottoms of her pants from the wet snow and for that, she was grateful. She hadn't taken the time to change out of her stupidly expensive pantsuit, wanting to simply get in the car and escape, but now she wished she'd been dressed a bit more casually, especially when the door was opened by Amy, who stood there in her sweats looking adorable and the slightest bit relieved to see she had finally arrived.

Kristin found herself immediately enveloped in a huge hug, which she tried to return despite her full hands.

"You made it." Amy's tone was unsuccessful in hiding the fact that she was actually surprised.

Kristin felt immediate guilt set upon her shoulders like a wet, cold blanket. "I did. It's good to see you."

They moved indoors and Jo took Kristin's bags and coat. The interior was just as warm and cozy as the outside glow had suggested and Kristin felt herself relax ever so slightly. She took in the faces of the four other women—well, the faces of three and the back of Molly's head as she concentrated on the video game she was playing on the television.

"Come in. Let me introduce you." Amy hooked her arm in Kristin's and escorted her farther into the cabin. Gesturing to the club chair, she introduced the dimpled blonde who was reading a book, a small dog curled in the crook of her knees. "Kristin, this is Laura Baker."

Laura smiled. "I'd get up, but…" She pointed at the dog, then reached out and shook Kristin's hand warmly. "Nice to meet you, Kristin."

"Same here." Kristin followed Amy to the living area where two women sat, one on the couch and one on the floor, both alternating between watching what Molly was doing and looking at the newcomer.

"This is Sophie Wilson. She created our logos."

"Guilty as charged," the woman on the couch said with a grin.

"That was really nice work," Kristin complimented her as they shook hands. "I loved both designs."

"Thanks." Sophie looked pleasantly satisfied.

"And this is Jo's niece, Darby," Amy went on.

Darby stood and Kristin didn't miss the quick once-over as Darby's blue eyes slid along her body. "Heard a lot about you."

Her handshake was firm and Kristin noticed a subtle clicking as she talked. She caught a quick flash of metal from Darby's mouth. *Tongue ring.* She refrained from making a distasteful expression. "All good, I hope."

Darby smiled, but didn't answer. The silver hoop in her eyebrow reflected the firelight as she sat back down next to Molly, not leaving a whole lot of distance between the two.

"Damn!" Molly heaved a sigh as the words "Game Over" flashed on the screen.

"Hey, you did great," Darby said, squeezing her shoulder. "Look. You're the number two high score."

"I'm going to beat you." Molly's voice was light, teasing. "Sooner or later, I'm going to beat you. You know it."

Playfully, Darby snatched the controls out of Molly's hand. "Promises, promises."

Kristin stood in minor discomfort as she waited for Molly to acknowledge her arrival, knowing this was her punishment for being so late and she had to take it like a big girl. Finally, Molly stood and turned to look at her, her face stern, but a faint flush in her cheeks. Kristin wasn't sure if she was happy to see her or still excited by the game. She didn't allow herself to dwell on the answer, just enjoyed the little jolt that she still got every time Molly focused those intense green eyes on her. After seven years together, she was still amazed by how attracted she was to her wife. Molly was beautiful, even when she was ticked off...*especially* when she was ticked off. Like now.

"Hi, baby." Kristin stepped forward and put her arms around Molly, ignoring the fact that the hug returned to her was halfhearted. "I missed you," she added softly, both hope and truth coloring her voice.

"I missed you, too," Molly said, giving in slightly, her arms tightening just a touch.

"How about some dinner and a glass of wine?" Amy offered. "We saved you some chicken."

"Oh, my God, that would be wonderful. I'm starving." Kristin slid her hand down Molly's arm and linked their fingers together, suddenly relieved to be with her. Molly was looking over her shoulder at the game Darby was playing.

"How was your drive?" Jo asked, returning from upstairs where she'd deposited Kristin's bags.

"Uneventful. It snowed pretty steadily, but nothing too scary."

Jo peered out the window. "That Lexus good in the snow?"

"It's not bad. I've been pleasantly surprised." At the sound of dishes in the kitchen, Kristin squeezed Molly's hand to get her attention. "I'm going to go up and change out of this monkey suit, okay?"

"'Kay," Molly answered distractedly, her eyes still focused on the television screen. "On the left, Darby! The left! Good."

Kristin headed upstairs, peeking in both rooms looking for her bags. Finding them on the queen-sized bed, she headed over to it, taking in the soft comforts of the room itself, feeling a little like she was at a bed and breakfast in the woods. The idea wasn't unpleasant and she gazed out the window at the snow sparkling in the moonlight. Breathing deeply, she tried to exhale all the stress of the past couple days, wanting to see it dissipate in the air like steam.

That was when her Blackberry buzzed from inside her briefcase.

"God damn it," she muttered, rifling through the leather case and pulling out the contraption. Reeves's number showed on the screen. "Son of a bitch," she said to the room, took another deep breath, and clicked on.

"Hey, Jack. What's up?" Quick and to the point, hoping he'd notice her clipped tone and take the hint.

"Just wanted to make sure you got Howard's e-mail. I told him you'd get right back to him." His booming bass voice vibrated in the pit of her stomach. She used to find him powerful and intriguing. Lately, he just annoyed her.

"Yeah, I got it. I'll give him a shout in the morning."

"He's working late tonight. You can catch him at his desk right now." His tone left no room for doubt about what he expected.

Kristin poked the inside of her cheek with her tongue. "Fine. I'll call him now."

"That's my girl." The line clicked off.

"I'm not your girl, you asshole," Kristin whispered as she dialed her client's number. Standing at the window, gazing out but not really seeing anything, she waited while the phone rang on the other end. Once, twice, three times…she allowed the hope for voicemail to creep in, thereby jinxing herself. The line was picked up. *Damn it.*

"Howard Felt." Her client's voice was gentle and friendly. She liked the guy and it irritated her that Reeves was making him the enemy.

"Howard. It's Kristin Collins. How are you?" As she listened to his response, she turned away from the window. Molly stood in the doorway, her face a combination of hurt, anger, and disappointment.

"Five minutes," Molly said. "You've been here all of *five fucking minutes.* Jesus Christ, Kristin." She turned and tromped back down the stairs, her footsteps reverberating against the hardwood.

Kristin closed her eyes and pinched the bridge of her nose with her thumb and forefinger, knowing she didn't stand a snowball's chance in hell of staving off the headache that was suddenly ripping through her mind like a freight train. "I'm sorry, Howard. Can you say that again? I think my phone cut out for a second there."

Thursday, December 29

THE GANG'S ALL HERE

I hate that I always let it get to me like this." Molly sniffed, determined not to cry, but still feeling the threat of tears welling up in her eyes. She swiped at her nose with her mittened hand and held tighter to Darby's elbow as they plodded through the new-fallen snow, their boots leaving a path of fresh tracks behind them in the woods.

"Why *wouldn't* it get to you? You'd have to be pretty cold and unfeeling for it not to. And I don't think that's who you are." Darby strolled casually, enjoying the feel of Molly beside her, holding fast to her arm.

It was early. Only Jo was awake when Molly had come down the stairs looking like she hadn't slept more than five minutes in a row the entire night.

"Hey, gorgeous," Jo had greeted her, the expression on her face a mix of sympathy and concern.

"Morning." Molly had kissed the top of Jo's head as she passed. "I need some air. Is there a travel mug around here? Me and my coffee want to go for a walk in the snow."

"I think there's one in the cupboard over the stove," Jo replied.

Darby had suddenly appeared out of nowhere, much to the surprise of both other women. "Want some company?" she'd asked Molly, ignoring the pointed stare from her aunt.

"You do know that the sun's not quite up yet, right?" Molly teased.

"Yes, I'm aware of that."

"Just making sure. Get dressed. I'd love the company."

"Be right back." Darby had disappeared into the bathroom to change and was back in record time.

"You can share my coffee," Molly said, holding up the mug after only finding the one.

They headed out into the silvery blue almost-light of the morning, the brisk, frosty air awakening their senses. Darby had asked about the previous night, knowing when Molly had returned from the second floor and made the remark, "She's on her damn cell already," that things weren't going to be smooth sailing for the couple. Molly had spilled it all without taking a breath.

"I don't know, Darby. I always thought when I was in a relationship with the right person, it would be easy. Effortless." She shrugged. "I guess I was wrong."

"Or you haven't found the right person." Darby consciously injected a tone of innocence into her voice.

Molly seemed to absorb that, not saying anything.

Back in the cabin on the second floor, Kristin watched the two of them as they headed off into what looked like a path cut into the woods at the end of the back yard. She'd felt, rather than heard, Molly get up and dress, but she'd been too exhausted to ask her where she was going so early. It seemed easier to just pretend to be asleep until she left. Kristin was actually surprised she had slept at all herself. Molly had given her the cold shoulder for the rest of the evening, generally keeping her distance in order to make it clear to Kristin that she was being punished, but refraining from open hostility in order to keep the rest of the group from being subjected to the weirdness and discomfort of an obviously battling couple.

Kristin knew the others were aware there were problems. Amy was Molly's best friend; she knew everything. And Kristin *was* two days later than she was originally supposed to be there. She was sure that hadn't gone unmentioned. She played it off, though, forcing herself to make conversation, crack jokes, and laugh with everyone. It was totally draining and she had fallen into bed next to Molly barely conscious. She'd drifted off within minutes. She was sure Molly was annoyed by that. She was also sure Molly had barely slept a wink, as was her tendency when she was upset by something.

Kristin watched the two figures disappear into the woods, arm in arm, and wondered absently if Darby was somebody she should be wary of. She snorted almost immediately, the piercing, the ratty, low-rise jeans and the tousled hair springing to mind. She fully expected there was more than one tattoo hidden beneath Darby's thrift store-clothing and she rolled her eyes, envisioning the typical, grunge-loving, lazy and irresponsible twentysomething of the current era. She despised their indolence, their cavalier, the-world-owes-me attitude and their arrogance. Darby was *so* not Molly's type. Molly was a doer, a go-getter, a volunteer, not the kind of person who waited for something to fall into her lap.

Still…

Across the hall, Sophie and the terrier were having a staring contest in the growing morning light while Laura slept on, oblivious. The dog was curled up at Laura's feet on the bed, his chin resting on her ankle, but his brown eyes were wide open and blinking at Sophie as she sat up and swung her feet over the edge of her own bed. They held one another's gaze for several long minutes before Sophie threw up her hands and asked, "What are you lookin' at?"

The dog blew out what sounded very much like an irritated breath and then closed his eyes, seemingly content to stay put as long as Laura did. Sophie rolled her eyes and headed off to the bathroom.

Jo was turning the page of the morning paper when she felt her wife approach from their bedroom. The next second, she was enfolded from behind, Amy wrapping her arms around Jo's shoulders as she kissed her cheek. Jo inhaled deeply, absorbing the just-awakened scent of her beloved into her very being, adoring the familiar smell that came as a blend of musk, citrus, and laundry detergent.

"Morning, sunshine," she said.

"Good morning, my love." Amy's voice was slightly scratchy, as it always was first thing.

"Sleep well?"

"That last hour…hoo. That was the best sleep ever."

Jo grinned knowingly. "A good orgasm always has that effect."

"Damn right." Amy let go of her partner and headed for the coffeepot. Noting its contents were at just above half, she glanced up and registered the empty couch. "Darby's up already? What happened? Was there a fire?"

"She went for a walk."

"Seriously?"

"With Molly."

Amy pondered that information for several seconds before asking, "Should we be worried?"

Jo turned to look at her pointedly. "I've been wondering the same thing."

"There's definitely the whole crush issue going on. That's painfully obvious." Amy lowered her voice. "But now that Kristin's here...I don't want things to get uncomfortable. There's enough trouble in that relationship without Darby tossing herself into the mix—which we know she tends to do without thinking about the consequences."

"Maybe I should have a little heart-to-heart with my niece."

Amy held up a hand. "You know what? Let's leave it alone for now. Let's not create a problem that may not even exist."

Jo nodded, and a subtly reluctant tone crept into her voice. "Okay. For now. But we need to keep a close eye on things."

"Agreed."

❖

Laura sighed. It was the deep, God-I'm-comfortable sigh of a person snuggled in a warm bed with no earthly reason to get up until she damn well felt like it. Absently, she thought how much warmer the atmosphere seemed once Sophie left the room. Then she rolled her eyes, disappointed in herself for thinking such unfriendly things. The terrier roused himself from the crook of her knees and picked his way across the quilt to settle down against her chest.

"I never thought the next time I spooned in bed, it would be with a dog," she said with amusement, burying her nose in the now-clean and soft fur at the top of his head.

She'd waited until late afternoon yesterday to be sure his system was sufficiently warm and healthy before subjecting him to the much-needed bath. He surprised her by not struggling or creating problems.

He just stood in the water, ears back flat against his head to express his disapproval, and let her shampoo his wiry hair. Now, he smelled like peaches.

Laura didn't know a lot about dogs and there was a large part of her that was afraid to get too attached to this one. It was the reason she hadn't given him any sort of name yet other than "little guy" or "hey, buddy." He had to belong to somebody. Wouldn't his owner be missing him by now? At the same time, she hoped nobody ever came looking. She'd never felt such unconditional love before and she was certain it was something she could get used to pretty damn quickly. The thought of him inhabiting her half of the duplex with her was not unpleasant.

"Be careful with the terriers," Jo had warned her, handing her one of the extra leashes and collars she'd found in the basement. "They're great dogs, but they tend to run." At Laura's questioning expression, Jo had elaborated. "They're bred to hunt vermin...squirrels, chipmunks, moles, rabbits. They use their noses and their ears and when they put that nose to the ground, they don't pay much attention to anything else. My uncle raised Westies. They were damn adorable and loving, but they couldn't be trusted off the leash. They'd be gone like little white shots."

Laura inhaled his cleanliness one last time before speaking to her newfound friend. "We should probably get up, huh, buddy? Do you have to pee? I do."

"So...why kindergarten?"

Molly took the time to honestly think about the question. She and Darby had been strolling for nearly an hour, arm in arm, walking over their own tracks, and there had yet to be a lull in the conversation. Molly was surprised to admit that she was thoroughly enjoying herself and couldn't remember the last time she felt so relaxed.

"It's the perfect age for molding," she said matter-of-factly. "For the most part, my students are too young to have been jaded by the world yet. If they've got decent parents, then the kids are usually still respectful of authority and of each other. They don't discriminate against each other because of race or money or gender. I get them before the real world does and I hope in the short span of time they're with me, I can teach them something to help them grow into good people."

Darby looked at her in amazement. "Wow."

"What?"

"That's…" Darby shrugged and shook her head, at a loss. "I'm just so impressed."

"By what?"

Darby bumped Molly playfully with her shoulder. "By you, dorkball. That was the perfect explanation. That's what every education student should say when asked why they want to be a teacher. You know? You didn't say 'so I can have summers off,' or something similarly superficial. You said something meaningful. I admire that. I admire you."

Molly blushed, feeling inexplicably proud at the words Darby bestowed upon her. "Well, you couldn't pay me enough to teach fourth or fifth grade. That's when brats happen."

"Do you want to have kids of your own?"

Molly shook her head. "I don't think so. It's crossed my mind, especially as I get older and the clock starts to tick a bit louder. But teaching is exhausting and I don't think I'd have the energy to deal with kids all day and then come home to my own. Maybe I'm simply not cut out for motherhood."

"I don't believe that. I think you'd be a great mother."

Molly squeezed Darby's arm. "Thanks. What about you? Do you want kids?"

Darby released a deep breath, watching the vapor dissipate in the chilly morning air. "I think I might. I'm not sure yet." She glanced at Molly with a twinkle in her eyes. "I do know that I don't want to do the carrying. No way do I want to be pregnant."

Molly laughed. "Really? If I wanted kids, I think I *would* do the carrying."

"Seriously? Gaining all that weight, having to pee all the time, not being able to sleep, constant backaches, weird midnight cravings? Why would you want to suffer through all of that?"

Molly shrugged. "Nine months goes by fast. I just think it would be amazing to have a little life growing inside me, that's all."

"Pregnant women are beautiful, I'll give you that."

When Molly looked up, the house was in view and she had a hard time believing they'd just kept walking. Three shrill barks broke the air as they cleared the woods into the open yard. She waved at Laura, who stood out in front of the house with the little terrier on a leash. He yipped again, his tail moving down each time, as if he were built like a water pump and pushing his tail toward the ground caused the bark to come out his mouth.

"Morning," Laura said with a smile as they approached. She rubbed her hands over her upper arms, wishing she'd been smart enough to grab a jacket on the way out the door. The long-sleeve T-shirt wasn't doing much to keep her warm. "Out for an early walk?"

"Nothing wakes you up like twenty-degree weather," Darby responded. Glancing at the dog, she asked, "Taking his sweet time, is he?"

"Apparently, the way it works is that he has to sniff every snowflake first. Who knew? I assume we'll get around to peeing in an hour or two."

Molly squatted near the dog and received a heartfelt lick for her efforts, the terrier's tail wagging happily back and forth. Giggling, she patted his head, then took off her own coat and set it over Laura's shoulders. "You're going to catch pneumonia standing out here like that."

Everybody looked up as Molly and Darby entered the cabin. The atmosphere buzzed with the goings-on of morning, the complete opposite of the hushed quiet when they'd left just an hour earlier. A fresh pot of coffee was brewing on the counter and Amy stood at the stove flipping pancakes. The fire was crackling with warmth.

Sophie, clad in plaid flannel pants and a red sweatshirt, sat on the floor in front of the television shooting at zombies before they had a chance to eat her, leaning to her left and then her right as she pushed the fire button as fast as she could. Muttered swear words could be heard every so often from her end of the room. Grinning, Darby ripped off her coat and boots so she could scoot over next to her opponent. In doing so, she missed the expression Kristin tossed her way from the dining-room table, a combination of suspicion, hurt, and anger. Molly, however, caught it.

Pasting a smile on her face, she shed her own boots and joined Jo and Kristin at the dining room table. Kristin fiddled with her coffee mug, studying its contents.

"How was the walk?" Jo asked.

"Brisk. Invigorating. It's so gorgeous here."

Amy leaned over the table and set down a plate with a large stack of pancakes on it. "That's why we love it." Turning her head to be heard by those in the living room, she announced, "Breakfast is served. Come and get it."

"See any deer?" Jo asked.

"No, but we saw several birds and a rabbit. Lots of deer tracks, though."

Darby appeared and began tossing pancakes onto a plate. "Aunt Amy, your salt licks are getting low."

Amy nodded from her post at the stove. "I think I might make a quick trip into town today. I'll pick up a couple more while I'm there."

"Can I go with you?" Molly asked.

"'A quick trip into town?' What is this, *Little House on the Prairie*?" Sophie asked from where she still sat on the floor, a teasing tone in her voice. "Can I tag along? Are we taking the wagon and horses?"

"I think we could probably squeeze you in," Amy said, teasing back by infusing her voice with a slightly Southern accent. "I hear the general store has this newfangled thing called 'sliced bread.'"

Sophie laughed and tried the same accent. "But...should I be worried about how all the white folks will look upon a single black woman? Especially one as devastatingly attractive as myself?"

"It's a chance we'll have to take," Amy responded.

"Of course," Sophie continued, "in this day and age, I should probably be more worried about being a lesbian. I wonder if our illustrious president would be happier if I just wore a sign that says 'Second-Class Citizen' and be done with it."

Snorts of agreement traveled the room.

"Don't you worry your pretty little heads about going into town," Darby said, jumping in. "I'll protect you."

"Oh, no, you won't," Jo countered. "You're staying here with me. We've got a couple things that need to be done outside and I could use your help."

Anyone who bothered to look in from the outside at that moment would most likely have laughed at the polar opposite expressions on the faces of Darby and Kristin. Darby looked crushed, like a small child who was just told Christmas had been cancelled and Santa wasn't coming. Kristin was smugly satisfied, like she'd just been informed that all her wishes would come true, but she couldn't tell anybody. Those were the expressions Laura saw when she came through the front door with the terrier, and she *did* laugh.

"Okay, what did I miss?" she asked, unclipping the terrier's leash. He promptly wandered over near the television and sat down next to Sophie, who pretended not to notice him.

"We were just planning the day," Jo informed her. "Amy, Molly, and Sophie are taking a trip into town. Want to go?"

Laura pondered for a second, casting a glance in Sophie's direction, thankfully only seeing the back of her head. "I think I'll stay here. I'm really enjoying my book. Plus, I should probably make some phone calls about him." She gestured with her eyes toward the terrier, who set his chin gently on Sophie's thigh.

"Okay, okay," Sophie muttered, massaging the dog's head. "Fine. I'll pet you. I'm about to get killed anyway. I think you jinxed me."

Laura smiled in spite of herself and headed to the table. Sophie wandered in a few minutes later, the dog following on her heels.

"Game over?" Darby asked smugly.

Amy watched with smiling eyes as six of the loves of her life ate, chatted, and joked. Despite her loyalty to Molly, her heart went out to Kristin as she noticed Molly offering very little of herself to her partner but laughing and teasing with Darby. She glanced at Sophie and Laura, who stood next to one another, not engaging each other in any sort of conversation at all. Their shoulders were actually touching, and it struck her immediately what a stunning couple they made, blonde and brunette, blue eyes and brown, pale skin and dark. She took it all in for several moments before standing behind Jo, who sat at the head of the table.

Laying a hand on her wife's shoulder, Amy held up her juice glass and said, "I'd like to offer a toast." When the table quieted and everyone had a mug or glass in hand, she continued. "To friends, without which we'd all be nowhere and lonely."

Glasses were clinked together. Sophie peered at her own. "Hey, shouldn't this be a mimosa? The holidays aren't officially over yet, are they?"

Jo and Amy grinned at each other, and Amy said, "I think we can spare one of the New Year's Eve bottles of champagne for this morning, don't you?"

SOPHIE

The ride "into town" wasn't nearly as long or desolate as it had sounded. In about twenty minutes, Sophie pulled her Jeep into the small town of Westover. "Tiny village" was a more accurate description, as it basically consisted of one street that ran down the middle of town, past the post office, the hardware store, the bank, the gas station, and the grocery store.

"Wow," Molly said from the backseat. "What a booming metropolis."

Amy chuckled. "It works for us when we forget to bring something from home. The people are nice and everything's cheap." She opened the passenger side door and slid to the ground, slinging her purse over her shoulder. "Coming?"

Sophie and Molly followed her into Hindman's, taking in the three lanes of cash registers and the total of nine aisles of groceries. A rotund man in a green apron waved in Amy's direction.

"Morning, Ms. Forrester."

"Hi there, Fred. How's life treating you?" Amy responded, a friendly sparkle in her blue eyes as she picked a blue plastic handbasket from the stack near the door.

"Can't complain."

"That's good to hear. Tell Connie I said hello."

"Will do."

Sophie and Molly exchanged glances. "My God, we *are* in Walnut Grove," Sophie whispered, causing Molly to clamp a hand over her own mouth to keep her laughter from bursting forth.

"Come on, you two," Amy said with a good-natured rolling of her eyes at the teasing of her friends.

Sophie followed Molly as they headed toward the produce, taking in her surroundings and especially the women in the area—the young blonde behind register three was particularly attractive, her friendly smile inviting and her long neck decidedly lickable. It was something Sophie had recently noticed about herself: she seemed to be constantly checking out the women. Not leering. She was too polite to be that obvious. But she looked. More than that, she liked to look. And more than *that*, she fantasized. A lot.

Sometimes, she surprised herself with the quickness of her imagination. She could look at a woman across a bookstore, for example, and no sooner did she register the fact that said woman was very attractive than her brain would immediately toss her an image of the woman naked and beneath her, head thrown back, throat exposed, voice straining. Sophie's face would flush a deep crimson and her heart would race and she'd look around in embarrassment, absolutely positive somebody nearby would be looking at her in disgust, as if the pictures from her head were projected onto the wall like a filmstrip from elementary school. This type of thing didn't start happening until two months after Kelly had left. Somewhere deep inside, Sophie knew it was her brain's way of telling her there were other fish in the sea and it was time to start noticing that fact, but she still resisted, feeling somehow unfaithful. Which was ridiculous and she knew it.

As if to drive the point home, Sophie found herself staring at Molly's ass as Molly walked in front of her. When she realized what she was doing, she nearly gasped out loud, and veered off in a different direction to collect herself. Finding the meat counter at the back of the store, she leaned against the glass and chewed on her bottom lip while two sides battled in her head, one telling her there was nothing at all wrong with looking and appreciating and the other side telling her she was a big fat pervert. She found herself zeroing in on the conversation between the butcher behind the counter and the heavyset, gravelly-voiced man in front of it some six or seven feet away. She feigned careful study of the Virginia baked ham and fresh lamb chops, hoping her eavesdropping wasn't totally obvious.

"She'd better hope she never comes back, I'll tell you that," the heavy guy said.

He was the epitome of the word "redneck" as far as Sophie was concerned and she almost laughed at his presence in the store because he was exactly what she expected the place to be filled with. His green and white John Deere baseball cap was filthy with greasy fingerprints. His flannel shirt was threadbare and worn at the cuffs, and the camouflage vest over the top of it created a color and pattern clash of eye-assaulting proportions. His battle-worn Levi's hung too low, probably due to the protrusion of his enormous beer belly, and she knew that if he squatted down or bent over, she'd be treated to way more of his most-likely-flabby ass than she ever wanted to see. His work boots were crusted with mud beneath the wetness from the snow and his hands were dirty. He was unshowered, unshaven, and reeked of cigarettes even across the distance between them.

The butcher nodded and gave a sort of grunt of agreement, a sound that told Sophie he didn't really want to be sucked into a conversation with this guy. Contrary to the redneck, the butcher was neat and clean, his face smooth, his silver hair precisely combed. He pulled four plump pork chops from the case and plopped them on the scale as the redneck went on.

"No note, no phone call, nothin'. Bitch just took her clothes and left."

"Imagine that," the butcher said.

"Didn't even take the damn dog. Yappy little thing ain't worth a damn anyway. Terriers ain't no hunting dogs."

"She left the dog, even? Boy, she must have really wanted to get the hell away, huh?"

The redneck completely missed the sarcasm in the butcher's tone, but Sophie caught it and suppressed a grin. The next thing the redneck said caught her attention, though.

"Well, I locked the damn worthless runt out and I haven't seen him since. Went running into the trees and prolly got eat by coyotes by now. Stupid thing. I ain't spending my hard-earned money on dog food, that's for sure. He can fend for himself in the wild for all I care."

"You locked that little thing out in this weather?" The butcher stopped what he was doing and stared straight at the redneck, accusation in his eyes. "What the hell's the matter with you, Carl?"

For the first time in the conversation, Carl faltered. Just slightly. "Well, I...you know, I didn't want the damn dog to begin with."

The butcher shook his head in apparent disgust. "You're a piece of work."

"Hey, *I* was the one who was left, here." Indignation colored Carl's tone. "My wife just ran out on me without so much as a good-bye. A little sympathy would be nice."

The butcher nodded as he tossed the white paper-wrapped package on the counter. "I'm sure the black eye she had last week had nothing to do with her leaving." He turned away, effectively ending the conversation.

Carl stood still for several seconds, apparently searching for some sort of comeback. Finding nothing, he grunted, snatched his pack of chops off the counter, and took his leave, lumbering up the aisle in his work boots, passing Amy and Molly as they came to take his place at the meat counter. Sophie watched in disgust as he tracked the two with a leering look in his eyes.

"You okay?" Molly asked.

Sophie blinked, filing away the information she'd just acquired regarding the dog. "Yeah. Yeah, I'm good." She gestured at Amy who was in conversation with the butcher. "I thought we came here to pick up a few little things. Don't tell me she's buying more food. There's enough in that house for all of us to survive for a month."

Molly grinned. "She's asking if there's more bacon in the back. The cooler on the wall is empty and she's afraid we'll run out."

Sophie snorted. "And what? There won't be anything else to eat?"

"You know how she is," Molly said with a shrug.

"You two do know that I'm standing right here, right?" Amy asked. "That I can actually hear you?"

The butcher grinned as he went to check his freezer in the back.

When they exited the store, the snowflakes had thickened in the air, falling slowly like fluffy cotton balls from the sky. Sophie started the Jeep, then ordered her passengers to sit tight inside while she brushed it off, feeling the snow settle gently in her hair. She looked off into the distance where the backdrop was nothing but trees. It was quite beautiful. She wasn't necessarily fond of the winters in upstate New

York. As a matter of fact, she liked to complain about them as much as the next native and was just as familiar with all the jokes. *There are only two seasons here: winter and construction.* But this kind of snowfall, quiet and pretty, almost made winter seem worthwhile.

Amy and Molly were chatting about one of Molly's students as Sophie climbed back into the Jeep. Her thoughts turned to Kelly, as they so often did, and she remembered how much Kelly had hated the snow and the winter. She complained incessantly—she was freezing, she was bored, she was fat. No amount of reassurance from Sophie ever seemed to make things any better. Sophie tried to get them involved in things, knowing activity was the key to surviving the cold, gray season. She signed them up for a volleyball league, a racquetball league, a book discussion group, and a movie club. Nothing seemed to satisfy Kelly until the gym membership Sophie got her for her birthday. That's where Kelly met *her* and that's when Sophie's life headed for the crapper.

No good deed goes unpunished.

Her thoughts turned to Laura's husband. Sophie felt a weird sort of kinship with him, having her own experience of her partner cheating on her right under her nose. She wondered if he had suspected anything at all, if he'd felt her slipping away from him and had no idea how to stop her departure. Had he suddenly felt like a spectator in his wife's life? Like she was doing her own thing and he just happened to be there? Had he watched her sleep at night, wishing he could see into her dreams, wondered if he made even the smallest appearance in them? Had he wondered what to say and how to say it, suddenly and inexplicably uncomfortable with everyday conversation with her? Would he have given his very soul to have things back the way they were the first time he'd felt Laura's love for him? Sophie wondered if he knew he was losing her before she actually went and if it had been a tangible pain in his chest, so piercing he'd often felt he might be having a heart attack.

She pressed her leather-clad hand to her own chest and rubbed it absently as she drove, remembering what it had felt like. It had been months before the constant ache had subsided, and still, every now and then, a particular recollection could bring it screaming back. Not nearly as often as it used to come, which was a good sign, she knew, but the memory of it was enough to make her stomach clench in anticipation and fear.

"What do you think, Sophie?"

Molly's voice startled her and she blinked rapidly as if returning from some sort of trance. She glanced into the rearview mirror and met inquisitive green eyes.

Enough reminiscing, she scolded herself, annoyed that she'd allowed herself to drift so far. "I…" She cleared her throat. "I'm sorry. I was daydreaming. What were you saying?"

KRISTIN

Kristin watched as Darby set a semicircular log on its end on the huge stump behind the garage. Jo swung the axe with the precision of Paul Bunyan and the log split neatly in two. Kristin picked up the two pieces and stacked them with the others on the neat pile along the edge of the woods. It was mindless physical labor, and Kristin was glad to have something like that to occupy her. It was perfect... until Darby started talking.

"So, Kristin," she said, her breath billowing vaporously in the air. "What's your company do?"

"Advertising," Kristin answered as succinctly as possible.

"And you are?"

"Vice president."

"Nice."

Kristin found herself counting the erratic clicks as Darby spoke. Finally, she couldn't hold it in any longer. "Doesn't that thing annoy you?"

"What thing?" Darby looked confused.

Kristin pointed to her own tongue. "That thing."

"Oh, this?" Darby stuck her tongue out. "Nah. You get used to it."

"The constant...banging against your teeth doesn't drive you nuts?"

Darby shook her head and shot her a grin full of mischief. "It's worth it."

Kristin looked confused. "Worth what?"

Darby's eyes twinkled. "Never been to bed with a woman with a tongue ring, have you, Kristin?" Then she winked.

"You know," Jo cut in smoothly as Kristin blushed, "Kristin started on the ground floor at her company." Her voice was tinted with a layer of pride that surprised Kristin. "She joined the company at the bottom of the totem pole. Now she's almost at the top." The axe swung and hit its mark with a satisfying crack.

"Wow," Darby said with a nod. "Impressive."

"That's the problem with the younger generation these days," Kristin commented as she stacked. "They don't understand what it means to work their way up. They want to *start* at the top."

"Yeah, but if the top is what's offered…" Darby let the sentence dangle.

"It's usually not."

"But sometimes it is. That's how it was for me at Langford." She set another log down on the stump. "I mean, it wasn't the *top* top, but it was far from the bottom."

"You work at Langford?" Kristin tried to hide the envy that colored her tone.

"Only for a few weeks. I didn't like it."

"You didn't like…wait. You mean you quit? You quit *Langford*?" She turned to Jo. "She quit *Langford*?"

Jo shrugged and swung.

"You don't get a job at a company as prestigious as Langford and then just leave. What's the matter with you?" Kristin gaped at Darby in disbelief.

"Why not?"

"Because you don't. Jobs there are too hard to come by. When they're offered you snap them up."

"Why?"

Kristin caught the shadow of a smirk on Darby's face and suspected that she was enjoying needling her. To her own dismay, though, she was unable to leave it alone. "Why? *Why?* Because, that's why. It's Langford. They've got a great setup. You'd move up the ladder steadily. You'd be pretty much set for life."

"But I wasn't happy."

"I bet you were making a ton of money. Right out of college. God, that's amazing. Most people would give their right arm for an opportunity like that."

"I was doing okay. But you're not listening. I wasn't *happy*."

Kristin groaned in frustration. "So what? Who is? If the money's good and the benefits are good and there's opportunity for advancement, you stick it out for a while."

Darby blinked at her and made a face. "That makes no sense. Why on earth would I 'stick it out' someplace if I hated it?"

"It's called responsibility. You pay your bills, you take care of your partner, you put money away for the future."

Darby's expression grew almost smug. "Wow, Molly was right. Money, money, money. Is that all that's important to you? Jesus, all you need is a penis and you'd be the typical American white male. Are you a Republican, too? I bet you voted for Bush, didn't you?"

Kristin's blood began to boil and she was almost thankful when Jo stepped between the two of them. "Okay, okay. That's enough." She shot a warning look at Darby. Kristin saw Darby's eye glimmer like she was enjoying the act of pushing Kristin's buttons.

"I'm going inside," Kristin said quietly, then took her leave and tromped through the snow to the house.

Molly was right…

What the hell did that mean? Had Molly been talking about her—about their situation—behind her back? To *Darby* of all people? The thought made her stomach churn with the unpleasantness of betrayal.

Money, money, money. Is that all that's important to you?

Was it? Kristin shook her head. Of course not. Of course that wasn't it. A lot of things were important to her, she just needed money to take the best care of them that she could. That only made sense. What did being happy have to do with making a living?

Kristin stopped in her tracks as if she'd been slapped by the ridiculousness of the statement.

"Jesus Christ, I hate that little bitch," she muttered to the snow at her feet.

❖

Inside, Laura was sitting at the dining room table, the cordless phone in front of her and the terrier curled up at her feet. The dog lifted his little brown head at the sound of the front door and gave a halfhearted yip.

"Hey," Kristin said as she shed her boots and coat. "Any luck?"

Laura grimaced and shook her head. "The nearest animal shelter is closed this week for the holiday. I called the police station to see if anybody had reported a dog missing, and nobody has."

"Maybe you've got yourself a new pet." Kristin ruffled the dog's fur.

Laura looked the slightest bit uncomfortable with that idea. "Somebody's got to be missing him. Look how sweet he is."

Kristin sympathized with the worried look in Laura's eyes. "It'll work out."

"I just think about somebody knowing he's gone and how scared they must be for him."

"He was very lucky to be found by you. Look at it that way. Without you, he'd be a pup-sicle by now."

Laura smiled at the dumb play on words. "I suppose you're right. I just can't help feeling like I'm stealing him, you know?"

"Think of it as dog-sitting." Kristin smiled and touched Laura's shoulder, hoping she was making her feel the tiniest bit better. Though she couldn't explain why, it bothered her to see Laura uncertain. She had such a great smile—those dimples were to die for—and Kristin just wanted her to smile again.

Glancing up and out the window, she saw Sophie's Jeep turn into the driveway. "Looks like the gang is back." It surprised her to realize that she was happy to see Molly return, had missed her while she was gone. The thought brought a smile to her lips, one that soon faded as Molly exited the Jeep and, rather than coming into the house, strolled behind the garage and stood chatting with Jo and Darby.

Kristin tried to swallow her disappointment. For the first time since her arrival, she seriously wished she hadn't come. She could be at home right now. Better yet, she could be in her office working on something that would take her mind off this crap. Why be here with people she didn't like? With people who didn't like her? Somewhere in the deep recesses of her mind, she knew that was a gross overgeneralization, but she didn't care.

Darby didn't like her and she certainly didn't like Darby. *Christ, my own wife doesn't even like me anymore*, she thought with bitterness. She didn't know Laura or Sophie well, so they didn't count as friends. Amy and Jo had always been sweet to her, but they'd been Molly's friends before Kristin had come along. During her stay, she'd felt their distance, felt that they were keeping her at arms' length. Jo's comments about her rise at work had been the first inkling she'd had that maybe she wasn't number one on their shit list.

Because we're all lesbians, we have to automatically like each other? Who made up that rule?

She headed upstairs to her room and sat heavily on the bed, feeling the stress drench her as though somebody had come along and dumped it over her head in icy, liquid form. Her heart began to race and a searing pain pierced her behind her right eye.

"Damn it."

The experience was almost familiar now. She tried to relax, to calm herself, to talk herself down, so to speak, as she'd been doing for the past six months since the panic attacks had started. Part of her knew she should probably go see a doctor about them, but logic always won out. She was tired. She was stressed. She was overworked. Was there a business executive in this day and age who *didn't* have panic attacks like this?

She leaned forward, dropped her head between her knees, and rocked, counting slowly from one to ten. Tears sprang into her eyes, which annoyed her more than anything else. She wanted nothing more than for Molly to come up the stairs, find her in pain, and wrap her up in her loving embrace. Kristin couldn't remember the last time they'd hugged for no other reason than because they loved one another.

"Molly," she whimpered as she stared at the braided rug beneath her feet.

But Molly was outside. Talking to Darby.

"Damn it," she said again, but this time, it came out as more of a whimper, and one half-sob escaped her lips before a distinct buzzing sound filled the air. Kristin whipped her head up—a bad idea judging from the way the room spun for several seconds. Her Blackberry was vibrating on the dresser.

Excellent, she thought as she pressed the palms of her hands against her throbbing temples and squeezed her eyes shut. Something to focus on was just what she needed. It was what she always needed when she felt like this. Taking a deep breath to steady herself, she got slowly to her feet and crossed to the dresser. She picked up the Blackberry and did her best to infuse her voice with a clipped, professional tone she didn't feel.

"Kristin Collins."

She listened, trying her hardest to focus on her client's voice while she massaged her forehead with icy fingertips. She didn't register the footsteps coming up the stairs.

Nothing's Trivial

Jo took a swig from the Heineken bottle as she watched the others settle into seats around the living room. She sighed inwardly, wondering what the hell her beloved had been thinking when she broke the group into teams. Jo totally understood the splitting up of partners—that was standard practice in any game—but teaming Molly with Darby was something she herself would never have done. She made a mental note to have a talk with Amy later that night, assuming the game went well and nobody was beaten to death with the game board. Then she was thinking that the discussion with Darby they'd debated earlier might actually be in order after all.

She arranged the question cards in piles she preferred on the TV tray in front of her—after all, she was the Quiz Master, a name she liked to call herself; she'd much rather ask the questions than play the game any day. Scanning a few of the queries, she let her thoughts dwell on her niece. Much as she liked to admit that it was amusing to watch her push Kristin's buttons—and she'd become a pro at it in an alarmingly short time—there was a line that Darby was coming dangerously close to crossing. Her attention to Molly was bordering on inappropriate. It was one thing to be harmlessly flirty—hell, they were all like that every now and then—but when it was pretty apparent that a couple was having issues, that type of behavior was unacceptable and the best course of respectable action was to step back.

Jo blamed Darby's age as well as her reckless personality for her failure to realize these facts. Or did she realize them, but not care? Jo was a little bit shocked to find herself feeling sympathy for Kristin. Molly wasn't cutting her any slack at all. Granted, Jo didn't live in their house, didn't see their day-to-day interaction, and might very possibly be missing something big. But from what she saw here in the past two days, Molly held the reins, pretty much all the cards, and pulled every string, and still she seemed miserable. Was it possible that she had no idea? No clue that she had all the control? That Kristin had handed it all over, maybe not even knowing it?

Across the room, seated on the couch, Sophie felt her nostrils flare as if her disappointment used them as an alternative route for escape. Amy had paired her with the cheater. *What the fuck?* She grabbed her glass and took a big gulp, then nearly choked. She'd mixed it herself and the ratio of vodka to tonic was distinctly backward. She managed to hold back the coughing fit, feeling her eyes water and her face redden, but nobody noticed, thank God.

Laura sat close to her on the couch, their thighs pressed together and Sophie caught herself inhaling deeply, taking in the scent of Laura's perfume, letting it absorb deep into her lungs. She absently wondered what brand it was. She tried to watch Laura out of the corner of her eye, peripherally without turning her head. It wasn't easy and gave her a headache almost immediately—or was that from the previous two drinks? God, she was going to be useless during this game.

Something she'd noticed about Laura that alternately softened Sophie and annoyed the crap out of her was the perpetual smile. It didn't matter what she was doing...eating, watching TV, reading, on the phone with various animal shelters...Laura always seemed to have a very slight grin, making her dimples almost constantly apparent. It gave her an air of friendliness, of gentle kindness. Sophie snorted aloud. *She should have to have the word "adulteress" tattooed on her forehead,* she thought with bitterness. *As a warning for future potential partners.*

She sipped again, squeezing her eyes shut for a second as she swallowed, and made a mental note to ease up on the next drink. When they'd returned from their shopping trip earlier in the afternoon, Laura had been feverishly scanning the phone book for more places to call about the dog. Sophie didn't know why, but she neglected to mention the guy at the store. It was pretty obvious that the terrier now lying possessively across Laura's feet was his, but something had kept Sophie from sharing that knowledge. As if sensing her train of thought, the dog shifted slightly and rested its chin on one of Sophie's socked feet.

Sophie ignored her self-deprecation. She told herself she enjoyed the worried look in Laura's eyes. She told herself it served her right to be uncertain. *Let her sweat it out.* She sipped again, willing the vodka to dull the realization that she was simply being mean for the sake of meanness, and tried not to feel the warmth radiating from Laura's leg against hers. Instead, she turned to her left and asked Kristin if she was any good at Trivial Pursuit.

Kristin blinked rapidly as if coming out of a trance. Dragging her pretty blue eyes away from Molly and Darby, who were giggling together across the room as they sat on the hearth, she turned to Sophie. "Depends on the category," she said, forcing a smile. "I'm sort of a science geek."

"Me, too," Sophie said. "And I like the geography questions."

"Good, because I stink at those." Laura joined the conversation. "I'm pretty good with the literature and entertainment categories, though. We might do okay."

Kristin leaned forward so she could see Laura around Sophie. "Molly rocks at entertainment. She might give you a run for your money."

Laura grinned at the challenge, her dimples deepening. "We'll see."

Over on the hearth, Darby was enjoying making Molly laugh as they bumped shoulders. "How's your drink?" she asked.

"Still half full," Molly responded as she peered into her rum and Coke.

"And you're laughing this much at my jokes? Man, you must be a lightweight."

Molly smiled at the truth of the statement. Kristin always teased her for her inability to hold her alcohol. She looked across the room at her girlfriend, but she was lost in conversation with Sophie and Laura. She turned her attention back to Darby, who was talking.

"Are you good at this game?"

Molly shook her head. "Not really."

They held each other's gaze in silence for several long seconds before they both burst out laughing.

"Terrific," Darby said. "We're going to get our asses kicked." She tousled Molly's hair playfully.

Amy entered from the kitchen, handed a new beer to Jo, another to Laura, then plopped down on the floor at Kristin's feet. Leaning back against Kristin's shins, she tipped her head backward and asked, "Ready, partner?"

Kristin had managed not to glare at Darby when she touched Molly's hair, but she was presently entertaining a very satisfying fantasy that consisted of breaking every one of Darby's fingers, one at a time. Slowly.

"Okay," Jo announced. "Here we go. Team One, you go first."

Molly leaned forward and rolled the dice, then moved their slice of pie the requisite number of spaces on the board that sat on the coffee table. "Green," she said.

"The category is Innovations," Jo told her. "What company, the makers of Rogaine, genetically altered a mouse to be bald?"

Molly and Darby put their heads together, whispering. Kristin gritted her teeth.

Darby looked up. "That would be Upjohn, Alex."

"That is correct."

Darby and Molly high-fived each other. Molly's smile was wide and sparkling as she rolled again. Kristin's stomach clenched and heaved as they answered another question correctly and slapped hands. Kristin exhaled in relief when they got the next one wrong, thinking she couldn't possibly take any more demonstrations of team celebration without going completely insane.

Sophie rolled for Team Two.

"The category is News," Jo said in her serious game-show-host voice.

Laura leaned forward and caught Amy's eye. "She gets into this, doesn't she?"

Amy snorted. "You have no idea."

"Here's your question," Jo continued. "Who was assassinated on November 4, 1995, in Kings of Israel Square?"

Laura looked at Sophie, eyebrows raised.

"Rabin, wasn't it?" Sophie offered.

"You think?"

"I do." Sophie nodded her certainty.

"I trust you," Laura said with a gentle smile. "Go ahead."

Sophie was surprised to find herself returning the smile. Then she focused on Jo and said, "Yitzhak Rabin."

"That is correct."

Laura bumped Sophie affectionately. "Nice work, partner."

They rolled the dice again. "Brown," Sophie said.

"The category is The Written Word. What beloved family dog died after rescuing little April in the comic strip *For Better or For Worse*?"

"Oh, God, I know this one," Laura responded. "I cried for a week." She turned to Sophie, who made a gesture that said "go ahead." "Farley."

"That is correct," Jo stated.

Laura bent forward to pet the terrier and Sophie patted Laura's back in congratulations. When the little voice in her head screamed, "You're touching the cheater!" she told it to shut the hell up.

Just over an hour later, all three teams were in the home stretch. Amy had carried her team, Kristin being unfocused and not answering a single question correctly, much to her deep consternation. Jo felt sorry for her, knowing that The Molly and Darby Show was bothering her a great deal. Sophie and Laura worked surprisingly well together, a fact that did not surprise Amy at all. Molly and Darby were out in front, though, followed closely by Sophie and Laura. Molly rolled a three that put them in the winner's circle.

"Okay, Team One," Jo said. "Answer this question correctly and you will be the winners. The category is Stage and Screen. Here is the question: What comics-page 'girl reporter' did Brooke Shields bring to the silver screen in 1989?"

Darby blinked and looked at Molly, whose face was scrunched up in a semblance of concentration. Laura began to hum the theme song to Jeopardy, which made the others chuckle.

"I have no fucking idea," Darby muttered to her team partner. "Not a clue."

Laura laughed. "What were you in 1989? Eight years old? Nine?"

Molly held up a hand, silencing them. "Hang on. I know this…" She stared hard at the floor, while Darby and Kristin both watched. Even the terrier had his eyes open and focused on Molly. Finally, Molly flinched as though she'd been poked and looked up.

"Brenda Starr."

"That is correct," Jo commended.

Darby gave a hoot of joy and jumped up. "Yes!" She did a little dance around the room while most of the others laughed and the terrier yipped. "That's my partner," she said, pointing at Molly. She pulled her to her feet and made her dance, too. "That's my partner!"

No, that's my *partner*, Kristin thought, feeling nauseated. She stood up and stepped over Amy. "Excuse me. I've got to use the ladies' room," she said quietly, heading upstairs.

Molly watched her go, her grin dimming several watts. Jo also watched. Turning her head, she made eye contact with her wife, whose lips formed a straight line. Then she shifted her gaze to pin Darby with a disapproving glare.

Darby didn't notice and continued to dance.

Friday, December 30

MOLLY

God, it was early.

Molly didn't even think the birds were awake yet. Nobody else was. She'd managed to sneak into her winter attire and out of the house making very little sound. She wasn't sure what time it was, but she guessed somewhere between five and six in the morning—closer to five, judging by the fact that Jo wasn't even up yet.

There was no sound but the crunching of her boots in the snow, and when she stood still, the silence was almost eerie. It was still dark and she wasn't terribly familiar with the area, so she wandered out behind the garage where she knew there was a big stump to sit upon and plopped herself down on it with a world-weary sigh.

"What the hell happened to my life?" she whispered into the stillness, the puff of her breath visible as it drifted away into the atmosphere.

Kristin hadn't said a single word to her for the rest of the night. When she didn't return right away from the bathroom, Molly went up to check on her. She was already under the covers in the bed and—Molly was sure—feigning sleep. Molly knew they were going to have to have a serious discussion, more likely several of them, but she just hadn't had the energy last night. She'd had a little too much rum, and the idea of arguing around and around in a pointless circle with Kristin was just too exhausting to entertain. Instead, she'd closed the door and gone back downstairs to laugh and joke with the others, telling them that Kristin wasn't feeling well and had decided to retire early.

It was something she felt decidedly guilty about now and it was probably the main reason she hadn't slept. The bed was cozy and comfortable and she'd sensed the familiar warmth of Kristin's body heat next to her and still, she'd never felt so cold and lonely in her life.

Now she was out in the dead of winter, in the freezing dark of the early morning, because she couldn't stand lying there for one more second. At least if she was moving, she'd feel like maybe she was getting the tiniest bit of exercise. She stood up again and began walking a large circle around the garage.

Am I being too hard on her?

It was a thought she had often, too often for her liking. It forced her to stop heaping all the blame for the failing relationship on top of Kristin and take some of it herself. Last night was a perfect example. Rather than settling into the bed next to her partner and talking about what was bothering her, what was bothering them, she had run away. It's what she did best and she inwardly cursed her mother for teaching her the fine art of never facing a problem head-on. *If you ignore it, it's not there.*

She loved her mother to pieces, but the woman was queen when it came to avoiding conflict. Oh, she'd be upset about something, lose sleep over it for weeks, even give the cold shoulder to the source, but she'd never face it directly. Her mother deferred all decisions to her husband without even knowing it. When Molly's father asked his wife for her input, her most common answer was to shrug and wave a dismissive hand and say, "Oh, I don't care," even when she did.

So her father was left to make all the decisions and to hear about it later when he made one that his wife suddenly didn't agree with. Molly had watched this behavior over and over as a child, as a teenager, and as a young adult. She vowed never ever to be that way, especially in her relationship. Yet here she stood, in the black of predawn in the middle of winter, pacing in the snow rather than facing her problems, hoping they'd all just disappear on their own if she ignored them. She was a carbon copy of her marshmallow of a mother.

The most frustrating thing, though, was that she *knew* it. She knew it and yet she couldn't find a way to make herself stand up, to say what she felt, to act like her opinion counted, like it mattered. When she and Kristin had moved into their house a couple years back, they were painting their bedroom. Kristin had two paint chips from the hardware store—a soft lavender and an earthy khaki. She'd asked Molly which one she liked better.

Molly had looked at them both, shrugged, and responded, "Oh, I don't care. You pick."

Kristin picked the khaki, and now Molly hated the color of their bedroom and blamed Kristin for it.

In her defense, though, it wasn't all her own fault. Of that, she was well aware. When had Kristin's priorities gotten so out of whack? On her way out of the bedroom that morning, Molly had glared insidiously at the Blackberry on the dresser and her fingers had literally itched to pick it up and whip it across the room. She suspected she'd feel an enormous wave of satisfaction to see it shatter into a million pieces and fall to the floor. If Kristin gave her half the amount of attention she paid to that stupid piece of electronic equipment, they'd be two much happier women, of that she was sure.

That's why Molly couldn't regret that she'd been having so much fun with Darby over the past couple of days. Darby *listened* to her. Darby *looked* at her. Darby didn't seem to be thinking about her job when Molly was talking to her. She actually made eye contact and seemed genuinely interested in what Molly was saying. Molly felt like she got *all* of Darby's attention when they were talking, not just a certain percentage of it. It had been ages since she'd felt what it was like to be the focus of somebody else. Somebody like Kristin.

Darby also flirted with her mercilessly. Molly knew it was something she should probably put an end to, but if she was going to be honest with herself, she'd have to admit that part of her—a big part of her—was enjoying the green tint of jealousy that Kristin had been sporting.

That's right. There are still women who want me, even if you don't anymore.

She immediately felt guilty for the thought. The gut-wrenching truth was, plain and simple, she missed Kristin. She missed her so much, it was like a constant, physical ache in her body as well as her mind.

She shook her head and continued doing slow, easy laps around the garage, willing it to get lighter out so she could take the path through the woods without feeling like she was being swallowed by them. She rounded the back corner of the garage, so lost in her own thoughts that she ran straight into another body. A thick-mittened hand clamped over her mouth and muffled her startled scream, pulling her body close and holding her tightly.

"Shh. It's me," Darby whispered as she chuckled. "You want to wake up the whole house?"

"Jesus Christ," Molly hissed when Darby removed her hand. "You scared the living shit out of me."

"Sorry. I was sure you must have heard me coming; it's so quiet out."

Molly inhaled deeply, bidding her racing heart to slow down. "No. I didn't hear a thing. Lost in my own head, I guess."

"Well, still. I'm sorry I scared you." Darby laid a hand on her shoulder and Molly looked up at her. Her dark hair was tousled, but Molly was learning that it always looked that way. She was wearing jeans and Jo's ski jacket, so Molly suspected she'd dressed in a hurry. Flattery closed in on her as she realized that Darby had probably seen her outside and had quickly donned whatever clothing was available so she could join her in the chill morning air. Molly had wanted to be alone with her ruminations, but Darby's presence was not unwelcome.

"Penny for your thoughts," Darby said as they automatically continued on Molly's circular path.

Molly tucked her hand in the crook of Darby's elbow and tried for a smile, but felt it appear as a grimace instead. "Thanks."

"Want to talk about it?"

"There's not really a lot to say."

"Okay." Darby nodded and they walked.

After a few minutes of silence, Molly blurted, "I just don't know what to do, Darby. I don't know how I got here and I don't know how to fix it and I don't know what to do. You know?"

Darby frowned. "Kristin obviously doesn't know what she has."

Molly sighed. "Thank you for saying so, but that's not quite true."

"Sure it is. I've seen the way she's treated you while you've been here. She's been on her damn cell half a dozen times even though she knows how you feel about it and she was already two days late."

Molly was impressed by Darby's observations and despite the fact that a small part of her wanted to defend her partner, a larger part welled with indignation. "I hate that damn thing."

"Why wouldn't you? She certainly hasn't allowed you to forget about it." Darby's tone was angry, like she was pissed off on Molly's behalf.

"She wasn't always like this, you know."

"Yeah, well, she's definitely like this now."

"I don't know what happened. I keep wracking my brain to pinpoint the moment when it all went to hell, but I can't find it."

"If I were you, I'd dump her ass."

Molly's eyes snapped to Darby's. "Don't you think that's extreme?"

"You're obviously not happy." Darby shrugged, as if she thought things were incredibly simple.

"But I was. I'd like to get back there."

"Do you think you can?"

Molly watched their feet, her voice a whisper. "I don't know."

"You deserve better."

"Maybe." Molly said without conviction.

"You do, Molly." Darby sounded adamant, firmly insistent. They rounded the back of the garage and started along the far side, away from the view of the house. Darby suddenly swung Molly around and pushed her backward against the wooden shingles. Molly blinked and then focused on Darby's blue eyes as they bored into hers from only inches away. "You deserve so much better," Darby whispered before her lips descended onto Molly's.

Molly was taken so off-guard that she was momentarily caught up in the moment and made no attempt to stop what was happening as her eyes drifted closed. Darby's mouth was soft and warm. *And talented*, was a thought that zipped through her brain as Darby slipped her tongue easily between Molly's willingly parting lips. The solid contact of Darby's tongue ring surprised her, but not in a bad way, and she felt herself sinking into the sensation. Molly couldn't recall the last time Kristin had kissed her like this, so thoroughly, with such intensity, every part of her communicating that there was so much more to come. Molly's body responded instantly, a flood of heat rushing to the juncture between her thighs as Darby pressed more firmly into her. *So good*, she thought absently. *It feels so good...*

Darby must have dropped her mittens to the ground because the next thing Molly felt was the cool skin of strong, bare hands on her face, then long fingers burrowing into her hair. "I'd treat you like a queen," Darby murmured, pulling her lips from Molly's only long enough and far enough to speak. "You deserve to be treated like a queen. Don't you know that?" She covered Molly's mouth again without allowing her any time to respond.

The kiss was deeper this time, Darby exploring every possible inch of Molly's mouth with great skill. When she pushed her jean-clad thigh against and then between Molly's, Molly gasped—partly in surprise and mostly in pleasure, vaguely noticing that her own thighs separated without any instruction from her brain. Darby applied the smallest pressure and a jolt of desire shot through to Molly's core, forcing a gasp up from her lungs.

Feeling the very last vestiges of her control slipping from her grasp like the string to a helium balloon swept up by a strong wind, Molly managed to plant one hand on Darby's chest and push feebly. Turning her head to the side—a task that proved to be more difficult than expected—she hissed, "Wait. Darby, wait."

Darby's hands were strong, cupping Molly's chin firmly and turning her head back around. "It's okay," she said. "It's okay." She kissed Molly again, and again Molly's conscience warred with her desire. After several more long seconds, she tried again.

"Darby," she uttered, wrenching her lips from the younger ones keeping her so occupied. "Just...wait. Stop. Please?" She was horrified to hear her own voice crack and mentally warned herself not to cry. "Please stop?"

Darby blinked several times as if waking from a dream. She smoothed a thumb over Molly's eyebrow, her cheekbone, her swollen bottom lip. "What's wrong?"

Molly gave a halfhearted swipe at Darby's hand, frightened by the dangerously primal pang it sent through her. "I can't do this."

"Why not?" Darby looked honestly confused.

"Why not?" Molly repeated with surprise. "Because I'm with somebody."

"Yeah, somebody who doesn't even notice you half the time."

Molly looked down at her feet, buried in snow. Despite the season, her body felt hot. She knew her cheeks were flaming and she was truly uncertain whether it was because of the kissing or the guilt that came with it. "Look, I know we don't have the best relationship right now, but—"

"You have *no* relationship," Darby interrupted, her eyes flashing. "Can't you see that? Any stranger looking in on this week would be very surprised to learn you and Kristin are together."

"I know." Molly rubbed at her forehead. "But we *are* together and I..." She was startled by the certainty in her voice. "I still love her." Darby snorted and Molly smacked her arm. "Hey," she snapped angrily. "You're entitled to your opinion, but as my friend, I expect you to show me at least a little bit of respect."

Darby's eyes dropped. "You're right. I'm sorry. It's just—"

"No. Don't." Molly held up her hand as Darby leaned forward ever so slightly, worried that she couldn't take it if Darby started to say any more of all the right things. Her body still thrummed with desire and she didn't know how long her defenses would last under another assault. Her expression softened. "Look. I like you, Darby. I like you a lot. But the bottom line is that I'm not ready to throw in the towel on my relationship yet and I'm not the kind of girl who can have an affair." She grinned wryly, trying to lighten the moment. "I'm Catholic. The guilt would eat me alive."

Darby leered at her for a moment, her face saying *she'd* like to eat Molly alive. Molly waited, hoping she'd gotten through. Finally, Darby nodded her assent. "Okay. I'm not bowing out gracefully, but I'll step aside. For now."

"That's all I ask."

Into the Woods

Jo sipped her coffee and looked expressively at her niece as Darby came in through the front door. She was disheveled, wearing Jo's coat, and her face was flushed. Jo poked the inside of her cheek with her tongue, reasonably sure of the cause of Darby's redness. No, it wasn't the cold. Jo had heard some quiet rustling earlier; Molly's boots and coat were missing from the rack. Part of her wanted to take her niece by the scruff of her neck and shake her, but she knew that was the wrong approach. Still, something was going to have to be said. Soon.

"Hey, Aunt Jo." Darby rubbed her hands together in front of the newly stoked fire and carefully avoided eye contact.

"Morning." After a beat, Jo asked, "You see Molly out there?"

Darby's head snapped up. "Um, yeah. Yeah, I think I did. She's walking around the garage." She shot her aunt a conspiratorial expression as she lowered her voice. "Trying to clear her head, I'm sure." Then she looked to the ceiling, indicating that the cause of Molly's troubles was on the second floor.

"Be careful, Darby," Jo said, a note of warning layering the simple words.

Before Darby could respond, Sophie came down the stairs, rubbing at her eyes as greetings were exchanged.

"A little early for you, isn't it?" Jo kidded as she poured her guest a cup of much-needed coffee.

"That damn dog decided licking my face was a good thing to do at the crack of fucking dawn." Sophie gratefully took the mug from Jo, sipping immediately despite the fact that it was too hot. She patted at her head, trying with little success to tame the wild hair that stuck out in all directions.

"He's a friendly little thing, that's for sure."

Surprising, given the way he was probably treated, Sophie thought as she recalled the bitter man from the store. Darby asked if Laura would be taking the dog home with her, but Sophie remained quiet.

"It's kind of looking that way," Jo responded. "Laura's a responsible girl, though. I'm sure she'll continue to make calls."

Responsible. Sophie barely managed to hide her snort. *Responsible for destroying a life, maybe.* Even as she mentally vilified Laura, she recalled the sight of her several minutes ago, lying on her side in bed. After licking Sophie awake, the terrier had curled into a ball against Laura's midsection as if protecting her. His big brown eyes blinked at Sophie, innocent and sweet, and she wanted to strangle him when she realized how early it was. Laura's straight blond hair was lightly tousled, her creamy complexion apparent even in the very first hints of dawn, her face relaxed. As Sophie had stared from her own bed, she'd felt a tingling, a small quiver of excitement that she hadn't felt in ages.

It had scared the hell out of her.

No way, she'd thought with determination. *Not this one.* She'd practically jumped out of bed. All she knew was that she had to get out of that room.

Now she stood in the kitchen against the counter, sipped her scalding hot coffee, and tried to act nonchalant—like she hadn't just fried the roof of her mouth and like she wasn't entertaining sexual fantasies about a woman she should, for all intents and purposes, despise. She hated the confusion that welled within her.

The front door opened and Molly came in, stomping the snow off her boots. Jo noticed that she made a point not to look at Darby.

"I'm going to grab a shower," Molly said, hanging up her coat and brushing the fresh snowflakes from her hair.

"What do you feel like for breakfast?" Amy asked

"Whatever you decide is fine with me." Molly gave a small smile and headed up the stairs.

Darby couldn't stop herself from staring after her. She tried to ignore the fact that she could feel Aunt Jo's eyes burning a hole into the back of her skull.

No sooner had the water for the shower kicked on than Kristin came down the stairs, looking bleary-eyed and exhausted. The sweats she sported didn't look worn to coziness; they just looked ratty. Amy noticed the dark circles under her usually bright blue eyes with concern. She was so worried about her friends and she hated that they were having problems now, at her house, when they were all supposed to be happy and celebrating the holidays.

"Coffee?" Jo asked Kristin.

"God, yes," came the hoarse-voiced response. Kristin passed Darby without looking at her and entered the kitchen to stand in front of the coffeepot and watch as it brewed, willing it to work faster.

The group was fairly quiet, it being earlier than most of them normally awoke. The time, along with the obvious tension that filled the air between Darby and Kristin, kept everybody looking innocently into their own cups.

"Snow's coming down pretty good," Jo muttered as she gazed out the window at the big, fluffy flakes falling from the sky. The silence continued, broken only by the occasional clang of a pan as Amy got the bacon sizzling on the stove.

Soon, the clicking of canine nails on the hardwood steps could be heard and Laura and the dog joined the bunch, the terrier wagging his tail furiously and greeting everybody individually. The atmosphere perked up immediately as the women cooed and scratched him. Sophie leaned against the frame of the front door and tried hard not to roll her eyes at the display. Instead, her gaze was drawn upward to the dog's adopted mother. Laura looked absolutely edible in her striped pajama pants and royal blue hooded sweatshirt. Her hair was in a ponytail and the sleep hadn't quite retreated from her sparkling blue eyes. As she smiled at the terrier, her dimples deepened, sending a pang through Sophie's lower body.

God damn it, she thought, annoyed by her body's betrayal.

The dog scooted her way next, standing on his hind legs and scratching at Sophie's thigh until she gave in and reached down to pet him. Then he jumped at the door to go out. Sophie simply opened it without thinking.

"No!" Laura cried as the terrier shot out the front door and into the snow, bounding through the yard and toward the woods like an escaped prisoner. She turned pained and angry eyes on Sophie. "What...*why*? Why would you do that?"

"I...I..." Sophie stuttered as she watched Laura step into the nearest boots and grab a coat off a hook. She shot one more hurt look at Sophie before plunging out into the icy morning, calling, "Here, boy!"

When Sophie looked back, the rest of the group was getting up and quickly dressing in outerwear. Jo and Amy both looked at her pointedly.

"I didn't...it was..." Nobody seemed to be listening. She sighed and began putting her own stuff on.

"You stay here," Jo said to Amy. "We've got it. You take care of breakfast, okay?"

Amy nodded and gave Jo a kiss. "It'll break Laura's heart if you don't find him," she said softly. Her worry about Kristin and Molly was one thing, but the tension between Sophie and Laura had been completely unexpected and Amy wasn't quite sure what to do with it.

"We'll find him," Jo reassured her. "Don't worry."

They all tromped out the front door. "Looks like Laura went that way, following his tracks," Jo said, pointing to the path in the back yard. Laura's footprints were obvious in the snow, but wouldn't be for long if it kept coming down as thickly as it was. They could hear her voice in the distance, calling for the dog. "Hopefully, he'll stay on the path, so we'll go this way and head him off." She indicated the other end of the path near the garage. Jo looked at Sophie and pointed in the direction Laura had run. "You go that way."

Sophie nodded guiltily. She knew she needed to apologize to Laura, and that's exactly what Jo was telling her to do. She turned and jogged off toward the fading sound of Laura's voice, irritated with both the situation and herself. "It was a goddamn accident," she muttered to nobody as she followed Laura's footprints. But even she wondered if that was the honest truth. Was it an accident or did something in her subconscious think it would be a good way to hurt the cheater? She groaned, knowing if she came up with that explanation so quickly, there was a good possibility it was exactly what had happened.

"Son of a bitch," she hissed, her breath dissipating in a puff of air as she noticed Laura up ahead.

Laura looked over her shoulder at Sophie's approach and her blue eyes were icy. "Leave me alone." She kept walking.

"I came to help find him."

"Don't you think you've helped enough?"

Sophie dropped her arms against her sides. Okay, she deserved that. "Look, I'm sorry. It was an accident."

Laura shot her another look, and her face had *I don't believe you* written all over it. She turned her back on Sophie and kept moving, making smooching sounds with her lips and calling "here, boy" as she diligently followed the meandering dog tracks through the snow. The flakes had gotten thicker, and even in the trees, they seemed to be falling at a very rapid rate. It wouldn't be long before the tracks were obscured completely.

Sophie scrambled along behind Laura, hating the idea that Laura thought she'd done this on purpose. She also hated that it was bothering her. She grabbed for Laura's arm and spun her around so they were face-to-face.

"Laura, please. Listen to me." Sophie's tone was pleading. "I swear I didn't mean for this to happen. I wasn't thinking."

Laura's blue eyes were crystal and cold, as she jerked her arm out of Sophie's grasp. "I am sick to death of being judged by you," she said with venom and continued walking.

Sophie flinched. "What the hell is that supposed to mean?" she asked the back of Laura's head.

"The scowls, the snorts, the eye rolling. Do you think I miss it all? Do you think I'm blind *and* deaf?" Laura wanted to sound angry, but she was annoyed by the undercurrent of hurt that so obviously colored her tone. "Here, boy!"

"I don't—" Sophie began, but was cut off by Laura's upheld hand.

"Shut up."

Sophie blinked in surprise.

Laura glared at her. "I know your girlfriend fooled around on you and I'm sorry about that. I know it hurt you terribly and I also know you're projecting your anger onto me because I did the same thing to my husband."

Sophie poked the inside of her cheek with her tongue and struggled to remain quiet, to stay in the same spot, to keep from turning on her booted heel and running away as fast as possible, leaving Laura standing in the snow alone in her pajamas. She didn't want to hear this. She didn't want to hear any of it.

"But you know what, Sophie?" Laura's voice dropped until she was practically snarling through her clenched teeth as she carefully articulated each word. "You don't know a thing about me. You don't know a thing about my life. You don't know a thing about my marriage. You have *no right* to judge me. No right at all."

They stood face-to-face among the trees, creating a dichotomy of light and dark. Snow fell silently onto their hair as Laura's chest rose and fell, the quickened pace a sign of her anger, something she kept banked like the glowing embers of a fire. She was so incredibly tired of having to explain herself, to defend herself. No, she wasn't proud of the way she'd handled things, but she'd had her reasons. It was over and done with and she'd moved on. She wished people would just leave her the hell alone about it.

She turned on her heel and headed deeper into the woods. "Come here, boy!"

Sophie saw the hurt, the resentment, the exhaustion in Laura's face before she turned away, surprised by how they made her feel. She wet her lips and spoke before she had a chance to think about it. "I was a crappy wife."

Laura stopped, her back to Sophie, feeling somewhat off balance at the remark. "What?"

"I was a crappy wife." Sophie couldn't believe she'd said it. Twice. "A crappy partner." She also couldn't believe how much better she felt, as if the fact had weighed an extra fifty pounds and by saying it, she was now that much lighter. "I was never around and when I was, I was a control freak. I was bossy. I worked too much. I was distant."

"Oh, Sophie…" Laura didn't know what to say. She sighed and looked at her feet.

"I drove Kelly to somebody else. It was my fault."

Laura turned to look at her, saw the anguish and the self-recrimination in Sophie's eyes. "Don't say that."

"It's the truth. Do you know why Kelly started going to the gym where she met her new love?"

Laura suspected this was the first time Sophie had talked about this and she didn't want to answer because she knew it would only exacerbate the pained expression on Sophie's beautiful face. At the same time, she guessed maybe Sophie needed to tell the story, needed to say the words out loud. All of them. "No. Why?"

"Because she was always complaining about being fat—which she wasn't. And so one day she said she was fat and instead of trying to convince her that she was beautiful, which any good partner would have done, I agreed with her. I told her she was right, that she was putting on weight, that she needed to get herself back into shape because she wasn't getting any younger." The memory horrified her and made her sick to her stomach. "Who says something like that to the person they supposedly love?" She shook her head and snorted. "I bought her the gym membership for her birthday. Serves me right."

Laura was quiet for several minutes. Looking at Sophie, she was surprised to note that all she wanted to do was relieve the hurt that came off her like waves of heat. "You know…it takes two to tango. It takes two to mess up a relationship."

"Sometimes it only takes one," Sophie said with a sad smile.

Laura took a deep breath and exhaled slowly, knowing she couldn't make this better, that only Sophie had the power to forgive herself, to learn from her mistakes and move on. "I'm sorry." It was the most fitting thing she could think of to say.

"No, *I'm* sorry. You're right. I've been a judgmental bitch and I had no right."

Laura grinned, surprised by the words. "Apology accepted." Her dimples deepened. "Do you think we can start over?"

Sophie held out her hand. "Hi there. Sophie Wilson. Nice to meet you."

Laura took the offered hand and shook it, warmed by the strength of the grip. A tingle zipped up her arm as she nearly became lost in the rich brown of Sophie's eyes, lighter now than they'd been earlier. "Laura Baker. It's nice to meet you, too." They held on for several long seconds before Laura reluctantly let go and asked with a smirk, "Think you can help me find my dog?"

By early afternoon, the snow had subsided and then started back up again. Bellies were full from the lunch of turkey sandwiches and vegetable soup Laura had prepared for the group, ordering Amy to take a meal off and just sit, not an easy feat. Wine and beer were flowing in abundance and the atmosphere in the cabin was one of general relaxation. Peals of laughter rang through the living room as Sophie and Molly battled video game zombies, squealing like little girls as they sat Indian-style on the floor.

Laura had reclaimed her chair and book. The terrier, located that morning by Jo and Darby with his nose stuck in the chipmunk hole of a dead tree, was curled up in the crook of her knee sleeping off the exhaustion from his adventure. Every so often, she'd glance up at the game players and catch Sophie's eye. Sophie would smile and they'd each return to their tasks, relieved to have gotten past the animosity. Amy was in the shower. Kristin sat at the kitchen table with her Blackberry and a beer, checking her e-mail. Jo and Darby were putting away the lunch dishes.

"How's your wine, Laura?" Jo called to her guest. "Ready for a refill?"

Laura glanced at her half-full glass. "Not yet, thanks. I'm good."

"Zombie warriors?" Sophie and Molly picked up their empty bottles and held them over their heads. Jo laughed. "I'll take that as a 'yes, could we please have more beer, Ms. Cooper?'" She retrieved two fresh bottles from the fridge and handed them to Darby for delivery. "Kristin?"

Kristin was absorbed in her e-mail, using her thumbs to type a response to a client as she became increasingly annoyed that Reeves continued to forward e-mail to her knowing she was on vacation. He could just as easily be handling it himself. Jo laid a hand on her shoulder, causing her to jump.

"Sorry." Jo reached for Kristin's beer. She handed it to her frazzled-looking friend. "Finish this last swallow and I'll get you another one. You look like you could use it."

Kristin did as ordered and handed her bottle over to Jo, who took it into the kitchen. Darby walked by with the empties from the living room. Looking at Kristin with thinly veiled disgust, she commented in a tone only Kristin could hear, "Jesus, look at you. In a corner away from the women, swigging beer and absorbed in your job while you're supposed to be on vacation. You might as well not even be here."

The muscles in Kristin's jaw clenched.

"You're practically invisible. Pretty soon, she won't see you at all."

Kristin's nostrils flared and she felt her face heating up. She knew if she didn't move, run, get away *right now*, she would very likely knock Darby on her ass. Hard. It would be embarrassing for everybody, Molly would be pissed, she'd ruin her friendship with Jo and Amy and succeed in hammering the final nail into the coffin of this "vacation."

She stood up so fast, her chair fell backward and crashed loudly to the floor.

The cabin got quiet as everybody turned to look at the two women staring at each other. Kristin's eyes were blue fire and if she could have shot laser beams out of them at Darby, she would have. Darby, on the other hand, had enough sense to look a bit fearful, knowing instinctively that she'd crossed a line. She stood her ground, swallowing hard and feeling not only Kristin's glare, but that of her aunt in the kitchen.

Her nostrils still flaring and her jaw clenched so tightly it was giving her an instant headache, Kristin managed to speak. "I need some air," she ground out.

Darby stepped back out of her path before she could be bodily pushed. Kristin didn't look at anybody as she stepped into her boots and donned her coat, hat, and gloves. She crossed to the kitchen and took the open beer bottle Jo had been about to bring her, then headed for the front door.

"Kristin?" Molly's voice was uncertain.

Kristin held up a gloved hand, forestalling any further conversation. "I need some air," she said again and then she was gone.

Nobody moved for what felt like several long minutes. The room was silent, save for the shrieking of the dying characters on the video game. Amy returned freshly showered and her gaze bounced around the room in confusion.

"What happened?" she asked and her voice seemed to free everybody, as if they'd been frozen and just waiting for a sound to break the spell. They all shifted at once, Sophie and Laura glancing at each other, Molly looking across the room at Darby in disappointment.

Before Darby could react at all, Jo grabbed a handful of her shirt and yanked her bodily past a bewildered Amy and into the back bedroom, where she slammed the door and pushed her niece roughly against the wall, keeping her pinned with a hand on her chest.

"What the hell was that about?" she demanded.

"What?" Darby tried to feign innocence, knowing it wasn't going to work. "She obviously can't take a joke."

"Why would she take a joke from you, Darby? You've been slobbering all over her girlfriend the whole week."

"You think she's actually noticed?" The sarcastic edge to her voice didn't do a thing to dissuade Jo's anger with her.

"Everybody else has."

Darby chuckled, but stopped immediately as Jo pulled her forward just enough to bump her back into the wall again, wiping the smirk right off her face.

"*Not* funny. Show some respect, God damn it. These are my friends and you're way out of line."

Darby couldn't remember the last time she'd seen Aunt Jo this angry with her. She blinked, honestly not following her aunt's train of thought. "How? How am I out of line?"

"How?" Jo looked at her in disbelief. "Jesus, your generation is just a fucking mess, isn't it?" She rubbed at her forehead in frustration as she realized she was actually going to have to spell things out. "They're in trouble, Darby. Molly and Kristin. Their relationship is in trouble and if you knew them the way Aunt Amy and I do, you'd know that they love each other enough to fix it." She eyed her niece, satisfied she was paying close attention. "Maybe you and your friends think it's okay to move in on somebody who's spoken for—though I want to believe you're not that cold-hearted—but me and *my* friends? We don't work that way. I don't know what your intentions are in this game you're playing with Molly, but I suspect you want nothing more than to get into her cute little panties so you can carve another notch into your bedpost." At Darby's gasp of indignation, Jo sneered. "Oh, come on, Darby. It's what you do. You cruise, you fuck, you move on. You know it and I know it. You talk about it all the time. And I've never judged you for it, have I?"

Darby grimaced and bit the inside of her lip as she shook her head. "No."

"Well, this time, I am. These are my *friends;* they're not a challenge put here for you."

"But I like her." Darby sounded like a small child.

"What?"

"I like her. Molly. I...you know...I *like* her."

Jo looked at her for several long seconds, seeing something in Darby's eyes she'd never seen before. *Son of a bitch. Why now? Why Molly?* No, it didn't matter. She shook her head. "That's too damn bad. You can like her. You just can't have her. She's a married woman who's desperate to fix her failing relationship. If you *do* like her, then you need to step back and respect her enough not to interfere."

Darby looked at her feet, feeling like she was eight years old all over again and being scolded by her aunt for messing with her tools.

"Do you understand?" When Darby looked back up at her, Jo, too, was reminded of a much younger version. She could vividly see her niece fifteen years ago, kind, smart, quick-witted. It was excruciatingly difficult to stay angry with her. She consciously softened her tone. "Look, I know you like Molly. It's not hard to, believe me. She's a good egg who's in a bad place right now. She's vulnerable and she's confused and she needs help from her friends, not more obstacles. Can you do that? Can you be her friend and not an obstacle?"

Darby grimaced, thinking back to that morning, of kissing Molly, of how good she felt under her hands, under her mouth. She also remembered being pushed away, being begged to stop, and the look of uncertainty in Molly's bruised green eyes—the look that told her she wasn't helping matters any, no matter how Molly had responded.

Darby wet her lips. "Yeah. I can do that."

Jo rubbed her hand over her face as if trying to wipe away the recent stress. "Good." She backed off, letting Darby move away from the wall. "Thank you."

Darby nodded once.

"Go." Jo gestured to the door. "Aunt Amy's going to bust in here any minute wanting to know what's going on."

"Okay."

As she watched her niece leave, Jo released a breath she didn't realize she'd been holding, her cheeks puffing out as she did so. She tried hard not to think of the week as having turned into a disaster of epic proportions. *It could be worse. Laura and Sophie could have killed each other by now and the stray dog could have been a rabid Rottweiler instead of a little terrier. Worse yet, we could be out of alcohol.* She chuckled and ran a hand through her curls, shaking her head in wonder. The door opened and Amy came in, concern on her face.

She touched a hand to Jo's cheek. "What the hell happened?"

KRISTIN

Kristin wanted to scream at the top of her lungs, and if she had been farther away from the house, she would have. The last thing she wanted was for all of them to come running out to see if she was okay. She wanted to be alone. She wanted to wallow in self-pity. She wanted to bawl her eyes out and shriek to the heavens, demanding to know how and why her life had become such a complete catastrophe.

She was so angry at everybody right now. She couldn't remember ever feeling such rage. It boiled within her like some sort of witch's brew, sour and hot. As she stomped through the snow and into the trees behind the house, she pictured the face of Jack Reeves. Then she pictured her fist punching him square in the nose with all her strength. She used to belong to a gym and she used to kick-box; he was a big guy, but she could clobber him pretty well, she was sure.

She took a slug from the beer bottle in her hand. In her mind's eye, while Jack was writhing on the floor and whining "my nose!" like Marcia Brady, Kristin turned her head and there stood Darby.

"Disrespectful little bitch," Kristin muttered out loud, clenching her teeth and wrinkling her lip in a snarl. "Who the fuck do you think you are?" And then her imaginary self punched Darby, too. Twice. Hard. It took her longer to go down than Reeves. No surprise there.

All you need is a penis and you'd be the typical American white male.

Where the hell did that little punk get off saying something like that to her? Kristin hated how much the statement had stung. Did that mean that somewhere deep down inside, she thought it was true?

Kristin swigged again, choking on the swallow of beer and then stopping to collect herself and catch her breath. She forged ahead, off the cleared path and straight back into the woods. The air was crisp and she was glad she'd grabbed the hat and gloves on her way out. She intended to stay outside for as long as she could. She didn't want to be near any of those women, not even Molly. Not now. She was too embarrassed, too ashamed.

You're practically invisible. Pretty soon, she won't see you at all.

That *was* true. God, what Molly must think of her. But really, did she have an option? Her job was stressful and demanding, Molly knew that. There were times when it was going to have to come first, right? There were bills to pay. There was a mortgage and two car payments and Molly's student loan and vacations to take...Kristin blinked snowflakes from her eyelashes. *When's the last time we went on a real vacation? Three years ago? Four?*

It had been Hilton Head. They'd rented a nice little bungalow and spent the week playing golf, lying on the beach, and eating fine food accompanied by expensive wine. She could still vividly recall the love on Molly's face as she sat across the dining table of the fancy restaurant, the candlelight flickering in her sea green eyes. Even now, Kristin's heart raced when she thought about it. How long had it been since Molly had looked at her that way? Since Molly had looked at her at all?

She trudged on as unwanted tears welled in her eyes and a small whimper escaped her throat. The ground sloped downward slightly as she stepped over a downed tree branch, slipping a little in the snow.

"I'm so lost," she murmured, her voice cracking. "God, I'm so lost." A tear spilled free and forged a path down her pinkened cheek. "I don't know what to do anymore."

She thought of her job and her bills and her clients and her boss and her house and her car and her wife and the pressure. God, the pressure. The pain flared up again just as it had the previous day, pressing on her as if a boulder had been set on her chest. She moaned and squeezed her eyes shut, determined to push ahead. If she just kept moving, the pain would go away. It always did. She just needed to keep moving.

On her next step, her boot landed on a jagged and snow-covered rock, throwing her completely off balance. She was falling before she even realized it. Her feet flew forward and her arms flailed, grabbing uselessly at the air to try and maintain her balance. She went down hard on her back, her head smacking against a fallen log. Her vision blurred, then went black.

When Kristin opened her eyes and saw only sky, she had no idea how much time had passed. "Son of a bitch," she grumbled, pulling herself to a sitting position in the snow. Much as she had wanted to stay away from everybody else, she now had no choice but to go back. Her jeans had soaked through and her legs and ass were freezing. She expelled an annoyed breath and hauled herself to her feet.

She followed her own tracks back to the path, then to the back yard and the house. She heard a high-pitched yipping and saw the terrier in the distance. "Damn thing needs a name," she muttered. He was heading toward the other end of the path near the garage, his leash held by Laura.

"Watch your step in there," Kristin called to her. "It's a little slippery."

Neither the woman nor the dog looked her way.

"Terrific," Kristin mumbled. "The silent treatment. Can't wait to go inside."

She knew she'd made a scene, knew most of the women probably wished she hadn't come at all. She was beginning to feel the same way and wanted nothing more than to stay outside in the snow and away from the rest of the gang. If she'd thought to grab her car keys before she'd stomped out, she could just hop in the Lexus, drive away, and leave all this crap behind her. The reality, however, was that her butt was numb and if she didn't get out of her jeans soon, they might end up frozen to her body permanently.

She trudged around the side of the house and up the steps to the front door. She stomped the excess snow off her boots and went inside.

Jo and Amy sat on the couch, Amy's feet in Jo's lap, Jo rubbing them absently. They were smiling as they listened to Darby relay a story in animated detail as she sat on the floor near the fireplace. Molly sat in the club chair, looking distracted and a little sad, but she pretended to pay attention to the story. Nobody looked up as Kristin entered.

In the dining area, Sophie stood near the window and looked out toward the garage.

"They went onto the path," Kristin said to her. "Walking's a little tricky." She gestured to her own backside. "I ought to know."

Sophie said nothing and didn't turn her way.

Christ, Kristin thought. *Is this how it's going to be? Now everybody hates me?*

She turned to glare at Darby, thinking that if people had heard what *she'd* said, how she'd said it, maybe they wouldn't be so quick to judge. Maybe they'd be ignoring her instead of Kristin. She unzipped and shed her coat and hung it up. Then she stepped out of her boots. The whole time, she looked at Molly. Molly never once met her eyes.

She flinched at the realization of how much it stung to have her own partner completely ignore her and she swallowed the lump in her throat. *This is ridiculous.* She crossed the living room to the chair and looked down at Molly.

"Can I talk to you? Upstairs? Please?" She kept her voice calm and low. Darby kept on with her story, something about a weird customer at the video store. Jo and Amy watched with rapt attention and smiles on their faces. Molly gazed wistfully out the front window, her chin balanced on her fist.

Kristin blinked and looked around the room. Everybody was doing their own thing, absorbed in their own thoughts and conversations. Kristin felt anger welling inside. "God damn it," she snarled as she stepped in between Darby on the floor and Jo and Amy on the couch. "Hello?" she said, sarcasm dripping from the word.

Darby continued on with her story as if Kristin wasn't there. Jo laughed at something she said. Kristin whipped her head around to face Jo, hurt. "Come on, you guys. This is mean." Jo and Amy both continued to focus on Darby. Kristin turned back around and growled at Darby. "Oh, my God, can you *shut up for two seconds*?"

Darby kept talking.

Kristin turned to Molly. She stepped back to the chair. "Molly? Honey, please? I'm sorry about earlier. I just want to talk to you."

Molly gazed out the window, her eyes sorrowful.

"Honey?" Kristin repeated.

Sophie approached from across the room and Molly looked up at her. "I'm going to make some hot chocolate. Want some?"

"That'd be great," Molly replied. "Thanks."

Kristin watched in disbelief as Sophie headed toward the kitchen. Molly was once again looking out the window.

"What the hell, Mol?"

Molly continued not to answer. Kristin was breathing heavier now, her anger and hurt causing her heart to beat more rapidly. She moved again so she was standing between Darby and her aunts. They continued to converse, seemingly oblivious to Kristin. Kristin said nothing, but watched carefully. After several minutes of watching Darby, then spinning and watching Jo and Amy, a kernel of fear formed in the pit of her stomach. Jo and Amy never adjusted their positions so they could see around Kristin. Kristin moved and stood directly in front of Darby, who also never shifted to look around the obstacle before her. The realization struck Kristin like a truck.

They're looking right through me.

"Oh, my God," Kristin whispered. She squatted down in front of Darby and waved a hand in front of her face, barely an inch away. Darby didn't even flinch. Her blue eyes were sparkling as she stopped talking and listened to what Amy was saying. Then she laughed and responded, never once moving aside; she spoke to Amy as if Kristin was *not* in her way, was *not* blocking her view. Kristin broke out in a cold sweat and stood.

"Oh, my God," she said again, her voice panicked this time. She looked at her wife. "Molly? Honey?" She leaned close. She could smell Molly, her apple-scented shampoo, her citrus perfume. She liked to joke with her that she smelled like a fruit bowl half the time, but now Kristin inhaled deeply, reveling in the scent that represented her love, her life. "Molly?" Her voice was barely a whisper. "Please look at me. Please."

As Molly gazed out the window at the freshly falling snow, Kristin reached out slowly, waiting breathlessly for the moment when her fingertips would touch the creamy-smooth skin of Molly's cheek. She whimpered in horror when her fingers passed right through, then touched the chair in which Molly sat. She tried again. It was as if Molly was made of mist. Kristin's hands simply passed through any part of Molly she tried to touch. She staggered backward, blinking in shock, and fell on her butt to the floor.

She sat there for several long minutes, her heart pounding, her hand pressed to her chest as the anxiety attack swept over her like a mudslide, burying her in its thick darkness. She squeezed her eyes shut and clenched her teeth, willing the pain to pass. When she was able to breathe again, she looked to her left. Darby sat not three feet away, listening with a grin as Amy prattled on about an unruly restaurant customer. Kristin blinked at Darby, then reached out to touch her socked foot. Her hand passed right through to the floor, and though it didn't surprise her, she still inhaled sharply when it happened. She looked back up at Darby, studied her face. That's when Darby's voice rang through her head.

You're practically invisible. Pretty soon, she won't see you at all.

"Oh, God." Had she actually become invisible? How? How was that possible? How had it happened? How could she fix it? *Could* she fix it? The questions raced through her head faster than she could grab onto one and concentrate on it. She looked up at her partner of so many years. "Molly?" Kristin knew she wouldn't hear her, wouldn't respond, but she said her name anyway, hoping to use it to ground herself. The feel of it on her tongue helped to steady her jangling nerves just a little bit.

"Molly?" she said again as she crawled back toward her wife. Molly's chin was still propped on her hand, her elbow balanced on the arm of the chair. She looked out the window at the day, but her eyes were unfocused. "What are you looking at?" Kristin followed her gaze but could see nothing of interest. "Are you daydreaming?" She sat down on the chair's matching ottoman, wanting so badly to touch Molly that she thought she might scream. She studied Molly's face, the lines etched around her mouth, the dark circles under those dazzling eyes. "You look so sad," she whispered, her throat constricting and her heart breaking at the sight. "Do I do this to you? Do I make you this sad?"

Tears welled in her eyes and she was powerless to stop them as they spilled over and tracked down her cheeks. The sob that raced up from her chest nearly choked her.

"Molly, please hear me. Please see me." She looked around the room as if somebody there might help her, but nobody even knew she was present. She turned back to Molly and looked at her. Just looked at her. "God, you're so pretty," she said. "You're so beautiful."

Molly's dark hair was loose and very wavy. She rarely let it air dry because she said the waves annoyed her, but Kristin often begged her to let the waves come. She thought they were sexy. Molly's sea green eyes were the definite focal point of her face, their color startling amidst the dark hair and olive skin. Her eyebrows were dark and neatly shaped and her eyelashes were long and lush, like those of a teenaged boy. Straight friends were always telling her they'd kill for eyelashes that thick. Her bottom lip was full and Kristin had the sudden urge to kiss it, to suck it into her mouth, to nibble it with her teeth. She couldn't recall the last time she'd felt such a primal, sexual pulse, and now she couldn't do a thing about it. It was torture.

"Molly, please." Her voice cracked and she dropped to her knees next to the chair, her face inches from Molly's. "We're a mess. I feel like I'm losing you and I don't know how to stop it from happening. Every day, I see you slipping further and further away from me and I feel like I can't reach you. And even if I could, I wouldn't know how."

She stopped to catch her breath, willed herself to stop crying. It didn't work. The tears continued to fall. The sobs were smaller, but still frequent. Kristin was losing control. She pressed the heels of her hands to her eyes for several seconds, then looked back at Molly and continued to say whatever came into her head, unable to stop the flow of words.

"This is my fault, Molly. *My* fault. I know I work too much. I know I place too much emphasis on my job. But I feel so stuck, so lost. I feel like I'm carrying so much weight and it's crushing me. Any minute, my legs are just going to give out and it's all going to flatten me forever."

She wiped angrily at the tears on her face. "You know what? I hate my job. I hate it. I hate Jack Reeves and I hate most of my clients and I hate having to go in there every day. I *hate* it, Mol. I want out. I *need* out, for my own sanity, and I don't know how to do it without disappointing everybody. I don't want to disappoint you. I promised to take care of you and I don't know how I can do that if I quit. I don't know what to do. I don't know what to do." She looked up at the oblivious face of her partner, searching it for answers and knowing with sudden clarity that she didn't want to do anything without her. "I need your help, Molly. Please. Please help me."

The blinding pain came screaming out of nowhere and took her by surprise, closing on her skull like a vise. Both hands flew to her head as she squeezed her eyes shut and clenched her teeth. Then there was nothing but black.

LAURA

When Laura and the terrier came in from their walk, the first thing Laura saw was Sophie smiling at her from the dining room table. It was such a surprising change from the sour expression Sophie usually shot her that she smiled back immediately. She unsnapped the dog's leash and he skittered right to Sophie, putting his front paws up on her thigh.

"How was the walk?" Sophie asked as she stroked his wiry head.

"Nice." Laura shed her coat. "It's starting to snow again, but it's the pretty, fluffy stuff."

"I like that kind of snow."

"Me, too."

"How about some hot chocolate to warm you up? I just made myself a cup."

Laura grinned at the offer, touched. "That would be great." She stepped out of her boots and listened with a grin as Amy recounted a story about an obnoxious customer she'd dealt with in the restaurant she owned. *Exactly why I stay in the kitchen,* she thought. She noticed Molly sitting alone in the chair, staring out the window at the snow, and remembered the scene between Darby and Kristin a little while earlier. She wondered what had been said. It was obvious Darby was pushing Kristin's buttons, and Laura had cheered internally when Jo had hauled her niece into another room for what she hoped had been some sage advice. Darby was so young. She had some lessons to learn.

"You look puzzled." Sophie's voice broke her out of her reverie as Laura sat down at the table.

Taking the mug from Sophie's grasp, Laura laughed. "I was just thinking that I can barely remember my twenties."

Sophie chuckled. "It seems like forever ago, doesn't it?" She followed Laura's gaze across the room to where Darby sat on the floor. "She's pretty damn young."

"Has Kristin come back yet?"

"No." Sophie sipped from her mug. The terrier jumped at her until she allowed him up on her lap. He curled up in a ball. "This boy needs a name, you know."

"He's probably got one."

"Then he needs a new one because we can't just keep calling him Dog."

"I'll think about it." For several long minutes Laura lapsed into listening to the conversation taking place between the others, then she asked quietly, "Do you think they'll be okay?"

"Who?"

"Molly and Kristin."

Sophie set down her cocoa. "Yes," she responded with certainty. "I do."

Laura was surprised. "What makes you so sure?"

"They love each other."

"A lot of people love each other. It doesn't mean they stay together forever."

"True enough. How can I explain this?" Sophie chewed on the inside of her cheek as she searched for the right words. "Those two have had their problems since they've been here. That's been obvious. But they've never once been mean to each other. They haven't disrespected one another in front of us. I think that's really important, and two people who love each other and want their relationship to work understand that."

Laura studied Sophie's face. Her coffee-colored skin was so smooth, Laura was surprised to find herself wanting to reach out and stroke it, just run her fingertips across Sophie's cheek. "That's an excellent point. You sound like you speak from experience."

"Respect is the most important ingredient in a relationship, aside from love, of course. I didn't have enough respect for Kelly," Sophie said wistfully. Then her face cracked into a wry grin. "Of course, she didn't have much for me either, so I guess we were pretty even."

"I think I was hit with some poetic justice myself," Laura said. "I obviously didn't respect Stephen enough, but Amanda didn't respect me. I think I may have gotten what I deserved."

"What goes around comes around, huh?"

"Evidently."

"You should keep the dog," Sophie blurted suddenly.

Laura blinked at the abrupt change in subject. "What?"

"The dog." Sophie stroked the brown fur as the words left her in a rush. "I heard a guy in the grocery store when we went to town yesterday. His wife left him and left the dog behind, but he hates the dog and locked him out of the house. He was a big, skeevy, gross guy and he doesn't want the dog back. And if he had him back, I don't think he'd be nice to him." She took a breath. "So you should just keep him. He likes you. And you're good to him. You should be together."

Laura stared at her with raised eyebrows, trying to absorb everything.

"I should have told you sooner. I'm sorry."

As if on cue, the dog lifted his head and looked at Laura, his brown eyes blinking at her with watery sleepiness. "He looks like a Ricky to me," she said finally.

Sophie smothered a relieved smile and glanced down at him. "He does, doesn't he?"

"Maybe we'll try that on for size and see if he likes it."

They sipped their cocoa in companionable silence, glancing at one another and grinning. Finally, Sophie spoke. "Can I ask you something?"

"Sure."

"It's kind of personal."

"I don't mind."

"How did it feel when Amanda called things off? I mean, how did you get over her?"

Laura spent a few seconds contemplating the most honest answer. "Well, first of all, I was completely shocked. Here I was, head over heels in love with this woman—my first woman, mind you—and in the process of leaving my husband for her. Now, in her defense, she didn't know I had told Stephen about us. She had no idea I was leaving him."

"Seriously?"

"I did it as a surprise for her." She snorted at the irony. "I thought of it as a gift. Little did I know that she had no intention of embarking on any sort of life with me. As far as she was concerned, we'd just go on as we were forever...married to our husbands and sleeping with each other on the side. She liked her life just the way it was."

"Damn. She sounds cold."

"I didn't used to think so. But you're right. She's very cold and I'm amazed that I fell as hard as I did for her." Laura glanced out the window at the falling snow. "God, she was gorgeous."

"Yeah?"

"Legs to die for." Laura didn't often allow herself to revel in the past, to reflect on how good it was with Amanda before it all came tumbling down. How many weekends had they spent together in bed while their husbands were away on business, leaving the bedroom only to grab some food so they'd have enough energy to have more sex? Laura had learned more about her body from Amanda than from anybody else in the previous thirty-plus years of her life. "So...back to your question. How did it feel? It felt...it felt like my world had been ripped out from under my feet while I stood there completely oblivious to what was going on. It felt like one minute I had two people that I cared very much about and the next minute, I had nobody. Nobody and nothing. I lost my house, my stability, my life. And I blamed her. Wrongly, but I blamed her."

Sophie nodded. "It's a lot easier to blame the other one than to look in the mirror, isn't it?"

"Way easier." Laura watched Sophie, who studied the contents of her cup. Her face had visibly softened since their earlier conversation. It was pretty amazing. Sophie's judgmental expression was gone, replaced by something different. Something gentler. Her hair was loose, falling around her shoulders in a mass of corkscrew curls. She seemed a little thinner than she should be, and Laura found herself wanting to cook for her, to fatten her up a bit with gourmet meals served by candlelight.

She shook her head and chuckled internally at how strange life could be. When she had arrived barely two days ago, she'd been quite solitary and perfectly okay with that fact. She had a great duplex, a job she loved, and the hope that she wouldn't be lonely for the rest of her life. Now it looked like she had a new dog and a woman who would be—at the very least—a friend. More specifically, a friend who understood what she'd been through over the past year. Laura couldn't remember the last time she'd met somebody she felt connected to. Well, Amanda, of course, but that had obviously been some sort of lapse in judgment on her part...

Amanda.

She had taught Laura all about the opposite extremes of feeling. Nobody had ever made her feel so much love and then so much pain within the space of a few months. If she hadn't been so damn beautiful, Laura would never have been so easily seduced. Would she? It was a question she pondered often, knowing now that she must have been a target for Amanda, a challenge. She could see Amanda's gorgeous face in her mind's eye, calculating how long she thought it would take for her to convince the naïve and married straight girl to sleep with her. How many other women had she seduced in the same way? Had they all thought Amanda was in love with them or had Laura been the only one to be that stupid? Did she have another conquest already? These were the questions that plagued her and probably always would.

The last day she saw Amanda was etched into her brain forever and no matter how hard she tried to forget it, she could still remember every detail, every word, exactly what Amanda was wearing and how she smelled and the precise second that she knew it was over. They'd met in the parking lot where Laura worked. She'd told Amanda that she was leaving Stephen, that she'd admitted their affair to him and had told him that she was in love with Amanda and Amanda was in love with her.

Amanda had looked at her with wide-open, wild eyes. "You told him what?" Her voice had registered disbelief and something else... finality? Resignation?

"I told him we're in love." Laura was giddy. She'd never felt so free in her life.

Amanda was looking edibly sexy, as always, in her black slacks and royal blue silk blouse, the simple gold chain Laura had given her as a gift sparkling invitingly at the base of her throat. She reached out to touch a strand of Amanda's silky, dark hair. She was wearing it loose that day, down around her shoulders the way Laura loved it and Laura wanted nothing more than to bury her face in it, soak in the scent of this magnificent creature. She wanted to take Amanda to bed right then and there, to lose herself in Amanda's body, to hear her begging

Laura for release. She'd been thinking about it all morning, hadn't been able to concentrate on work at all, her hands trembling and her panties uncomfortably damp.

Amanda caught Laura's wrist before she could touch her, and pushed her away. "God damn it, Laura." She said it quietly and then she turned and opened the car door. She dropped into the driver's seat with a weary sigh.

"What? Honey? What is it?" Laura was confused and an inexplicable panic had suddenly seeped into her system like dry ice as she watched Amanda's movements, felt her retreating. "I thought you'd be happy. We can be together now. Where are you going? Amanda, please."

Amanda paused, her hand on the ignition. She turned to look at Laura, her normally mischievous and glittering eyes showing nothing but sadness and disappointment. "Can't you see? You've ruined it. It was perfect and you had to go and ruin everything."

The quiet and almost monotonous manner made the words even more painful than if she'd shouted them at the top of her lungs. She started the car and pulled away, leaving Laura standing in the middle of the lot at a complete loss, floundering like a small, empty rowboat that has drifted out onto the choppy ocean waves. It was the last time she'd ever seen Amanda.

In that moment, as she watched the black BMW turn a corner and disappear, Laura had known that she had just lost everything familiar to her. Everyone and everything comfortable was now gone. She was alone.

"Hello?" Sophie's gentle voice cut into her reminiscing as she tapped a fingertip lightly on the back of Laura's hand. "You okay?"

Laura looked up to meet concerned brown eyes and laughed. "You know, it's sort of freaking me out having you look at me with worry instead of disdain."

Sophie laughed with her. "Disdain is much easier for me. I'm a pro at disdain." She tilted her head to the side. "Where'd you go just now? You seemed really far away."

"I was just remembering the moment when I realized that my entire life had changed and nothing would ever be the same."

"When you left your husband?"

"And then Amanda left me."

"Was that, like...on the same day?"

Laura nodded slowly and sipped from her mug.

"Oh, wow." Sophie grimaced. "That'll wake you up, huh?"

"You aren't kidding."

She remembered the panic that had set in, as she stood in the empty parking lot. She actually wondered then if she could somehow make it up to Stephen, tell him she'd been mistaken, that Amanda had been a weird phase of some sort and she wasn't in love with her after all, that she really loved him and could they just go back to the way things were and pretend none of the morning's conversation had ever happened. That thought process had only lasted a few seconds. She'd known immediately that even though she wouldn't have Amanda by her side, she had discovered the *real* Laura, the one who'd been hiding deep inside all this time...and she *liked* her. She wasn't about to let go of her so soon.

"It's a weird feeling, finding out that somebody you love is leaving you and there's nothing you can do about it, isn't it?" Sophie asked. It was more a statement than a question and there wasn't even a hint of accusation in her voice.

Laura had a sudden flash of Sophie's partner telling her she was leaving, of the pain that must have sliced across Sophie's smooth features, creasing her flawless skin, forcing her to accept the fact that life as she knew it was over. The image made her want to comfort her new friend, to smooth away the lines of worry and stress. She gripped her mug tightly to keep from reaching across the table. "Damn right."

IN FROM THE COLD

Kristin opened her eyes and blinked up at the clouded sky, the snowflakes falling like tiny pinpricks on her skin. She was shivering.

What the hell time was it?

She sat up from her position of lying on her back on the cold ground, and a sharp pain stabbed the back of her head. She winced and rubbed at it, noting a small goose egg. She vaguely remembered slipping and falling and realized that she very well might have knocked herself out cold. She was surprised to see that her legs were completely covered in new-fallen snow and she wondered again what time it was and how long she'd been out there. Turning slowly to look behind her, she noticed her tracks had been covered.

Her body shook and she knew she needed to get herself back to the house and warm up. She stood slowly, bracing herself against a tree, breathing deliberately as she allowed her body to adjust to being upright. Her jeans were soaked through and her fingers were numb. She closed her eyes and inhaled deeply as she stood up straighter and let go of the tree, trying to balance on her own and remember what the hell had happened.

The exchange with Darby came racing back to her and she grimaced. A split second later, though, she had a flash of sitting directly in front of Darby, waving a hand in her face, and having Darby look right through her. Kristin flinched and her hand flew back out to steady her against the tree as adrenaline flooded her system.

"What—?" Memories hit her hard and fast, faces of her friends, of

Molly, none of them looking at her, none of them *seeing* her. "Oh, my God," she said aloud. "What the hell happened to me?"

She looked around wildly, frightened now. She knew which way would get her back to the path; she'd always been good with directions, something Molly couldn't say. She had another flash of Molly's face, the sadness, the pain, the loneliness etched across it. She wanted nothing more at that moment than to see Molly and have Molly see her. She turned and headed back the way she had come, using the trees to help her maintain her balance. God, she was cold. She trudged slowly, thinking only of Molly, wanting only Molly, and making clean, fresh tracks in the snow.

"What time is it?" Molly's voice held a tinge of worry as she paced back and forth in front of the roaring fireplace.

"It's five minutes later than the last time you asked," Darby said, her thumb pushing periodically on the remote in her hand, scrolling through the channels on the television. "I can't believe this," she muttered. "Three hundred and fifty channels and there's not a damn thing on."

"Should I be worried?" Molly asked Amy in a small voice as she sat down at the dining room table next to her dearest friend. "She's been out there a long time and it's gotten awfully cold. What if she's lost?"

Amy smiled and rubbed Molly's shoulder, hoping to alleviate some of the worry. "She's fine. She doesn't get lost, remember? Now you, on the other hand..." Molly didn't smile at her attempted humor. Lowering her voice and cutting her eyes toward Darby, Amy added, "I bet she just wanted to be alone for a while."

Molly looked into Amy's blue eyes. They were soft and gentle, friendly with love and concern. She felt Amy's warm hand squeeze her shoulder.

"She probably ran into Sophie and Laura and decided to walk with them." Jo touched the back of Molly's head affectionately, her voice sounding certain and reasonable. "Tell you what," she said. "We'll give her another twenty minutes and if she's not back by then, I'll go find her. Okay?"

Molly nodded, knowing she was worrying needlessly. Kristin was just upset; Molly had seen it in her eyes when she'd left. The hurt, the anger, the helplessness. It was in that moment, those three seconds of eye contact, that Molly had realized Kristin was floundering, that she had no idea what to do to fix any of their mess, and that she felt like she was alone. The sudden understanding of that fact had sliced through Molly like a razor blade, leaving her raw.

How did we get here? It was a question she asked herself often lately. Her life now was so far away from what she'd expected it to be after so many years with Kristin. *How did this happen? How did we get so far apart?*

She shook her head almost imperceptibly, unable as usual to come up with any acceptable answers—at least not answers she was prepared to deal with.

Amy's voice cut into her thoughts. "I'm going to start on dinner. Come and talk to me in the kitchen and have a glass of wine with me. It'll take your mind off things."

Molly scratched at her eyebrow, knowing Amy was right. She needed to think about something else or she might very well go insane. As she stood up, the front door burst open and Molly whipped her head around. Her eyes widened at the sight.

Kristin stood in the doorway, drenched to the skin. Her shoulder-length blond hair was wet and matted to her head. Her jeans were soaked completely through, darkened with the wetness. Her boots had snow spilling out the tops. Her skin was deathly pale and her blue eyes were wild and darting. The vision of her made Molly's heart pound and she ran to her.

"Jesus, honey. Where the hell have you been?" Molly gave her a once-over and immediately began unzipping her coat. "You're freezing, baby. Come on, let's get you out of these wet clothes."

Amy, Jo, and Darby all hung back, sensing somehow that this was a private moment. Jo watched carefully, noticing that Kristin's eyes focused on Molly and stayed there.

Molly grasped the gloves and pulled them from Kristin's hands. As she caught Kristin's fingers in her own, she gasped. "God, Kristin, your hands are like ice." She wrapped her smaller ones around Kristin's and blew hot breath on them. "What happened? Why are you all wet?

Where have you been? I was worried about you." Her voice was not loud, and it was more concerned than angry as she looked up into Kristin's face.

Kristin studied her, looking directly into her green eyes—the most beautiful eyes she'd ever seen. "Molly?" Her voice was a whisper so only Molly could hear.

Molly held eye contact and waited for Kristin to continue.

"Can you see me?"

Molly's forehead crinkled at the strangeness of the question. "What? Can I...? Of course I can see you. What do you mean?"

Kristin's eyes filled with tears. "You can? You can see me?"

"Yes, honey." Molly tried to ignore the weird desperation in Kristin's voice, somehow understanding that the answer to this question was very important. She stated matter-of-factly, "I can see you."

Kristin sucked in her breath and her chest jerked as a sob burst forth. "Oh, thank God. Thank God." She leaned forward, pressing her forehead into Molly's shoulder as she cried, unable to understand how it could possibly feel so good to have Molly rubbing feeling back into her frozen fingers.

Molly glanced over Kristin at Amy, who gave her a shrug that said, "Don't look at me, I have no idea." She brought one hand to the back of Kristin's head and held her as she wept. Her fingertips came in contact with a sizable bump. "Honey, what's this? You've got a lump back here."

Kristin stood back up, sniffing. She reached back, following Molly's fingers. "Yeah, I know. I fell."

Molly's eyes widened. "You fell?"

Kristin nodded and wiped her tear-stained face.

"Are you okay?" Jo and Amy approached and Amy was looking at her with concern.

Kristin nodded vigorously, one hand still holding tightly to Molly's. Molly's fingers were so warm, Kristin thought she might swoon just from the feel of them.

Molly continued to poke and prod in her wet hair. "Are you sure?" Her face was worried.

Kristin nodded again and wiped her nose with the back of her hand.

"Come on," Molly said, and it wasn't a request. It was an order.

"Take those boots off. Let's get you upstairs and into some dry clothes. Then I want you to sit by the fire until you warm up. Okay?"

Kristin lifted Molly's hand to her lips. "Okay." She pressed her mouth against the warm skin there, rubbed her lips against it gently as she closed her eyes and swallowed down the emotion that was threatening to consume her. Molly was here. She was here and taking care of her, and she could *see* her.

Molly squatted down to unlace Kristin's boots. Kristin held tightly to her hand. When Molly tugged gently to extricate it, Kristin didn't let go. "Honey, it's kind of hard to do this one-handed," she commented.

When Kristin still didn't let go, Molly gazed up at her. There was something very different about her…something behind her eyes. She didn't know what it was, and it worried her a little bit because it seemed so…*not* Kristin. She worked on the boots with one hand.

Once upstairs, Kristin let Molly continue to lead and be the caretaker. She stood still obediently while Molly stripped her of her wet clothing. Molly tsked and shook her head.

"I can't believe how wet you got." Kristin's skin was pale and clammy. "How long did you stay on the ground?"

Kristin shrugged and cleared her throat, her voice hoarse. "I think…I think I might have been unconscious," she said sheepishly as Molly tugged her cold, damp panties down her legs.

Molly stood quickly, horror on her face. "My God, Kristin. What if you'd been out longer? You could have frozen to death." She reached up for Kristin's head. "Let me see that bump again."

Kristin caught Molly's hands. "I know. I'm okay. Don't worry."

"But…" Molly regarded Kristin's face carefully. "What is going on with you?"

Kristin looked…changed somehow. Molly couldn't explain it, but her entire demeanor, the softer expression on her face, the fact that she seemed here, but still far away—it was weird. Weird in a way that Molly had no idea how to clarify.

Still naked, Kristin dropped down onto the bed and sat there staring at nothing. Molly shot little glances in her direction as she zipped around the room collecting dry clothes. It wasn't unusual for Kristin to be off in another world when they were together—she often ended up lost in thoughts about work or clients, and Molly could go on and on without realizing that Kristin hadn't heard a word of it. This was different, though. Kristin was not only somewhere else, she seemed… younger? Vulnerable? Sad? Molly couldn't put a finger on it and wasn't sure how to bring it up without sounding paranoid.

Instead, she squatted in front of Kristin's knees so she could look up into her face. "Honey?" she asked softly. "Are you sure you're all right?"

Kristin took Molly's face in her hands and pressed a kiss to her forehead, inhaling the scent of the apple shampoo and getting a quick flash of her…dream? Hallucination? What the hell *had* happened to her out there? Shaking off her own confusion for the time being, she answered quietly, trying to keep her voice light despite the fact that her lower lip was chittering nonstop. "I'm freezing is what I am." She reached for the dry clothes. "Will you help me get dressed?"

DARBY

Darby had hoped the mindless channel surfing would help her ignore the fullness of her head, but it was actually serving the opposite purpose, especially after Kristin's return. On her back on the couch, she continued to toggle buttons on the remote, absently watching the TV picture flit from news to sitcom to animation to infomercial. She supposed no one would be surprised to see her demonstrating the simple, typical behavior of anybody her age, focused on the nearest electronic device and paying no attention whatsoever to the outside world.

Inside, however, was a different story, for Darby Cooper was anything but a simple and typical woman. Much as she wanted to be able to say that the various events of the day hadn't affected her, they had. Big time. She tried to focus on *The Simpsons*, but her restless mind refused to cooperate. There were too many other subjects to think about.

The chewing-out she'd gotten from Aunt Jo featured prominently. She knew she should just move past it, that Aunt Jo had only been trying to set her straight, so to speak, but she could still feel the painful embarrassment of knowing the others had seen her hauled out of the room by the scruff of her neck like a misbehaving puppy. Thank God Kristin had already gone by that point. Darby didn't think she could bear knowing her nemesis had seen her treated like a child.

Nemesis? Is that what I think she is?

The thought sent a bit of a frightened chill through her. If Kristin was Darby's nemesis, that would mean that Darby actually thought she stood a chance of winning Molly's affections. After the display she'd just witnessed upon Kristin's return, she knew that was never going to happen.

She replayed the moment in her mind, despite having no desire to do so. Kristin banging into the house looking like a frightened animal—and yet somehow still stunning, at least to Darby's critical eye. *How the hell is that possible?* The last thing in the world she wanted to admit to was Kristin's good looks, but there they were, glaringly apparent even as Kristin stood in front of her, dripping wet and wild-eyed.

Her soaked, clinging clothing only accentuated a great body, and the matted state of her hair did nothing but prove that she was, in fact, a real blonde with no dark roots and several different shades of gold sparkling in the firelight. The cold had given her cheeks a rosy red glow, which advertised how creamy and smooth her skin really was. The alarmed and confused darting of her eyes only forced onlookers to notice what a gorgeous shade of blue they were. If Darby had wanted the pleasure of ripping her apart for her physical shortcomings as well as her emotional ones, she was way out of luck.

When Molly ran to her, Darby's stomach churned. *Don't go to her. Come to me.* It was a silly command, given telepathically in some childish hope that it might be heard. But the concern and tenderness in Molly's incredible green eyes had nearly crushed Darby with its intensity…an intensity that was directed at somebody other than her.

Come on, Cooper. Did you really think she'd just throw away her seven-year relationship with a VP, her home, and her financial support to hop into a ten-year-old rattletrap car with the manager of a Blockbuster? Seriously?

But deep down, she knew there was part of her that *had* hoped, that *had* wanted, that thought maybe, just maybe, she *did* stand a chance.

And what was that about? Where the hell did this desire for more than a quick, juicy fuck come from? It was as if something had changed overnight, which was out of the question because people didn't change overnight. They didn't change at all, especially people like her. Once a lothario, always a lothario. She wasn't cut out for relationships, for commitment. She'd known that fact for years, since her very first, and only, girlfriend. Oh, she had no shortage of women. She was a pro at the pick-up, at the take-home, at the brush-off the morning after.

Always drive. Always go to her place, never yours. Always leave before daybreak.

Those were the three rules she lived by. It kept her free and easy, without clinginess, without unwanted attachment or responsibility. It was the way she lived and she'd always been very happy. She was the envy of many a woman stuck in the boring routine of a relationship, picking out paint, staying home on weekends to do yard work, and visiting the in-laws. Those women wished they had the carefree, easy life that Darby did, and Darby didn't envy what they had at all. Not even a little bit.

Until Molly.

Damn her.

Damn her and her piercing green eyes and her intoxicating laugh and her invigorating scent and her sexy mouth. Darby's mind took her back to the other side of the garage, back to the early morning and the snow and the intensity of pressing into Molly's body. The sensation of physically pushing her up against the shingled wood, of holding her a willing prisoner, was almost tangible. Darby could feel her own muscles twitch at the memory and at the fantasies she'd harbored since that moment, of all the things she wanted to do to that hot, tight little body. The visions ran the gamut from the simple tameness of making slow, passionate love to Molly to the erotic polar opposite of tying her to the bed and teasing her for hours on end.

That image was nearly her undoing and she squeezed her eyes shut tightly, wishing for nothing more than to have the ability to scrub it clean from her mind, to make it disappear like wiping fingerprints from a windowpane. She tossed on the couch and settled on her side, heaving an annoyed breath as *The Simpsons* blended into *Entertainment Tonight*.

"Damn tabloid news," she muttered, thumbing the channel button, wishing she had a similar remote for her whirling thoughts.

Part of her was irritated at the rest of the group for going about their day as usual. *Can't anybody see that I'm in turmoil here and don't know how to pull myself out?* She wanted to scream at them, to plead for help because she really was feeling lost and alone and confused. Somewhere in the deep recesses of her brain, she knew there was a good chance she was falling in love with Molly. She clenched her teeth at the thought. God, Julie was going to have a field day with this. Why couldn't she have had these feelings for Rebecca? It would be a hell of a lot easier and make so much more sense. Rebecca wanted her. Rebecca would be ecstatic to think Darby was in love with her. She'd squeal with joy and throw herself into Darby's arms, the giddiness oozing out of her like oil.

And then we'd be picking out paint and staying home on the weekends to do yard work and visiting the in-laws.

Darby closed her eyes, wanting to black the image out of her mind. And that's when she knew it was true, that she had fallen hard for Molly. That despite her reputation and her usual behavior and her unwillingness to settle down, this one woman had wormed her way in. She knew because suddenly picking out paint and doing yard work and visiting the in-laws didn't seem like they'd be so bad if she was doing those things with Molly by her side.

Son of a fucking bitch.

Darby rubbed viciously at her temple and cursed the gods or the Fates or destiny or whatever the hell was having a good laugh at her expense right now. Of all the women she'd been attracted to, of all the women she'd smooth-talked, of all the women she'd bedded, for Christ's sake, the one she finally ended up having real, honest-to-God feelings for was off-limits. She thought of her conversation with Aunt Jo earlier.

"I like her. Molly. I...you know...like her."

"That's too damn bad. You can like her. You just can't have her. She's a married woman who's desperate to fix her failing relationship. If you do like her, then you need to step back and respect her enough not to interfere."

Careful to keep her frustration disguised as laziness, Darby hauled herself off the couch and went into the kitchen, where Aunt Amy was preparing dinner. She opened the refrigerator and pulled out a beer.

"I'm making your favorite." Aunt Amy indicated the chicken breasts and ingredients for the breading to the chicken cutlets Darby had loved since she was a young teenager.

Darby managed a weak smile before twisting off the cap and downing half the bottle in three long gulps.

Aunt Amy arched an eyebrow at her. "Everything okay?" she asked with knowing concern.

Darby nodded. "Peachy." She kissed Aunt Amy's temple and went back into the living room, flopping down onto the couch in much the same position she'd been in previously.

"...If you do *like her, then you need to step back and respect her enough not to interfere..."*

The concept of respect was a new one for Darby, but she suddenly had a crystal clear understanding of what it meant. As much as she wanted Molly for herself, she wanted Molly to be happy more, and despite her penchant for the disrespectful life of love-'em-and-leave-'em, she was relieved to note that she *did* respect Molly enough not to interfere.

Maybe people do change.

She shrugged, took another slug of her beer, and flipped the channel.

BLACKBERRY PULP

Later that evening, everybody was on the first floor, stomachs stuffed with the chicken cutlets. As always, Amy had taken great joy in preparing them by hand, using the mallet-shaped meat tenderizer to pound them into submission. Jo had recognized her wife's subtle manifestation of all her frustrations. *What a freaking chaotic week,* she thought in amazement. When they'd come up with the brilliant idea of inviting their closest friends over for the holidays, they certainly hadn't bargained on all this Dyke Drama—though with seven lesbians in the same house for a week, the chances were pretty good. She felt like she and Amy had been plopped into the middle of a soap opera.

Now, from the vantage point of her leather club chair, Jo sipped coffee laced heavily with Bailey's Irish Cream and tried to get a fix on everyone and everything that was going on.

Kristin sat on a floor pillow in front of the fire and stared into the flames. She was finally dry and—Jo hoped—warm, bundled in a pair of black sweatpants and a thick gray hooded sweatshirt with the insignia of the school where Molly worked emblazoned in blue across the front. Her hair was dry and there was finally a little natural color back in her complexion, just the slightest hint of rosiness across her cheekbones. Her face remained fairly expressionless, yet her eyes seemed worried, tinted with confusion. Jo wanted to talk to her, to find out what was going on in her obviously working-overtime brain, but at the same time, she sensed Kristin needed to be alone. She seemed to be working through some stuff in her head and, curious or not, Jo was loath to cut in on her private musings.

Across the room, stretched out on the couch, Darby had her earphones in. She listened to her iPod while reading a graphic novel, her eyebrow piercing reflecting the firelight. Jo seriously wondered how much reading was getting done, as her niece hadn't turned a page in more than fifteen minutes. Every so often, Darby threw surreptitious glances in Molly's direction but Molly's only concern was Kristin, it seemed. She sat at the dining room table and looked up periodically from her hand of cards to check on Kristin, a mixture of wonder and apprehension on her face.

Jo had a smidgen of sympathy for her niece, but at the same time hoped she was learning a valuable lesson. Given the look on Darby's face when she'd said she "liked" Molly, Jo suspected it was the first time in ages—maybe ever—that Darby had felt genuine interest in somebody...beyond the sexual. It was sheer dumb luck that she hadn't fallen for Sophie or Laura—the *available* women. Jo heaved a sigh of frustration, aimed at life in general.

Across the dining room table from Molly sat Amy, her partner in their game of euchre. Amy was wearing one of Jo's button-up denim shirts, and Jo found herself prey to a sudden vision of unbuttoning it very slowly to reveal what lay beneath the fabric: creamy-smooth, freckled skin just aching for her touch. She literally shook the image from her head, internally chuckling over her ridiculously active libido and vowing to save those thoughts for later.

The other two seats at the table were occupied by the other set of partners, Sophie and Laura. Nobody had surprised Jo more this week than those two and she actually did chuckle when she thought of them. *What a turnaround.* Rather than scowling at one another and avoiding close proximity, as they had for the first two days of their stay, they now looked to be friends—friends who shared custody of the little terrier who moved back and forth between the two of them, giving equal amounts of love. Not twenty-four hours ago, they had hated each other—or at least disliked each other immensely. Now they were laughing and joking and winning at cards. Jo shook her head. *Life is so strange.*

"Way to go, partner," Sophie said with a smile. She slapped Laura's hand in a high-five across the table.

Molly grimaced at Amy. "We're getting our asses handed to us, Ames."

Amy sighed. "I know."

Laura grinned. "And they're such nice asses." Looking to Sophie, she said, "Maybe we should hang on to them for a little bit before we hand them over."

Sophie nodded with enthusiasm. "I like that idea. Can we touch them and play with them, too?"

Jo's voice boomed across the room. "I've got a little bit of a problem with that."

The table erupted in laughter.

"Thank you, honey," Amy said, her voice managing to rise among the mirth of the rest of the table. Then she furrowed her brow. "What's that?"

"What's what?" Sophie asked.

"That humming."

The four of them looked around until Molly's eyes settled on the Blackberry Kristin had left behind earlier that day. It had been moved to the kitchen counter to make room for the card game and was now lit up as it buzzed in place, indicating a call or an e-mail coming through.

Molly sighed inwardly, vowing not to let the annoyingly familiar interruption upset her tonight. She was enjoying herself too much. "Kristin?"

Kristin continued staring into the fire.

"Kristin." Molly's voice was firm and this time Kristin flinched and blinked rapidly as if returning from a dream.

"Hmm?"

"Your Blackberry's ringing." Molly indicated its location with a jerk of her chin.

Kristin followed Molly's gaze until she saw the item in question. "Oh."

She stood up and walked into the kitchen, following the buzzing. Her face devoid of any expression, she picked the device up, noted the caller, then set it back down. Without preamble, she grabbed up the nearby mallet-shaped meat tenderizer Amy had used on the chicken earlier, and with one vicious whack, smashed the Blackberry into useless plastic fragments.

There was no sound at all from anybody else in the room as she set the tenderizer back down and returned to her seat near the fire, running a gentle hand across Molly's shoulders as she passed her. Back in her previous position, she resumed staring into the flames. The others simply gaped in astonishment.

Life is so strange, Jo thought again, feeling the sudden urge to burst out in giddy laughter. A sense of pride in Kristin welled up within her. *Even after fifty years on this earth, I still don't get it.*

Saturday, December 31

MOLLY

The only reason Molly opened her eyes was because of the loss of body warmth, the realization that she was alone in the bed. It was morning and the sun was shining brightly. It was the first time all week she hadn't woken up at the crack of dawn, and when she thought back on her night, she couldn't remember the last time she'd slept more soundly. Watching through slitted eyes while Kristin dressed, she also couldn't remember the last time they'd slept so closely together. Kristin had fallen immediately asleep, as though her body had been worn out from the day's activities. Any time Molly had rolled over or adjusted positions, she felt Kristin—a hand on her hip, her leg thrown over Molly's, her head on Molly's shoulder. Now her body was protesting the cold, wanting that proximity back again, having gotten a taste of something it had been missing for months.

"Where are you going?" Her voice was hoarse with sleep as she questioned Kristin softly, not wanting to startle her.

Kristin looked up from her foot, sock in hand. She whispered, "I'm sorry, sweetie. Did I wake you up? I was trying to be quiet."

Molly stretched, reaching her arms over her head to grab the headboard as she willed the sleep out of her system. "I just didn't hear you get out of bed."

"Did you sleep okay?"

"I slept great."

Kristin smiled. "Me, too."

She looked amazing, Molly noted. The lines of stress that usually marred her creamy skin had eased and her blue eyes had softened, showing only a fraction of the worry that had glazed them the previous night. She'd pulled her blond hair back into a ponytail and it shimmered in the morning sun that sliced through the window, golden highlights winking at Molly. She was wearing a pair of jeans, a white turtleneck, and a navy blue sweater. She looked like she'd just stepped out of an L.L.Bean catalog.

Molly sat up in bed. "So, where are you going?"

"I'm going to take a walk, get a little fresh air."

"Do you want some company?"

Kristin hesitated. "Would you be okay if I said 'not yet'?"

Molly tried to ignore the small prickle of hurt that poked at her. "Sure."

"I just...I need to roll a few things around in my head, that's all." Kristin's face was clouded with a slight unease. "I wouldn't be terribly good company."

"Okay. I understand."

"I'd like to walk with you later, though. If you want to."

Molly could feel her own smile light up her face. "That would be great. I'm going to hold you to it."

"Good." Kristin approached her and bent forward. She stopped several inches from Molly's face and simply looked at her for a few long seconds. Molly held eye contact, reveling in the feeling of being Kristin's sole focus, something she'd become very unused to. Kristin kissed her softly on the mouth. "I'll be back soon."

"Do me a favor?" Molly asked as Kristin moved toward the door. "Sure."

Nodding at the dresser, she said, "Take my cell phone?" At Kristin's questioning look, she shrugged. "In case you fall on your head again."

Kristin grinned. "Okay." She clipped the phone to her jeans, waved, and left the room.

Molly lay in bed for a while longer, listening to the sounds of her friends and thinking about the previous day.

She still couldn't believe Kristin had smashed her Blackberry, or "Crackberry," as Molly liked to call it because of its addictive tendencies. It was her lifeline, her tie to her work, her boss, her clients. And now it was in several small chunks sitting in the wastebasket in Amy's kitchen. Not to mention that it was Jack Reeves's connection to Kristin. What would he do when he couldn't reach her? When she didn't return his calls or e-mails?

Molly, like the rest of the group, had no idea what to say after the meat mallet descended. They'd all stared at Kristin in stupefied silence and then had gone back to whatever activities they'd been a part of. It had been surreal. Molly had kept a watchful eye on Kristin for the remainder of the evening, but she did nothing more than stare expressionlessly into the fire. On their way to bed, Molly had asked if she was all right.

"I think maybe I will be," was Kristin's rather cryptic answer. And that's all she'd said.

Now she was off wandering in the woods alone again and Molly wasn't sure whether she should be worried or relieved by her behavior.

Downstairs, a short while later, everybody looked up as Molly approached, smiling hellos and offering coffee. The smell of bacon was mouth-watering.

"God, I'm going to be a blimp after this week," she commented, grabbing a slice and nibbling on it with delight.

"That makes two of us," Sophie said with a smile. "Maybe a gym membership should be my New Year's resolution."

"I'm a member of the club over on Panorama Trail and I love it," Laura offered. "You should try there. They have so many different things that it never feels like a waste of money. There's always something to do."

"I've driven past there a million times," Molly said, taking a seat at the table. "I know a lot of people who belong."

"It's great," Laura went on. "If you don't want to lift weights, you can swim. If you don't want to swim, you can play racquetball. If you don't want to play racquetball, you can shoot baskets. There are yoga classes and step classes and spin classes. It's a great place."

A small smile touched Molly's lips at the way Sophie's eyes lit up and she hung on every word Laura said. Molly recognized the beginnings of attraction blossoming and wondered if the two could put aside their differences long enough to see how good they'd be together. A tiny pang hit her chest as she recalled the initial zaps of attraction the day she'd first been introduced to Kristin. The crystal blue eyes and sparkling golden hair had mesmerized her. Molly had wanted nothing more than to reach out and touch Kristin's face.

A voice in her ear startled her. "How was Kristin this morning?" Amy was behind her, her warm hands on Molly's shoulders.

"Quiet. A little distant, but smiling." She looked up at her dear friend as she tried to put her thoughts into words. "It's weird. She seems...different somehow. In a good way. I think. Maybe she just needs a whack on the head more often."

"Did you talk about yesterday?"

"No." Before Amy could scold her, she rushed on. "She was tired and seemed so...inside her own mind. I just didn't want to bother her, you know? I really get the feeling she'll talk to me when she's ready."

Amy looked skeptical but dropped a kiss on the top of Molly's dark head.

Across the table, Darby sat with a Coke and the business section of the paper. Molly caught her blue eyes as they darted up then dropped back to the paper just as quickly. Molly knew they should probably have a chat, not only about what happened between Darby and Kristin the previous day—Molly was sure something had been said, though she honestly wasn't sure if she wanted to know exactly what—but also about that kiss behind the garage the previous morning. Despite the fact that it had felt so good at the time, Molly was appalled with herself now. The Catholic guilt was in full swing.

Of course, she wasn't at all surprised that her butt remained fused to her chair and her legs did *not* force her to stand and cross the room to ask Darby if they could speak in private. Annoyed, but not surprised. She sipped her coffee instead and then reached for another slice of bacon.

RESOLUTIONS

By late morning, everybody was full and happy. Jo and Darby went outside to grab wood for the fire so nobody would have to go out later. Amy was in the kitchen working on hors d'oeuvres for the rest of the day and getting things ready for dinner that night. She mixed a dip while Molly stood at the counter cutting vegetables to go with it.

"Sit, Ricky." Laura stood before the terrier in the dining room, a small tidbit of bacon left over from breakfast held in her hand. "Can you sit?"

Ricky cocked his head and his furry brown tail wagged furiously. He continued to stand.

Laura squatted in front of him, held the bacon to his nose, and gently pushed down on his backside while simultaneously lifting the bacon, forcing his head up. His butt plopped to the ground. "Good!" Laura exclaimed, letting him have the bacon. "Good boy."

Sophie watched from her seat at the table where her crossword puzzle sat in front of her, full of blank squares. "Nice job," she commented.

"I think he's really smart," Laura said with delighted enthusiasm. "He's going to learn fast." She repeated the task a few more times with the remainder of the bacon. On the final try, Ricky sat on his own. After rewarding him, Laura swooped him up in her arms and allowed herself to be bathed in dog kisses.

Sophie laughed at the spectacle. "Do you have stuff at home for him?"

"What do you mean?"

"Bowls, toys, a crate. That sort of thing. Dog food?"

"I have nothing at all." Laura grinned. "I guess I've got some shopping to do."

"Well…I was thinking…" Sophie hesitated slightly before finding her nerve. "My good friend from college owns a pet store in the city. I'm sure they're closed tomorrow, but I bet they're open on Monday and, um, I'd be happy to go with you."

"You would?" Laura was surprised and pleased at the same time.

"Sure."

"I'd like that."

Neither Sophie nor Laura saw Amy gently nudge Molly with an elbow and wink at her, nor did they see Molly's responding grin.

The front door opened just then, a chilling burst of winter air whipping through the small cabin. Kristin stomped her feet on the mat and smiled. "Morning, all."

"Hi, there," Molly said as she abandoned her vegetables to help her wife out of her winter garb. "I was about to send out a search party."

Kristin's cheeks were winter-weather red and her eyes looked bright. "No falling on my head today. Just a great hike." Looking into the kitchen, she said, "Amy, this place is beautiful. I was amazed. The sun was shining and the birds were singing and there was fresh snow on the ground. Gorgeous."

Amy smiled with pride. "Now you know why I love it here so much."

"Absolutely." She fished in the pocket of her ski jacket as Molly hung it on a hook. Withdrawing her hand, she said, "Here. I found something for you."

Molly held out her hand and Kristin placed her treasure in Molly's palm, suddenly feeling as shy as a schoolgirl.

When Molly looked down, there was a perfectly shaped heart resting in her hand. She looked more closely, seeing that it was actually a rock, but its shape was unmistakable. "Oh, wow," she said, her own heart soaring. "Where'd you find this?"

"There's a big stand of evergreens back a ways off the path and there's no snow under a lot of them. That caught my eye and…I thought of you." Kristin didn't add that she'd felt inexplicably drawn to the spot, that she wasn't really walking anywhere near the particular tree under which the rock was nestled.

"You did?"

Kristin nodded.

Molly reached up and wrapped her arms around Kristin's neck, enveloping her in a warm hug. "Thank you," she said softly. "I love it." She tucked the rock into the pocket of her jeans. "I'm going to keep it with me all the time."

The huge grin that split Kristin's face was something Molly decided then and there she wanted to see more often, every day if she could help it.

Kristin kissed her quickly on the mouth. "I'm going to grab a shower."

"Okay. I'll be in the kitchen with Amy. Sadly, the vegetables won't cut themselves."

Back in the kitchen, Molly pulled the rock back out of her pocket and showed it to Amy, then to Sophie and Laura, who came to look. It was swirled gray in color, round and full, solid and weighty.

"That is so cool," Laura breathed, touching the rock with one finger.

"How the hell did she manage to find a rock in the woods in the dead of winter?" Sophie asked.

Amy grinned smugly and when Molly noticed, she slapped playfully at her arm. "You're not going to launch into a Magic Acre story, are you?"

"I wouldn't dream of it," Amy replied as she plunged a piece of celery into her dip and tasted it. She grinned as she chewed. "Besides, none of you would believe me."

❖

"Aunt Jo?"

"Yeah?"

"I'm sorry about yesterday." Darby gave the apology while pulling logs from the pile and stacking them into the carrying sling. She was embarrassed and couldn't bring herself to look her aunt in the eye. She hadn't been scolded by Aunt Jo like she'd been the previous day since she was a preteen. She'd deserved it then, too.

Jo stopped what she was doing and stood up straight to regard her niece. Darby had been fairly quiet since their run-in the day before. Jo didn't know how parents did it, how they scolded their kids and went on with their lives. Jo felt so bad, she had to catch herself on several occasions before she tried to sweet-talk Darby, to apologize, to make herself feel better and to wipe that hurt, chagrined look off her face. Her words had been harsh, but Darby had needed to hear them and it took all Jo's strength to let it sit, to leave it alone. Now Darby had done the apologizing. Jo felt a sudden, fierce pride in her niece.

"It's okay," she said simply.

When Darby looked up, her blue eyes were troubled. She opened her mouth as if about to say something, then closed it again and reached for more wood.

"What?" Jo prodded gently.

"I just…" Darby took a deep breath and blew it out in frustration, the puff visible in the chilly air. "I'm so good at noncommitment." She grimaced at Jo. "I'm good at the pick-up, I'm great at getting her home, but I suck at anything beyond that."

Jo studied her niece. "Don't you want more, Darby? Don't you want more than just great sex? Not that there's anything wrong with that," she added with a wink. "But don't you want somebody to wake up with? Somebody to come home to? Somebody to talk to or not talk to or a lap to rest your head in when you have a bad day?"

Darby answered honestly. "You know, I never did. I always thought what you and Aunt Amy have is really cool, but I also thought it just wasn't for me. I never thought of myself as the settling-down type. I'm not good at it and I've never wanted it." She sighed. "Until I met Molly."

Jo nodded, surprised by the admission, but at the same time, not. She knew that the day would come eventually when her niece would meet a woman who would finally be The One—the person who got Darby to relinquish her hold on a life of one-night stands and weekend clubbing. What she hadn't counted on was that person being one of Amy's dearest friends, and married to boot.

"Molly's in love with somebody else," Jo said with tenderness, not wanting to hurt Darby but wanting to be sure she understood the score.

"I know that."

"She's been with Kristin since you were a senior in high school."

"I know that, too." Darby looked up at the bright blue of the winter sky. She didn't want to hear these facts. She was aware of them, but having Aunt Jo say them out loud made them that much more real.

The wood was loaded and ready to be hauled into the house, but both women stood unmoving. Darby continued staring off into space. Jo watched her intently, wishing there was something she could do to help her niece through the confusion.

"I don't know how this happened," Darby said softly. "I don't fall for women at the drop of a hat. It's silly and it's not me."

"Things change." It was the most fitting explanation Jo could think of. "Maybe it *is* you and you just didn't know it."

Darby snorted.

Trying a different tack, Jo suggested, "Maybe it is you *now*. And falling for somebody isn't silly. Falling for somebody who's spoken for is. And not knowing when to back off is even sillier." Jo looked at Darby pointedly.

"Yeah. I know," Darby agreed, her face coloring slightly. "You're right. But that doesn't mean it doesn't suck."

Jo chuckled. "Sometimes, it does. Sometimes, it sucks *a lot*." She picked up one of the canvas slings full of logs and studied her niece. "It's the last day of the year, Darby. Tomorrow, you get to start fresh. Think about that."

Darby watched as Jo walked toward the house. For the first time since she could remember, starting fresh actually sounded like a good idea.

At precisely eight o'clock, dinner was served and it smelled unbelievable. Amy had cooked the beef tenderloin to perfection—her love of red meat made her thank her lucky stars none of her present friends were vegetarians—and her guests oohed and ahhed as it was sliced before them. Jo circled the table, filling everybody's glasses with a deep burgundy-colored Merlot that smelled almost as good as it tasted.

Laura pulled her nose out of her glass long enough to comment, "There's nothing quite like a good red wine to warm you up in the winter."

"Absolutely," Sophie agreed, her glass already to her lips.

"Hey, wait," Jo ordered. "We have to toast first."

Sophie caught herself and lowered her glass, looking sheepish. Laura grinned at her.

Jo stood at the head of the table where Amy's seat was, one hand on her wife's shoulder. "First of all, I want to thank you all for being here. Amy and I feel there is no better way to spend the holidays than with those you love."

Murmurs of agreement traveled around the table.

"I'd also like to say that friends like you are hard to come by and when you do find them, you need to hold on tight. So I stand before you and say, with all my heart—and I think my wife would agree—that our New Year's resolution is to spend more time with all of you. You're too important to us to let the everyday world of work and shopping and whatever keep us apart."

From Jo's right, Laura spoke up. "I'd like to add my own resolution to that. Starting with the New Year, I'm going to stop feeling guilty about things I've done in the past and promise to forgive myself." Nods and words of encouragement filled the air. "And I'm going to be a good mommy to Ricky," she added with a grin, smiling down at the terrier near her chair.

Sophie promptly raised her glass and said, "I'm going to stop wallowing in what was and start concentrating on what will be."

Darby was next. With a glance at Jo, she stated simply in a quiet but assured voice, "I think I'm going to open my eyes this year." Amy smiled up at Jo, both acknowledging the change in their niece this signaled.

Kristin studied her plate as she organized her thoughts. When she lifted her chin and spoke, her eyes sparkled, their color arresting. She placed a warm hand on Molly's knee under the table. "I'm going to try to finally fix my whacked-out priorities and focus on what's really important in my life." She looked at Molly.

Molly's eyes teared up and she laughed as she tried to wave the moist drops away, her friends *aww*ing at her. Pulling herself together, she spoke softly. "I have a couple resolutions that I'm going to try my hardest to stick to. First, while Darby's busy opening her eyes, I'm going to work on opening my mouth." Gentle laughter rounded the table. "Second, I want to start thanking the people who help me grow." At this statement, her eyes cut quickly to Darby and then away. "It's not always easy to understand yourself. Even the simplest things can elude your grasp. When somebody helps you make a connection or put a puzzle piece in place, they deserve some gratitude." Molly looked at Darby once again and mouthed a silent "Thank you."

Kristin looked at Darby as well, but her face was expressionless and it actually freaked Darby out a bit. She averted her eyes and took a swig from her water glass.

"I'm all misty now," Amy said, and her friends smiled at her. Holding up her wineglass, she waited for the others to follow. "I love you all and I'm so glad you're here. Happy New Year, my friends."

Seven glasses plinked together over the table filled with food. The women sipped, humming their overwhelming approval of the wine. Then they dug into the food, laughing and carrying on several conversations at once. Bowls were passed. Garlic mashed potatoes, green beans, squash, homemade rolls—the list of choices was endless. Amy had outdone herself, which surprised nobody. Ricky sat at Laura's feet, watching closely, no doubt hoping some tantalizing morsel would slip from her plate and fall on his head. He eventually moved so he was between Laura's chair and Sophie's, once he realized that, of the two, Sophie was the bigger softie. Several small morsels of beef found their way to him throughout the course of the meal.

Though the atmosphere was the friendliest, the most relaxed it had been all week, each woman had something on her mind. Though she'd attempted to put it aside, it scratched at her brain through the evening. Musings about life, about changes, about her own behaviors and about the others' swirled around in each head.

Amy worried for everybody at the table. She desperately wanted Molly and Kristin to be all right. Too many of her lesbian friends had gone through breakups in the past couple of years, and she was concerned that they hadn't tried. She thought breaking up was too easy, especially with no legal binding. She often felt it was easier for couples to split than to go through the effort of fixing the problems. Fixing things was hard and many just didn't have the stomach for it. Throwing in the towel was often the simpler solution.

She knew Molly and Kristin were strong and she was certain their love for each other was even stronger. She hoped they knew so, as well. She also realized with surprise that she'd love to see Sophie and Laura hook up. It wasn't something that had even crossed her mind when she'd extended the invitations for the week, and she was a little disappointed in her own usually adept matchmaking abilities for not seeing what a great pair they'd make. But she also knew they each had their own demons to exorcise before they'd be ready to give themselves to somebody else. Still…they were so damn cute together.

Before they could catch her smirking at them, she scanned down the table until her gaze settled on Darby. Poor Darby. She sympathized with her young niece, knowing being hauled out of the room by Jo hadn't done a lot for her self-esteem. But Jo was very wise and Darby knew it, so Amy hoped she took something beneficial from the experience. She still looked with puppy-dog eyes at Molly—a look Amy hadn't seen on Darby before, ever. She thought how strange life's timing could be…that the first time Darby met someone who might really matter to her, that someone was unattainable. Amy wondered what might have happened between the two if Molly had been single.

To Amy's right, Laura put a forkful of potatoes into her mouth and thought about her resolution as she chewed. Forgiving herself wasn't an easy feat for her. It never had been. She'd felt guilty for so long now, it was as if the guilt was a part of her, like a limb or an organ. She was afraid cutting it away would leave a hole so big she'd never be able to fill it. She glanced over and noticed Sophie covertly slipping a piece of meat to Ricky. She smiled and said nothing.

The thought of moving forward and leaving the past behind terrified Sophie almost as much as letting go of her guilt terrified Laura. Who was Sophie if not the woman Kelly left? It was her entire identity now, and she didn't know if she could exist as anything else. She didn't think she knew how. She swallowed hard and concentrated on fattening up the terrier.

Darby tried hard not to look at Molly at all through dinner, but it was painfully difficult. When she did look, her heart constricted in her chest because the look of love and hope in Molly's green eyes was focused solely on Kristin. *Damn, that is one lucky woman.* She hoped Kristin knew what she had, because Darby wanted nothing more than to snatch it away from her and if she had less respect for Molly, she would do just that. She did a mental double-take at her own thoughts and chuckled to herself. For the second time that day, she wondered when she had ever had a feeling that even slightly resembled respect for a woman she was interested in. Maybe Aunt Jo was right. Maybe she was evolving after all.

Kristin was hiding her panic like a pro. Despite the fact that she felt she'd made some huge progress in understanding herself and her issues and making realizations about her own life, the impending changes scared the living hell out of her. She knew that a complete shift in lifestyle, in mental processing, in behavior, was the only way she was going to make things right. Totally changing her way of thinking and acting with regard to work versus Molly was the end-all, be-all solution to fixing the mess she'd helped make of their relationship, but she had no idea if she held even half enough strength to accomplish such a feat. True, she'd changed her attitude over the last twenty-four hours without a lot of difficulty, but she knew it had been easy because of the atmosphere. She was away from home, away from work, and not alone with Molly. When they returned to their normal life was when they'd see if her promises and resolutions would hold any water. It was easy for her to say she wanted to change while she was far away from her own reality. But once they got home? The thought made her physically shudder with anxiety.

Kristin's hand was warm on her knee, but part of Molly was still cold inside. It was the part that harbored all the worry she was pretending she didn't have. She was concerned that Kristin might not be able to hold up her end of this unofficial bargain they'd made to fix their partnership. In addition, there was the guilt she had for not having enough faith in her wife. Plus, she worried that she couldn't hold up her own end. It was very easy to say she was going to start speaking up, but one doesn't go from passive-aggressive to assertive in a matter of hours. It was going to be very hard work for her. She'd had over thirty years of watching and learning from her mother and nearly twenty of her own adulthood. She'd been very good at putting the lessons she gleaned from her mother into practice in her own life. How the hell was she going to manage a complete personality change? She closed her eyes briefly, trying not to let the terror show on her face.

Jo lifted her wineglass to her lips and took a look around the table at each of her friends. She smothered a grin and indiscernibly shook her head from side to side as she dug into her food. She felt sympathetic, but knew all of this was part of life. Everything her friends were going through, each individual problem or concern or issue was part of living and they'd all figure out how to deal. All she could do was be there if they needed her, and that wasn't hard. She looked at their faces as they conversed, smiled, laughed. Her grin grew a little wider as she thought about the positions they'd put themselves in. Making big resolutions was one thing. Making them in front of six other people was something else entirely. Now, failure would be very visible and potentially embarrassing.

Every single one of them is crapping her pants right now.

"Only fifteen more minutes, guys," Amy said, folding her poker hand. "I'm going to pop the champagne." She grimaced as Darby raked yet another pot of chips to her spot at the table. "Are you cheating somehow?" She playfully slapped her niece's head. "Are there aces up your sleeves?"

"I'll help," Molly called, leaving Kristin in the living room. Kristin was reluctant to let go of her hand, and Molly grinned as she extricated herself, kissed Kristin on the forehead, and then followed Amy into the kitchen.

Sophie shook her head, throwing down her cards in mock disgust. "It's a damn good thing we're not playing with real money. My landlord would not be happy if I told him I lost next month's rent in a poker game."

"I told you to watch out for her," Jo said from the living room. "She's a whiz kid. Always was."

Darby grinned smugly, stacking her chips. "What can I say? I'm lucky."

"Lucky, my ass," Sophie muttered. "That's it. I'm done. I can only take so much loss in one night. It's bad for my ego." She joined Jo in front of the television. "My God, is he ever going to croak?" she asked when Dick Clark came on the screen. Jo slapped at her, making an appalled face, and Sophie laughed. "Seriously, what is he, a hundred and ten?"

"The man's immortal," Laura said from the sofa where she sat with Ricky curled up on her lap. "I'm convinced of it."

A muted pop sounded from the kitchen and a smattering of applause filled the air. "Ten minutes," Jo announced.

Molly returned with two glasses of champagne and handed them to Laura and Sophie. She got two more from the counter and supplied

Jo and Kristin. The next went to Darby, who was still counting her chips at the dining-room table. She looked up as Molly held out the glass.

"Here you go," Molly said.

"Thanks." Darby smiled, trying not to revel in the heat when their fingers touched.

"Are you okay?" Molly asked softly, concerned.

Darby thought about it for a moment, and then nodded with assurance. "Yeah. Yeah, I think I am."

Molly felt relief flood her system. "Good. That's good." Amy was suddenly at her elbow, handing her a glass. Molly took it with a grateful nod. She looked back at Darby and then headed into the living room where Kristin was waiting.

"Coming?" Amy asked as she, too, headed for the television.

"Yeah." Darby sighed and followed.

The last five minutes of the year flew by and soon all seven women were counting out loud.

"Five! Four! Three! Two! One! Happy New Year!"

The strains of *Auld Lang Syne* filtered through the room as Jo planted a loving kiss on Amy's mouth.

Kristin held Molly tightly and looked into her eyes for what seemed like ages before whispering, "I love you." Their kiss was soft and sweet.

Laura kissed the top of Ricky's head. "Happy New Year, little buddy. We're going to have a great time, you and me." When she looked up, Sophie was watching with a grin, despite the age-old discomfort of having no one to kiss at midnight. Laura slid the terrier from her lap to the couch and stood. She crossed the room to Sophie, took her face in her hands, and kissed her softly on the lips. "Happy New Year, Sophie," she said with a smile.

Sophie stood completely flummoxed as Laura turned to Jo and Amy, wrenching them apart so she could give them each a kiss. She brought her fingers to her lips, certain she'd feel heat radiating from them. She jumped when Darby spoke from right next to her.

"Yeah, I'd get me some of that if I were you," she stated simply and pecked Sophie on the cheek. She squeezed Sophie's shoulder before moving on to the others.

Molly hugged Amy. Jo wrapped Kristin in an embrace that said more than words could. Jo wasn't a big talker and Kristin knew it. She also felt the message in the hug. It said *you can do this*. Kristin tightened her grip on her friend.

Amy moved to Sophie, chuckling at her seemingly frozen state. She wrapped her in a warm hug and whispered something in her ear.

Darby and Molly found themselves face-to-face.

"Happy New Year, Darby," Molly said.

"Happy New Year to you." They stood awkwardly for several seconds before Darby found her nerve. "Can I hug you? Would that be all right?"

Molly swallowed. "Yeah. I think so." She opened her arms.

Darby held on for dear life, knowing this was the last time she'd get this close. She tried to imprint everything she could in the few short seconds she had: the smell of Molly's hair, the feel of the muscles in her back, the warmth of her thighs and her breasts as they pressed into Darby's own. She squeezed her eyes shut and concentrated until she felt Molly's grip relax and she knew she had to let go, too.

Darby couldn't meet the green eyes as she murmured, "Thanks," and searched for her champagne glass.

The cabin was loud—louder than one would think given there were only seven women. But it was the beginning of a new year, a chance to start over, to mend fences and heal old wounds. Laura held Ricky in her arms and carried him from woman to woman, each one gamely accepting his kisses, knowing he was in some ways their new mascot. He would always remind them of this week together.

Champagne flowed freely and the group spent another hour laughing and joking and celebrating before the yawning came and the gradual trickle to bed began. Some were anxious to get to sleep and others were hesitant, but for the same reason: tomorrow meant starting anew and making fresh tracks in the snow.

KRISTIN AND MOLLY

The house had grown fairly quiet. Somebody—either Laura or Sophie—was in the bathroom getting ready for bed, but other than that, there was very little sound. The moon was full and shone brightly through the window in the bedroom where Kristin and Molly were. Molly thought about closing the curtains, but decided she liked the bluish cast in which the room was bathed and left them open.

Kristin smiled as she took in Molly's winter pajamas. The two of them were so different that way. Molly was clad in soft pink flannel pants and a matching long-sleeve, button-up top, as usual. She was always cold, though her skin was more often than not hot to the touch. She always claimed that she was cold because she "gave her heat away" instead of keeping it to warm herself up. Kristin, on the other hand, was consistently warm and slept in a tank top and panties. She liked to joke that if she got too chilly during the night, all she needed to do was simply to curl up next to Molly the Human Radiator—who was giving away her heat as usual—and she'd be warm again in a matter of minutes.

She lifted the covers and made room as Molly approached the bed. Molly cuddled up beneath the thick quilt, tucking her head under Kristin's chin. She threw an arm over Kristin's stomach and a leg over Kristin's thigh, effectively trapping her. Kristin didn't argue; they hadn't slept this close on a regular basis in a long, long time and it felt good. It felt right. She'd missed it. She tightened her grip on Molly's smaller body, surprised to feel a small jolt low in her own when Molly's knee pushed into her.

They lay quietly, listening to the occupant of the bathroom as

Kristin toyed with Molly's hair and Molly drew small circular patterns on Kristin's chest with her fingertips. After many long, silent moments, Kristin spoke.

"Molly?" Her voice was the softest of whispers, barely audible.

"Hmm?"

"I'm sorry." They were only two small, simple words, but they carried such weight and emotion that they deposited an instant lump in Molly's throat when she heard them.

Molly nodded against Kristin's shoulder. "Me, too, honey. Me, too."

"I don't know what's happened to me. To us."

The anguish in Kristin's voice caused Molly to lift up slightly and look into her face. Kristin's blue eyes were plainly visible in the moonlight, and they were boring into her, as if pleading for her to understand.

"It's okay," Molly said, trying her best to sound reassuring as she stroked a fingertip over Kristin's pale brow. "We're going to work things out. We're going to fix it."

Kristin studied Molly's face. Her smooth skin looked like olive-tinted porcelain and her green eyes sparkled with the kindness and love that overflowed her heart. Kristin was reminded all over again why she'd fallen for her in the first place. She gave in to the urge and reached up a hand to touch the face looking down at her with such affection. The skin was warm, soft.

"Are you scared?" she asked, her voice cracking.

Molly smiled. "Yeah. You?"

"Terrified."

"That's okay. Don't you think? I think we're going through some big changes here and it's normal to be afraid."

Kristin absorbed the logic of the statement. "Doesn't make it any easier."

"No."

Molly settled back down against Kristin's shoulder and they lay cuddled against each other once again. The bathroom light went off and the door across the hall clicked shut. Then there was only silence and the sound of Kristin's heart beating steadily beneath Molly's ear. She listened to it, felt it against her head, the unchanging thump-thump as it pushed Kristin's life force through her body. Kristin's fingers were moving in Molly's hair, gently scratching at her scalp and twisting locks here and there. She felt a tingling in her limbs, a sensation that was both comforting and arousing. She snuggled in closer, hugged Kristin's body to her more tightly. As she adjusted her legs, she heard the tiniest gasp, the smallest intake of breath from her partner and the tingling intensified. It was amazing to her what a visceral effect a simple sound could have on her. She raised herself up slowly until she was just high enough to look down at Kristin's face.

No words were exchanged. There was only eye contact, deep and steady. *The eyes are the windows to the soul,* Kristin remembered reading as she found herself lost in sea green. *If that's true, then this woman loves me with everything she has.* The realization was so clear to her that she almost began to cry. Molly's feelings were written so plainly on her face, Kristin couldn't believe she hadn't seen them, was astounded that Molly could hide something so obvious. She concentrated on pouring every ounce of feeling she had into her stare. She wanted Molly to feel the same way when she looked into Kristin's eyes that Kristin did when looking into Molly's.

Molly lowered her head slowly until her lips were scant millimeters from Kristin's. She searched the blue eyes carefully, thoroughly, before settling her mouth onto Kristin's. She kissed her softly, the gentleness of their contact masking the underlying lust that had begun to burn deep in her belly. She increased the pressure slightly and felt Kristin's mouth open beneath hers. An inadvertent moan escaped her and she shifted her position so she was lying directly on top of Kristin, her knees on either side of Kristin's thighs. Kristin's hands were on her face, holding her head as she pushed her tongue into the warmth of Molly's mouth. They kissed for what felt like years, lips and tongues melding together until it was impossible to tell who began and ended where.

Molly finally wrenched herself away, air becoming a must. She pushed up on all fours, surprised by the heat their bodies were generating. She sat up on Kristin's hips and shrugged the covers off her shoulders, smiling down at Kristin.

"Warm?" Kristin asked.

Molly nodded. "Your fault."

"I don't think so. You're the hot one here." Kristin caught the lapel of Molly's pajama top with her fingers and tugged Molly forward so she was on all fours again. As she unfastened the buttons down the front of the shirt, she whispered, "I want to see you."

Molly's heart skipped a beat at the sheer primal need in the words. Her arousal cranking up another notch, she held her breath as Kristin pushed the flannel open, revealing her breasts, now covered in gooseflesh despite the warmth of the room. She gasped when she felt Kristin's fingers working at the waistband of her pants.

"All of you," Kristin said, a pleading note lacing the demand. "I want to see all of you." She tugged at the flannel and the panties beneath it, using her hands and then her feet to pull the fabric off her wife. Molly sat up again, still straddling Kristin, her bottom half now naked and her shirt hanging open. Kristin's breath hitched in her throat as she looked at the vision poised above her. She watched as Molly's nipples hardened under her scrutiny, then she pushed the shirt off Molly's shoulders. It left more gooseflesh in its wake as it slipped down her arms.

Sliding her hands back and forth over the skin of Molly's hips, Kristin stared, struck speechless by the beauty laid bare before her. Molly often complained of her shortcomings—her breasts were too small, her hips were too wide, she was too short. But Kristin never agreed with any of it. Molly was a beautiful woman, wonderfully proportioned and gloriously feminine. Kristin loved her compact size and used to joke about how it was easier for her to reach every part of Molly that way.

Ever since their first night together, Kristin loved to simply look at her. She could still remember the exact moment when she'd removed the last article of Molly's clothing and had seen her naked for the very first time. It had been like unwrapping a gift...an exquisite and breathtaking gift. Now, she felt that same joy. She couldn't pull her eyes away—she could barely blink—as she watched her own hand trail upward and capture one breast, kneading it in her palm, feeling the solidness of the nipple pushing into her. Molly's small intake of breath and the twitch of her hips only served to excite Kristin further, and she squeezed more firmly. Her other hand occupied the opposite breast and soon Molly was arching her back slightly. When she threw her head back and pushed her chest commandingly forward, her body bathed in the ethereal blue of the moonlight, Kristin thought Molly was nothing short of a goddess. Hot and unexpected tears filled her eyes.

Molly gasped when Kristin's fingers zeroed in on her hypersensitive nipples. Despite what they'd gone through over the last months, Kristin obviously hadn't forgotten how responsive her body was when it came to her breasts. The pinching and pumping and rolling forced guttural sounds to push their way from her throat. She was conscious of others in the house and tried to control herself, but the feeling was almost too much. She concentrated so hard on keeping quiet that she didn't notice Kristin's slight change in focus until fingers slipped between her thighs, sliding through the hot, silky wetness she was sure she must be leaving in pools. A cry did escape her then; she couldn't help it. She clamped a hand over her own mouth as Kristin smiled up at her. She fell forward so she hovered over Kristin, propped on her knees and one hand.

"Shh," Kristin warned with a grin. "You want to wake the whole house?"

Molly's breath caught as she tried to respond—Kristin's fingers hadn't stopped their gentle probing, slicking along her engorged flesh with maddening precision. "Your fault," she said for the second time.

Kristin's expression softened. "I can't help it. You're so fucking beautiful, I just can't help it."

"Kristin…" Molly's eyes drifted shut and she caught her bottom lip between her teeth as Kristin's fingers explored her, and she rocked against the touch.

"Come here." Kristin hooked the back of Molly's neck with a wicked grin. "Maybe if I can keep that mouth busy, you'll stay quiet." Pulling her down, Kristin kissed her roughly, with reckless abandon, suddenly sure she couldn't possibly get enough. She slid her hand down Molly's smooth back, cupping her ass tightly and pressing her closer. As she did so, she parted her own knees, which forced Molly open farther and allowed Kristin's fingers better access. Molly groaned and Kristin swallowed up every sound, every breath, never wanting to break their contact. God, how she'd missed this! She'd been such a fool, such a blind fool. Before she could berate herself further, Molly lifted her mouth away.

"Oh, God," she hissed as she squeezed her eyes shut. "Oh, God, Kristin. Yes…oh, my God…"

Kristin knew the chant well and knew what it meant. She felt a rush of wetness fill her own panties in response as she pulled Molly's head to her shoulder, holding tightly and relishing the anticipation of what would happen next as she pressed more solidly with her fingers.

Molly's body exploded, her muscles spasming tightly. She grabbed a fistful of pillow in each hand and buried her face in Kristin's shoulder as she ground herself down onto Kristin's hand.

"Shh…" Kristin whispered in her ear. "I've got you. I've got you, baby."

Silence was impossible and she knew it, though Molly did her best to muffle what she could. The climax was intense, the most intense she'd experienced in a long time and a hundred times better than when she'd taken care of herself, which she'd been doing a lot lately. The contractions continued periodically even as the rest of her body began to relax. And as each muscle eased, Molly suddenly felt emotion. It was raw and it was powerful and it raced up through her until her eyes filled with tears. She kept her face buried in Kristin's shoulder, hoping the feeling would pass, but a sob escaped, tattling on her.

Instead of panicking, Kristin held her tighter as Molly tried not to cry. She'd suspected they were coming, the tears of relief, joy, fear, love. She'd felt them herself and now they ran out of her eyes and down the sides of her face as she held her sobbing wife.

"It's okay," she murmured in Molly's ear, still next to her lips. "It's okay, baby. I love you. I love you so much and I've missed you so much. We're going to be okay. I promise."

She felt Molly nod against her shoulder, and the sobs eventually subsided into occasional hiccups. Molly shifted her body so she slipped sideways and settled against Kristin.

"We can do this," Kristin said.

Molly nodded again. "You think so?"

"If we love each other, I think we can." It was a simple statement, and it would have never scared Kristin before. She'd never wondered about Molly's feelings for her until this week. But even after seeing the unmistakable look on her face earlier in their lovemaking, she felt fingers of doubt, of anxiety, tickling up her spine. Before Darby, it had never occurred to Kristin that she might have driven Molly too far away to ever get her back.

Molly pushed herself up enough so she could look Kristin squarely in the eye. Their tears sparkled in the moonlight and they stayed like that, just looking at one another, for long minutes.

"Do you still love me, Molly?" Kristin's voice was barely audible, her worry nearly choking her as she stroked Molly's bottom lip with her fingertips.

Molly captured and kissed the fingers. "With all my heart," she said. "I always have."

The breath Kristin had been unconsciously holding left her in an enormous whoosh and she pulled Molly against her, squeezing her eyes shut, sure she could never get her close enough. *Thank God,* she thought. *Oh, thank you, God.*

"We're going to be okay," she said, repeating her reassurances. "We are. We can do this." And for the first time in many, many months, she actually believed it.

SOPHIE AND LAURA

Sophie wasn't sure what woke her up. A sound? A dream? She had no recollection of anything other than opening her eyes. It was dark, late. She felt for the nightstand, grabbing her watch and hitting the button that lit up the face.

3:12.

She groaned quietly, feeling suddenly awake. She shifted her position in the twin bed and was surprised to feel weight near her feet. Lifting her head, she noticed Ricky curled up near the foot of the bed. The moonlight was bright enough to allow her to see his brown fur. He snuffled in his sleep and Sophie smiled, inexplicably happy that he'd chosen to bunk with her. Despite her best efforts to remain cool and detached, she was really developing a soft spot for the little guy.

Laura stirred in her sleep in the next bed. Sophie looked, but didn't see much more than a mass of blond hair spilling across the quilt, though she knew from memory exactly what Laura wore to bed: Winnie the Pooh boxer shorts and a *very* clingy white tank top. She licked her lips at the recollection.

With a sigh, Sophie flopped her head back against her pillow and thought about the week. It had been an unexpected whirlwind of emotions, realizations, alcohol, food, fun, discomfort, anger, and self-awareness. None of it was what she'd signed on for, but if she was to be honest, she had to admit it had been an enjoyable experience. For the first time in many months, she felt alive, like she might really be ready to move forward with her life. It was clear to her now that she'd been oblivious to how stuck in a rut she really was. She had always despised women who wallowed in their own self-pity, but she now knew that's exactly what she'd been doing for a good six months. It was a new year. As good a time as any to start fresh.

Laura stirred again, her legs moving under the covers, and whimpered quietly. Sophie watched and waited, wondering if her bunkmate might be having a nightmare. Then she inhaled deeply and exhaled slowly.

Laura.

The midnight kiss came screaming back into her mind. It had been simple. Innocent. *Hadn't it?* It was midnight on New Year's Eve, after all, and neither of them had a partner to kiss. It only made sense that they'd kiss each other, rather than standing there twiddling their thumbs. Laura had simply been braver and faster. Sophie would have done the same thing, given more time. *Wouldn't she?* She brought her fingers to her lips, absolutely certain she could still feel the warm press of Laura's. It had only lasted a second or two, but Sophie felt as if the kiss had been imprinted on her mouth for all eternity, as if she could look in the mirror right this moment and see the faint shadow of where Laura's lips had touched hers.

Movement came from Laura's bed once more and this time, she kicked off most of the covers. Sophie stared with her heart in her throat as her eyes roamed over Laura's newly exposed form as she slept, however fitfully. Her skin was pale, made even more so by the light of the moon. Her legs were long and toned. Sophie thought about Laura's job and how she must be on her feet all day. Even relaxed, her muscle definition was apparent. She had nicely rounded hips, a slim waist, and modest breasts. All in all, Laura's body was beautiful, but it was her face that seemed to capture Sophie's attention the most. It was her creamy-smooth complexion, the kindness in her eyes, and those damn dimples.

Sophie was startled out of her reverie by Laura's sharp intake of breath as she awoke with a jolt. Her chest rising and falling with the rapid pace of her breathing, Laura put a hand to her eyes and pressed with her fingers as a subtle whimper issued from her throat. Worried, Sophie was surprised to feel herself getting out of her own bed and taking the few steps across the small room.

Laura watched her approach, her eyes drilling holes into her makeshift roommate, uncertain whether or not she was fully awake or still clinging to the remnants of the dream.

Sophie sat on the edge of Laura's bed. "Hey," she whispered. "Are you okay?"

"Sophie."

Laura's eyes were black. Sophie could tell so even in the darkness of the night, and it sent a twang through her body that was not unpleasant. "I'm right here. Did you have a bad dream?"

Laura took Sophie's hand. When she spoke, her voice was raspy and hoarse with need. "Please, Sophie. Finish me. Please?"

"What?" Sophie blinked, completely confused, thinking Laura couldn't possibly mean what it sounded like she meant.

"Please?" Laura pleaded once more. She guided Sophie's hand under the waistband of her boxers and before Sophie could make any sense of what was happening—or stop it—her fingers were pushed past Laura's coarse hair and into the warm, moist flesh between her thighs.

"Jesus Christ," Sophie gasped out as her fingers were immediately coated with a shocking amount of Laura's arousal. She'd been having a dream, all right.

Laura's other hand came up and hooked around the back of Sophie's neck.

"Laura?" Sophie whispered the name, alarmed that her fingers had begun moving in the silky wetness all on their own. She knew she should say something more, but no words would come. When Laura pulled her head down, Sophie didn't—couldn't—resist. Their lips crushed together in a bruising kiss that sent fire shooting through Sophie's body, short-circuiting any and all rational thought stemming from her brain, trying to force her to do nothing but *feel* for a change. Letting go mentally was something she had never been good at, but she tried it now. She pulled back, wrenching their lips apart so she could look Laura in the eye. They held one another's gaze, searching, trying to understand what was happening.

Am I just a vestige of a dream? Does she want me *or* this? *Does it even matter?* Sophie pushed the thoughts away. No, none of it mattered. They were two grown women, both lonely, both needy, both in a position to offer pleasure to the other. *And I've wanted her since the second she shook my hand that first day*, Sophie admitted. It was the truth and she decided she should run with it for once in her life. She lowered her head and set about devouring Laura's mouth.

They fit surprisingly well together. Laura held tightly to the back of Sophie's head and used her other hand to guide Sophie's. As Sophie nipped and sucked her way along the side of Laura's neck, Laura glanced down and her arousal ratcheted up another notch at the sensual dichotomy the two of them created: Laura's light skin on top of Sophie's dark as their forearms led down her torso and their hands disappeared into her shorts.

Sophie couldn't get enough. She felt wild, like a captive animal suddenly uncaged. She pushed Laura's tank top up, wanting to see her breasts, to touch them and taste them. The pink nipples stood erect and inviting. Laura gasped as Sophie closed her lips over one, sucking it in deeply, raking her teeth across it. The only thought in Sophie's head was that she wanted more. More, more, more. To a whimpered protest from Laura, she withdrew her hand from the wet warmth and curled her fingers around the waistband of the shorts. Looking up into Laura's face, she tugged at them.

Laura obediently raised her hips, watching in flushed excitement as Sophie slid the shorts down her legs and tossed them to the floor. In a haze of arousal, she propped herself up on her elbows to watch as Sophie pushed her thighs apart and draped Laura's bare legs over her shoulders. Her eyes never left Laura's as she lowered her mouth to Laura's drenched core and tickled the swollen flesh with barely the tip of her tongue. Laura's breath hitched and caught, the hair-light touch sending a wave of electricity through her limbs.

Sophie knew the power she possessed at that moment and she loved it. She repeated the barest of touches, brimming with satisfaction as Laura's head dropped back between her shoulder blades and a sensual groan rose from deep in her throat. It had been so long since Sophie had felt this way, been this turned on just from watching the sexual arousal of another woman and knowing she was responsible. Her time with Kelly seemed eons ago now as she focused instead on somebody else, somebody new, somebody different.

She touched her tongue to Laura's silky wet skin once more, using a hint more pressure. The combination of Laura's musky scent and her salty-sweet taste was making it difficult for Sophie to take her time. In the back of her mind, a little voice was pushing her, egging her on, cheering for her to plunge in, to take what was being offered and to take it now, fast and hard. She tamped down the desire, wanting to take her time, wanting to savor every moment, every taste and touch and twitch. It had been so long. She didn't want it to end too soon.

Using her thumbs, she spread Laura open farther, exposing the hidden pink flesh that was normally protected, and ran her tongue along its smoothness. Laura groaned, her breathing ragged now as she dropped flat onto her back. She was pleading in the softest of whispers, a constant stream of begging. Sophie could barely hear her, but when she did, she felt a surge of excitement hit her low in her own belly.

"Oh, Sophie. Oh, please. Please. You're driving me crazy. My God, you're driving me crazy…"

Sophie smiled against the slick wet and let her tongue skirt around teasingly, enjoying the endless flow of imploring dialogue coming from her prey. Then she decided to up the ante and slipped her fingers into Laura's waiting entrance. Laura's entire body convulsed and Sophie felt fingers fisting her hair roughly. The pain was delicious.

Clamping her arm down across Laura's stomach to keep her in place, Sophie went to work in earnest. She pressed with her tongue and matched the rhythm of her fingers as she slid them in, then pulled them out slowly, letting the tips dance lightly before pushing back in with more force. She kept it up, listening with elation as Laura continued to beg for release, her head tossing from side to side, one hand still in Sophie's hair, the other pressing the pillow into her own face to stifle the gasping and pleading.

Laura was sure she was going to spontaneously combust at any moment, that Sophie was trying to kill her. Death by sex. It was possible, wasn't it? She felt as if she'd been in this position with Sophie countless times. Sophie seemed to know her body too well, know exactly what to do and how. She was putty in Sophie's hands. She was Play-Doh. Sophie could mold her and shape her any way she wanted.

She tried to direct, to push her hips more firmly into Sophie's mouth, but Sophie's arm was pressed down tightly on her stomach, on her hips, not allowing her to move. She was Sophie's prisoner and only Sophie would decide when she would be released. Fingers thrust into her roughly and shockwaves sizzled through her body. They were pulled out and skimmed maddeningly over the sensitive skin at her entrance. Without warning, Sophie plunged them in again, stealing the breath from Laura's lungs. Sophie's tongue pressed and probed and stroked, feather-light, until Laura could barely remember her own name, let alone where she was. It was bliss…tortured, uncontrollable, sob-worthy bliss.

Just when Laura was sure there was no way she could take any more, that she was quite simply going to die from the pleasure, Sophie took mercy on her. Finally, thankfully, she sank into her and covered Laura's center with her entire mouth.

Laura's groan of relief rumbled through the pillow and Sophie almost laughed when she heard it. She used the flat of her tongue to stroke the oversensitized flesh beneath it and circled her fingers inside. She felt the contractions begin almost immediately, grabbing at her fingers and trying to hold them within Laura's body. Laura let go of Sophie's hair, using both hands to keep the pillow clasped tightly over her face as she cried out her orgasm, her thighs clamping warmly over Sophie's ears as her hips rose off the bed.

Sophie remained still as Laura relaxed. She could still feel the aftershocks pulsing against her tongue, her fingers. She gradually withdrew, grinning at the small gasps Laura let out as she did so. She sat up, running the palms of her hands along the outsides of Laura's thighs, reluctant to stop touching her. She felt like something that had been locked up within her had just been set free. Laura's chest was heaving as she pulled the pillow away from her face, dropping her arm to the bed like the dead branch of a tree. Her face, neck, and chest were flushed, the rosy tint visible even in the moonlight. Sophie continued to stroke her flank and when Laura's eyes met hers, they were full of gratitude and contentment. She smiled, giving Sophie a shot of her dimples. Sophie couldn't remember the last time she'd seen something so gorgeous.

"Wow," Laura commented, her voice a whisper.

"I'll say," Sophie replied, smiling down at her. She reached back and pulled the disheveled covers up from the foot of the bed.

"I can't move any of my limbs," Laura said with wonder in her voice.

Sophie chuckled. "I'll take care of it." She gathered Laura in her arms and shifted their bodies so Laura was cradled along her side in the small bed. She pulled the quilt up over their bodies.

"Wow," Laura said again.

"Feel better?"

"Better? I feel unbelievable. That was amazing. *You* were amazing."

Sophie felt her cheeks heat up and was glad Laura couldn't see her face. "I was just obeying orders."

"You follow direction well."

"That's what all my old report cards say."

They lay quietly for a long while, listening to the silence of the wilderness around them. Ricky dropped to the floor from Sophie's bed and then she felt him jump up onto the bed the two women now shared. He turned in a circle several times before settling between Laura's ankle and Sophie's.

"Laura?" Sophie whispered after a while.

"Hmm?"

"Thank you."

Laura lifted her head from its spot on Sophie's shoulder and looked into the rich, brown eyes as best she could in the moonlit darkness. "For what?"

"For trusting me to…help you." At Laura's embarrassed grimace, she rushed on. "It's been a really long time since I was able to just let go, to just focus on the moment. You know? It felt good."

Laura nodded. "I should be thanking you." She smirked. "I think I got the better end of the deal."

"Oh, I don't know about that."

Laura blushed and settled back down into Sophie's arms.

"Laura?" Sophie whispered again and she felt Laura smile against her skin.

"Hmm?"

"What were you dreaming about?"

Several beats went by before Laura finally asked, "What do you mean?"

"You were having a dream just before I came over here. You were whimpering and kicking the covers. What were you dreaming about?"

Laura pushed herself up once more and gazed down into Sophie's face. "You really want to know?"

Sophie blinked several times to focus, still amazed to be holding such a beautiful creature in her arms. She stroked the warm, smooth skin of Laura's arm as she nodded. "Tell me."

"I was dreaming that I was in bed with you, that you were making love to me and taking your time and driving me absolutely insane."

"Seriously?" Sophie couldn't keep the shock from her voice.

"Seriously. And *just* when I was about to have an orgasm…"

"You woke up."

"I woke up."

"Man, that sucks," Sophie sympathized, shaking her head.

"Actually, it worked out quite well, thank you very much."

Sophie chuckled and rolled her eyes at herself. "Oh, yeah. I forgot for a minute."

"Well, then, allow me to refresh your memory." With that, Laura leaned forward and kissed Sophie with such tenderness and passion that it made her toes curl.

Ricky snuffled in disgust and made his way back over to Sophie's empty bed.

Sunday, January 1

FRESH TRACKS

Jo stood in the dining room holding a hot mug of coffee and looking out the window as the recently stoked fire crackled in the fireplace. A fresh blanket of crisp, white snow covered the land and made everything look sparkling and new. The sun had just broken over the horizon and the virgin snow glittered like tiny diamonds had been sprinkled across the ground. It was the one thing about winter that Jo loved the most…waking up to such beauty, as if the world had been scrubbed clean overnight. She sipped, watching the tail end of a doe disappear into the woods, and felt her heart swell as it always did for her love of nature.

She felt Amy's approach before she heard her, so she was not surprised when arms wrapped around her from behind. Amy stood on her tiptoes and kissed the side of Jo's neck, then rested her cheek against Jo's shoulder blade and squeezed.

"Happy New Year, baby," she said quietly, not wanting to disturb Darby, who was still sleeping on the couch.

Jo shifted her mug to one hand and turned slightly so Amy could duck under her arm and tuck herself snugly against Jo's side. "Happy New Year to you." They stood together, wrapped up in one another, gazing out the window. Jo kissed the top of Amy's tousled red head.

"God, it's beautiful, isn't it?" Amy said. "I know I complain about winter sometimes. That I don't like the cold or the driving. But it's so pretty…it takes my breath away when it looks like this."

She took Jo's mug from her hand and sipped, not wanting to leave the view or the warmth of Jo's embrace to get her own coffee. They watched a pair of chickadees at one of Amy's many birdfeeders stuff themselves with a breakfast of sunflower seeds.

After a companionable silence, Jo commented, "Our friends all leave today."

Amy sighed. "I know. I'm kind of bummed about it."

"Me, too."

"You are?"

"Sure. I've liked having them here."

Amy squeezed her wife. "So have I. Do you think they had a good time?"

Darby's voice surprised them both as she spoke from her cocoon of blankets on the couch. "If the noises I heard last night are any indication, they *all* had a good time."

Jo laughed and Amy turned to regard her niece. Darby sat up and stretched, her dark hair sticking up at all angles. "What do you mean?" Amy asked.

"What do you mean 'what do I mean?' I mean there was a lot of sex going on in this house last night. You didn't hear it?" Darby stood in her sweatpants and T-shirt and began folding her blankets. "Apparently, I'm the only one not getting any," she muttered, making a face.

Amy crossed the room so she could interrogate Darby without others in the house hearing her. Jo rolled her eyes and went to get more coffee.

"What did you hear?" Amy demanded, her voice hushed. She huddled close to Darby as if about to receive a cryptic, secretive message.

Darby grinned and shook her head. "You are such a gossip, Aunt Ame. You're worse than my mother."

Amy slapped at her shoulder. "Tell me!" she hissed.

"Two of them were going at it right after we went to bed. Then when I got up around three thirty to get a glass of water, somebody else was doing some heavy breathing."

"Who do you think it was?"

"I don't know!" Darby feigned indignation at the line of questioning. "It's not like I was watching. But the math isn't that hard. Add up the panting and squeaking bed springs…a groan here and there." She shot a look at Aunt Jo when she returned from the kitchen with a fresh cup of coffee. "And when you two started in, I wanted to kill myself." She shuddered. "Please. It's like listening to my parents. Blech! Thank God for thick pillows." With a teasing glance at Aunt Amy, she said, "*You* make a lot of noise."

Amy had the good sense to blush and scratched her forehead in the hopes of covering it up.

Jo laughed outright. At Amy's glare, she shrugged. "Sorry, honey. Truth hurts."

The expression on Amy's face told the other two that she was searching hard for a witty comeback. Failing, she sighed and headed for the kitchen to make breakfast. Jo followed.

Darby smiled and shook her head as she continued to neaten up the couch. She supposed it was a good sign that her aunts apparently had a healthy sex life. They'd been together forever and a day and she didn't see any hints of the dreaded *lesbian bed death* that her older friends had mentioned or suffered from. It was easy for Darby to imagine becoming tired of the same woman day after day, night after night, and she wondered what that said about her. Her aunts evidently didn't have that problem. *Good for them*, she thought with unexpected pride.

The sounds from the previous night really hadn't bothered her all that much. What was so awful about listening to a woman's pleasure, after all? She did wince when she'd picked out Molly's, though. Darby had found herself torn between the stinging fact that it wasn't her causing Molly to make such sounds and the fantasy of pretending she *was* causing it. She simultaneously envied and hated Kristin.

Rifling through her duffel bag, she thought about her cell phone for the first time since her arrival. It made her shake her head in wonder when she realized that she'd barely thought about Rebecca—the reason she was hiding out here at the cabin in the first place—at all in several days. Her cell phone was like an extension of her body, and it was highly unusual for her to just put it out of her head like she had. She was sure Julie must have left her a message or two.

"Or twelve," she muttered in disbelief as she powered up the cell and noticed how many missed calls she had. Julie was going to skin her alive. She took a deep breath and dialed, resigned to her fate, as Kristin and Molly appeared from the stairs, hand in hand. Darby looked away, their tousled appearance and the glow on Molly's face too much to take in at the moment.

"Morning," Molly said cheerfully as she and Kristin entered the kitchen.

"Happy New Year," Amy said, hugging one and then the other.

"Yes, it is." Molly grinned as Kristin pulled her closer.

"Coffee?" Jo asked, holding up the pot. At the nods of consent, she pulled down two mugs and filled them.

"Looks like we got a little bit of snow," Kristin observed, pushing some blond hair out of her eyes as she gazed out the window.

"Not a lot. Couple inches," Jo said. "I'm going to go out and snow-blow in a few minutes. Do you two have a time in mind that you need to head out?"

Molly and Kristin looked at one another and Molly frowned. "We've got two cars. I totally forgot."

"That's okay," Kristin said. "I'll probably start out fairly soon. I have a couple stops to make." Feeling Molly stiffen next to her, she squeezed her hand. "Don't worry. It's okay. I'll get a head start, make my stop, and still beat you home. It won't take ten minutes."

"Promise?" Molly's voice was soft and her voice imploring.

"I promise." Kristin kissed her tenderly on the mouth and her body sent her several sizzling flashbacks in quick succession...Molly waking her earlier by whispering in her ear, Molly's knee nudging Kristin's legs apart as Kristin lay on her stomach, not quite awake yet, Molly's fingers slipping over Kristin's ass and down to the wetness that awaited them between her thighs, Kristin pressing her face into the pillow to muffle her sobs of ecstasy.

It certainly was a hell of a way to welcome in the New Year. It also made Kristin 100 percent sure that it was the way she wanted to be with Molly from that moment on. Close. Playful. Sexy. Loving. All the things they used to be. She'd missed Molly so much. She hadn't even truly realized it until that morning, and she was going to do everything in her power to keep from missing her again, even if that meant stomping into Jack Reeves's office on New Year's Day and telling him she quit. Which was exactly what she planned to do on her way home.

She was scared to death.

"Molly?" Kristin's voice was barely audible, quiet enough for only her wife to hear her.

"Hmm?"

Kristin took a deep breath. "I need your help." There. She'd said it.

"Sure, baby. With what?" Molly's green eyes were open, curious.

Just the sight of her gentleness and willingness to offer assistance made Kristin's eyes well with tears.

"We'll talk about it tonight."

Molly studied her carefully, squinting and then nodding. "Okay. Tonight."

Kristin let out a breath, surprised by how *not* hard it had been to ask Molly for help. She shook her head. *God, I'm an idiot.*

The ticka-ticka of canine nails coming down the bare steps interrupted any further conversation and suddenly, Ricky was jumping at Kristin's legs. Then Molly's. Then Amy's. The group chuckled, each woman squatting to the level of the dog to lavish attention on him. Amidst the cooing and fur-scratching, Laura appeared, looking tired, disheveled, and smiley.

"Morning, everybody," she said, her voice hoarse. She grabbed a jacket off the hook and stepped into her boots.

"Good morning, Laura." Amy eyed her suspiciously.

As Laura and the dog headed out into the sunny, snow-covered morning, Jo nudged Amy and said, "You were staring at her."

"Did you see the red mark on her neck?"

Jo burst into laughter.

"Told you." Darby's voice held a smile as she finished checking her messages and joined the group.

"Told you what?" Molly asked.

Jo raised her mug to her lips and just before sipping, said, "Apparently, you and Kristin weren't the only ones getting it on last night."

"Getting it—oh, God." Molly clamped a hand over her eyes. Cheeks flushed bright red, she buried her face in Kristin's shoulder.

Kristin held her tightly, enjoying the moment. Over her head, she regarded Jo and Amy. "Laura and Sophie? No way!"

"Unless you two were making the rounds up there last night," Jo said with a wink.

Kristin laughed. "Afraid not. Good for them," she said with satisfaction.

When Sophie came down the stairs a few minutes later and approached the chatting cluster, all five women did their best to look at anything but her. Sophie furrowed her brows. "All right. What's going on?"

At the various murmurs of "nothing," the five scattered in different directions. Amy and Molly hit the kitchen to start breakfast. Jo and Kristin dressed for outdoors. Darby busily dialed her cell. Sophie's eyes darted around the room and she pressed her lips together to stifle a grin. *We must have been louder than I thought.*

She glanced out the window and saw Laura and Ricky wandering in the snow, leaving twin tracks in the otherwise untouched white. Surprisingly, waking up in the same small bed, wrapped up in one another, hadn't been at all embarrassing. As a matter of fact, it had been nice. Very nice. The truth had given Sophie a minor bout of heart palpitations, but Laura's reassuring smile had put her at ease.

"I'm not going to ask you for a thing, so don't worry," she'd said gently as if reading Sophie's thought. The dimples were prominent in the morning light. "I just want to say thanks and that I've really, really, *really* enjoyed the past three or four hours with you. Happy New Year, Sophie."

Relief had flooded Sophie's system, along with…something else. "Happy New Year to you," she'd said, kissing Laura warmly on the forehead.

"And right now, I really, really, *really* have to pee." With that, Laura had struggled out of the too-small bed, hit the bathroom, and then taken Ricky downstairs.

Now, as Sophie finally tore her gaze away from the window, Darby was chatting on her cell. They made eye contact and Darby winked at her with a knowing smile.

Yep. Definitely louder than I thought.

Molly tried to tamp down the hint of panic that began to surface the second Kristin keyed the ignition of her Lexus. The window of the driver's side slid down silently and Kristin smiled at her, blue eyes twinkling in the bright sunshine.

"You look worried," Kristin pulled off her leather glove and stroked Molly's cheek with her fingertips. "Trust me?" she asked quietly.

"Always."

"Good." She pulled Molly's head partway through the window and kissed her soundly on the mouth. "I love you. I'll be home before you get there. Please drive safely, okay?"

"You, too. Precious cargo."

Molly stepped back as Kristin donned a pair of black sunglasses and rolled up the window. She looked so damn sexy, her blond hair loose around her shoulders and her face seeming more relaxed than it had in months, she took Molly's breath away. Kristin followed the freshly cleared driveway in reverse out to the road. As she shifted into drive, she waved through the window at Molly and at her friends, who were gathered in a clump at the front door. She tooted the horn twice and was gone.

Molly let her hand drop to her side and blew out a deep breath, the visible puff floating away and then dispersing into nothingness. She heard the crunch of snow underfoot and felt Amy's presence behind her. Amy wrapped her arms around Molly from behind and rested her chin on Molly's shoulder.

"You okay?" she asked with tenderness.

Molly nodded, placing her arms over Amy's where they crossed her stomach. "Yeah. I think so."

"Then how come you look like you just lost your best friend? You were glowing this morning. Why the change?"

Pressing her lips together in a thin line, Molly honestly contemplated the question. The answer was plain and simple, but no less scary to admit. "I'm afraid."

"Of what?"

Molly turned, threaded her arm through Amy's, and led her on a slow stroll back toward the house. "I'm worried that once we're home and the influence of"—she made an all-encompassing gesture—"this place is behind us, things will go right back to the way they used to be."

"And why does that scare you?" Amy asked gently.

"It scares me because..." She dropped her eyes to her boots. "I don't think I can stand going back to the way it was," she said so softly Amy could barely hear. "Not after seeing and feeling how good it can be between us again."

They reached the front door and stopped. The others had gone in, so just the two of them stood on the stoop. Amy regarded her friend with great affection. "All I can say, Primo, is you have to have faith. It's a lame piece of advice, I know, but it's all I've got. And I think it's the truth. You have to have faith—faith in Kristin and faith in the two of you together. If anybody can pull through this, it's you guys."

"You're right," Molly said, wrapping Amy up in a grateful hug. "It *is* a lame piece of advice."

They entered the house laughing and hung up their coats. "Where are the girls?" Amy asked Darby, who sat on the floor killing zombies.

"Upstairs packing, I think. Aunt Jo's in the shower."

Amy nodded and excused herself to the bedroom. Molly stood uncertainly, then turned to look at the back of Darby's dark head. She felt a mixture of emotions that she wasn't quite sure what to do with: sympathy, guilt, longing, regret. She sat down on the floor next to Darby, Indian-style, and watched her play. They didn't speak for several long moments.

"You doing okay?" Darby asked finally, not taking her eyes from the screen.

"Yeah," Molly replied. "You?"

"I'm good."

Silence settled upon them once again. Darby swore under her breath and leaned to her left, willing her character in the game to do the same, but it didn't help. "Game Over" flashed onto the screen. The irony was not lost on Darby as she looked down to study the controls in her hands.

"You two...fix things?" she asked softly, trying hard not to absorb the scent of Molly sitting so close.

"I wouldn't go that far." Molly caught herself, immediately feeling guilty for her dismissive tone. "But we're working on it."

Darby still didn't look up and her voice remained quiet. "And that's what you want?"

"Yeah," Molly said hoarsely. "It's what I want."

Darby finally lifted her head, her blue eyes boring directly into Molly's, intense, imploring. "Does she make you happy, Molly?" It was a simple question, but it meant everything.

Molly's gaze never wavered, even though she was surprised by the query. She had to consciously keep herself from breaking into a huge grin, but she did allow a kind smile to peek through. "I love her, Darby. Despite everything she and I have been through...and despite what you and I have been through, I love her with all my heart and I'd be a fool to let her go without fighting for her." She felt like she should say something more and she shifted her position on the floor. "I'm sorry."

"No," Darby stated firmly. "Don't say that. Don't be sorry. I'm not. Do I wish things had turned out differently? For me, yes. For you?" She paused, briefly lost in her own thoughts about what might have been. "I don't think so. I think you're right where you're supposed to be. You're an amazing woman, Molly, and you deserve to be happy. If it's Kristin who can give that to you, then more power to her. She's a lucky girl." Molly flushed a light shade of pink that Darby thought was adorable and she bumped Molly's shoulder affectionately. "And stop with the blushing or I won't be able to control myself."

"I think you're the amazing one," Molly said with sincerity. "You're going to make some woman very lucky one of these days."

Darby grimaced with disdain. "I doubt that. I think maybe I'm not cut out for a real relationship."

Molly's voice was strong as she surprised Darby by grabbing her chin and forcing her to make eye contact. "Don't do that. Don't sell yourself short. You're a wonderful woman. You're smart and sexy and kind and you *will* find the right person. I guarantee it."

The beginnings of a small grin crept across Darby's face and she was touched by Molly's sincerity. "You guarantee it, huh?"

"Absolutely."

Darby's voice dropped to a whisper. "Thanks, Molly."

"No," Molly said as she leaned over and kissed Darby tenderly on the cheek. "Thank *you*." She patted Darby chastely on the thigh and pushed herself to her feet with a groan. "I suppose I'd better get my stuff together, too, and get my butt home. Back to work tomorrow." Despite the fact that she'd always loved her job, the idea of getting the attention of a classroom full of five-year-olds still riding their holiday highs made her physically shudder as she mounted the stairs.

Darby watched her go, cursing her eyes for sliding down to settle on Molly's ass. She looked away and shook her head with a self-deprecating chuckle. As she was about to reset the video game so she could take out more of her frustrations on the zombies, her cell phone rang. She pulled it off the clip and looked at the screen. She bit her bottom lip as the phone rang again and continued to stare, trying to balance the pros and cons of answering. On the third ring, she made her decision and flipped the phone open. She took a deep breath and put the phone to her ear.

"Hey, Rebecca. Happy New Year, babe. How you doin'?"

❖

Ricky lay on the bed and watched with large brown eyes as Laura folded clothes and stuffed them into her duffel bag. His furry head moved with her hands, from the left to the right and back as she worked. When she stopped and looked at him, he met her gaze with adoration, causing her to put down the shirt she'd been folding and clasp his head in both hands while she rained kisses on him and told him how cute he was.

"That poor dog has no idea what he's in for," Sophie commented wryly, smiling and shaking her head. She was packing her own bag on the opposite bed.

"Love," Laura said, kissing the dog again. "Love, love, love. That's what he's in for."

Lucky bastard, Sophie thought without bitterness. "When I die, I want to come back as a lesbian's dog."

Laura laughed, and the sound alone made Sophie's smile widen. "That would be a pretty perfect life, wouldn't it?"

"Damn right."

They went back to packing in silence for a while. Sophie got their things from the bathroom and handed Laura hers as if they'd been packing for trips together for years. Laura thanked her, trying not to register any feeling at all when their fingers brushed and failing miserably.

Sophie went back to her side of the room and sat down on the edge of the bed, watching Laura's back as she worked. There were things she wanted to say, things she wanted to tell Laura, things she wanted to ask her. But she sat in silence, just watching, unable—or unwilling—to do anything but that. Just watch. Dozens of words sped through her head, handfuls of things she could say, but she couldn't figure out which one to grab or how to say what she wanted to in some sort of coherent fashion. So she sat.

Laura turned to get her books off the nightstand and noticed Sophie in her stillness. The look on her face was...odd, like she was trying to figure something out, like she was puzzling over a problem. Cocking her head to the side, Laura asked, "What?"

"Have dinner with me." The words flew from Sophie's mouth

before she was even aware that she'd been about to say them. She flinched as though somebody else had said them and startled her.

Laura suppressed a grin and glanced at her watch. "Now?" she asked teasingly. "It's a little early for dinner, don't you think?"

Sophie swallowed, knowing Laura was joking with her, but unable to latch onto some semblance of ease as more words tumbled from her mouth. "No, not now. But some time. Any time. This week? Wednesday? Friday?"

Laura opened her mouth to answer, but Sophie went on, looking surprised that she was doing so. The words poured from her lips in an endless stream. "Look, I know we're both still licking our wounds and I know we didn't get off on the right foot and I know that neither of us is ready for another relationship, which is perfectly okay because that's not what I'm asking for, but we've been so good together the last couple of days and we were *so* good together last night and I think we have a lot in common and I really like talking with you and I'd really like to see you again."

Sophie took a breath and blinked, as if she was unsure whether or not she was done talking. Her breathing had become rapid and now she was very nearly panting. She rubbed at the back of her neck, embarrassed.

Laura sat down next to her on the bed and licked her lips. Sophie's words had surprised her, but she expected to be frightened by them and she wasn't. And *that* surprised her more. She felt such a connection to Sophie, but she'd been afraid to say anything about it, knowing Sophie's hurt was still fresh, still close to the surface, that her wounds were still open and sore. Those wounds had been made by an adulterer, which is exactly what Laura was. It was a fact. There was no denying it, no way around it, and Laura honestly wasn't sure if it was something Sophie could handle.

But here she was, asking for more. Just a little more, but more, and Laura was inexplicably proud of her. Sophie had taken a huge step and Laura had at least an idea of how hard it must have been for her to do so. She looked at Sophie now, dark hair pulled back from her face, cocoa skin tinted with a hint of red at each cheekbone, announcing her consternation to anybody who looked. Her deep brown eyes darted around the room and then settled on her own hands clasped in her lap as if waiting for her fate. Laura placed her own hand over Sophie's, once again struck by the contrast of their coloring. She waited until Sophie found the strength to look up and meet her eyes. Then she smiled and squeezed Sophie's hands.

"I'd love to have dinner with you."

❖

At almost exactly three o'clock, Amy closed the front door and leaned against it with a pout. Jo smiled at her from the couch and held up a glass of red wine.

"I saved a bottle of that Merlot for us," she said. "It's back to work for you tomorrow, so let's enjoy the rest of today. Come sit with me."

Amy flopped down next to her wife and they sat in silence for a long while, cuddled in each other's embrace in front of the fire, just enjoying being together.

Speaking quietly so as not to disrupt the peace, Jo finally said, "So, how do you think the week went?"

"I think it went really well, considering how it *could* have gone," Amy responded. "I mean, Molly and Kristin? They were a mess. I was really worried. But I think they're going to pull through."

"Me, too."

Amy smiled at the straightforward response. Jo didn't say a lot, but she had very strong feelings about those she loved. Amy knew her wife had been just as worried about their friends' relationship as she had been. "I have to admit I was a little concerned about Darby fixating on Molly the way she did, but I think she ultimately helped rather than hurt."

"She hurt herself a little bit, but it was a lesson needed." Jo still felt pretty guilty about it and she gazed into the flames that crackled in the fireplace.

"Sweetie," Amy said softly as she laid a hand on Jo's thigh. "Don't feel bad. I know you're worried that you hurt Darby's feelings, but it's okay. You did what needed to be done and you would have done the same thing to somebody who was not a blood relation."

"She's so damn young," Jo said, almost wistfully.

"And she has lots of things to learn about life and love. The people who care about her, like you and me, are here to help her with those lessons so she doesn't have to learn them from strangers." She kissed Jo's warm cheek. "That's what being family is all about."

Jo turned loving brown eyes on her wife. "As always, my love, you're right."

"The sooner you accept that, the better off we'll all be," Amy said with a grin. A few more minutes passed in silence before Amy remembered the surprise of the entire week. She whipped her head around to look at Jo and exclaimed, "And how about Sophie and Laura?"

Jo laughed at the mention of the two. "Holy shit. Who saw *that* coming? I know I didn't."

"Me, neither. I was more afraid that they'd kill each other. I was trying to decide the best method for getting blood out of my hardwood. I never expected the hook-up."

"No way."

Amy sipped thoughtfully. "They are very good together, you know? They actually have a lot in common. I'm surprised I didn't think about it sooner."

"So am I, given your penchant for matchmaking."

"Maybe I'm slipping in my old age."

"I doubt that."

Amy leaned her head on Jo's shoulder. "I don't know that they'll end up happily ever after, but regardless, I think they *will* end up friends. You can never have too many of those." After a beat, she added, "Think they'll share custody of the dog?"

Jo's eyes widened with incredulity. "Seriously! What the hell with the dog? Just showing up out of nowhere like he did? How weird was that?"

Amy laughed as she nodded in agreement. "Molly and Kristin on their way to repair, Sophie and Laura hooking up, Darby learning an important lesson or two, the dog finding a new and loving home…"

Jo began to chuckle as Amy's voice trailed off. "Oh, no. Don't say it."

"I'm going to say it."

"Don't. Don't say it."

"You know I have to say it."

"*Please* don't say it. I'm begging you."

Amy grinned widely as she poked Jo in the ribs. "The Magic Acre, baby. The Magic Acre."

"Ugh." Jo slapped a hand over her eyes. "You said it."

"It's the only logical explanation for everything that's happened. My grandmother would agree wholeheartedly, I'm sure."

"Your grandmother was a little bit wacky, wasn't she?"

Amy slapped playfully at Jo as she laughed. "Hey. Watch what you say about my grammy. She might be here right now."

Jo looked around in mock fear. "Oh, I hope not. I wouldn't want her to have to witness this." Then she pressed her lips to Amy's and kissed her into silence.

They felt so right, so good, so *perfect* together, the two of them. They always had. How was it feasible? Was it luck? Was it fate? Why was she chosen to be with her perfect mate and so many others seemed to spend their entire lives searching and searching, but never finding— or worse, settling for a life with somebody so completely and utterly wrong for them, spending their whole existence never knowing what it feels like to be with a soulmate?

Jo didn't consider herself an emotional person at all and she despised the use of words like "soulmate," but there was really no other way to describe how well she and Amy fit. Like they were meant to be. Was that possible? She pondered these thoughts as she poured all of the love in her heart into the act of kissing her wife, knowing that Amy felt every bit of it.

Maybe magic does exist...

About the Author

Georgia Beers was born and raised in Rochester, New York. After high school, she attended college in Pennsylvania at Mansfield University, where she earned a bachelor's degree in mass communications. Always believing she wanted to be involved in television or radio somehow, she tried her hand at both after graduation and decided rather quickly—and much to her own horror—that she didn't like either one.

For as long as she can remember, Georgia has written stories. After discovering the Internet and the surprisingly large world of writing that exists on it, she met a fellow writer in the year 2000 to whom she felt close enough to share her first attempt at a manuscript for a novel. One thing led to another, Georgia was introduced to a publisher, and the next thing she knew, she was an actual honest-to-goodness novelist. To this day, she still has trouble believing it.

Georgia is the author of the romance novel *Too Close to Touch*, has selections in several anthologies, including *Erotic Interludes* 2&4, and is currently at work on her fifth novel. She still resides in Rochester with Bonnie, her partner of twelve years, and their two dogs.

Books Available From Bold Strokes Books

Fresh Tracks by Georgia Beers. Seven women, seven days. A lot can happen when old friends, lovers, and a new girl in town get together in the mountains. (1-933110-63-5)

Empress and the Acolyte by Jane Fletcher. Jemeryl and Tevi fight to protect the very fabric of their world...time. Lyremouth Chronicles Book Three (1-933110-60-0)

First Instinct by JLee Meyer. When high-stakes security fraud leads to murder, one woman flees for her life while another risks her heart to protect her. (1-933110-59-7)

Erotic Interludes 4: Extreme Passions. Thirty of today's hottest erotica writers set the pages aflame with love, lust, and steamy liaisons. (1-933110-58-9)

Storms of Change by Radclyffe. In the continuing saga of the Provincetown Tales, duty and love are at odds as Reese and Tory face their greatest challenge. (1-933110-57-0)

Unexpected Ties by Gina L. Dartt. With death before dessert, Kate Shannon and Nikki Harris are swept up in another tale of danger and romance. (1-933110-56-2)

Sleep of Reason by Rose Beecham. Nothing is at it seems when Detective Jude Devine finds herself caught up in a small-town soap opera. And her rocky relationship with forensic pathologist Dr. Mercy Westmoreland just got a lot harder. (1-933110-53-8)

Passion's Bright Fury by Radclyffe. When a trauma surgeon and a filmmaker become reluctant allies on the battleground between life and death, passion strikes without warning. (1-933110-54-6)

Broken Wings by L-J Baker. When Rye Woods, a fairy, meets the beautiful dryad Flora Withe, her libido, as squashed and hidden as her wings, reawakens along with her heart. (1-933110-55-4)

Combust the Sun by Andrews & Austin. A Richfield and Rivers mystery set in L.A. Murder among the stars. (1-933110-52-X)

Of Drag Kings and the Wheel of Fate by Susan Smith. A blind date in a drag club leads to an unlikely romance. (1-933110-51-1)

Tristaine Rises by Cate Culpepper. Brenna, Jesstin, and the Amazons of Tristaine face their greatest challenge for survival. (1-933110-50-3)

Too Close to Touch by Georgia Beers. Kylie O'Brien believes in true love and is willing to wait for it. It doesn't matter one damn bit that Gretchen, her new and off-limits boss, has a voice as rich and smooth as melted chocolate. It absolutely doesn't... (1-933110-47-3)

100th Generation by Justine Saracen. Ancient curses, modern-day villains, and a most intriguing woman who keeps appearing when least expected lead archeologist Valerie Foret on the adventure of her life. (1-933110-48-1)

Battle for Tristaine by Cate Culpepper. While Brenna struggles to find her place in the clan and the love between her and Jess grows, Tristaine is threatened with destruction. Second in the Tristaine series. (1-933110-49-X)

The Traitor and the Chalice by Jane Fletcher. Without allies to help them, Tevi and Jemeryl will have to risk all in the race to uncover the traitor and retrieve the chalice. The Lyremouth Chronicles Book Two. (1-933110-43-0)

Promising Hearts by Radclyffe. Dr. Vance Phelps lost everything in the War Between the States and arrives in New Hope, Montana, with no hope of happiness and no desire for anything except forgetting—until she meets Mae, a frontier madam. (1-933110-44-9)

Carly's Sound by Ali Vali. Poppy Valente and Julia Johnson form a bond of friendship that lays the foundation for something more, until Poppy's past comes back to haunt her—literally. A poignant romance about love and renewal. (1-933110-45-7)

Unexpected Sparks by Gina L. Dartt. Falling in love is challenging enough without adding murder to the mix. Kate Shannon's growing feelings for much younger Nikki Harris are complicated enough without the mystery of a fatal fire that Kate can't ignore. (1-933110-46-5)

Whitewater Rendezvous by Kim Baldwin. Two women on a wilderness kayak adventure—Chaz Herrick, a laid-back outdoorswoman, and Megan Maxwell, a workaholic news executive—discover that true love may be nothing at all like they imagined. (1-933110-38-4)

Erotic Interludes 3: Lessons in Love ed. by Radclyffe and Stacia Seaman. Sign on for a class in love…the best lesbian erotica writers take us to "school." (1-9331100-39-2)

Punk Like Me by JD Glass. Twenty-one-year-old Nina writes lyrics and plays guitar in the rock band Adam's Rib, and she doesn't always play by the rules. And oh yeah—she has a way with the girls. (1-933110-40-6)

Coffee Sonata by Gun Brooke. Four women whose lives unexpectedly intersect in a small town by the sea share one thing in common—they all have secrets. (1-933110-41-4)

The Clinic: Tristaine Book One by Cate Culpepper. Brenna, a prison medic, finds herself deeply conflicted by her growing feelings for her patient, Jesstin, a wild and rebellious warrior reputed to be descended from ancient Amazons. (1-933110-42-2)

Forever Found by JLee Meyer. Can time, tragedy, and shattered trust destroy a love that seemed destined? When chance reunites two childhood friends separated by tragedy, the past resurfaces to determine the shape of their future. (1-933110-37-6)

Sword of the Guardian by Merry Shannon. Princess Shasta's bold new bodyguard has a secret that could change both of their lives. *He* is actually a *she*. A passionate romance filled with courtly intrigue, chivalry, and devotion. (1-933110-36-8)

Wild Abandon by Ronica Black. From their first tumultuous meeting, Dr. Chandler Brogan and Officer Sarah Monroe are drawn together by their common obsessions—sex, speed, and danger. (1-933110-35-X)

Turn Back Time by Radclyffe. Pearce Rifkin and Wynter Thompson have nothing in common but a shared passion for surgery. They clash at every opportunity, especially when matters of the heart are suddenly at stake. (1-933110-34-1)

Chance by Grace Lennox. At twenty-six, Chance Delaney decides her life isn't working so she swaps it for a different one. What follows is the sexy, funny, touching story of two women who, in finding themselves, also find one another. (1-933110-31-7)

The Exile and the Sorcerer by Jane Fletcher. First in the Lyremouth Chronicles. Tevi, wounded and adrift, arrives in the courtyard of a shy young sorcerer. Together they face monsters, magic, and the challenge of loving despite their differences. (1-933110-32-5)

A Matter of Trust by Radclyffe. JT Sloan is a cybersleuth who doesn't like attachments. Michael Lassiter is leaving her husband, and she needs Sloan's expertise to safeguard her company. It should just be business—but it turns into much more. (1-933110-33-3)

Sweet Creek by Lee Lynch. A celebration of the enduring nature of love, friendship, and community in the quirky, heart-warming lesbian community of Waterfall Falls. (1-933110-29-5)

The Devil Inside by Ali Vali. Derby Cain Casey, head of a New Orleans crime organization, runs the family business with guts and grit, and no one crosses her. No one, that is, until Emma Verde claims her heart and turns her world upside down. (1-933110-30-9)

Grave Silence by Rose Beecham. Detective Jude Devine's investigation of a series of ritual murders is complicated by her torrid affair with the golden girl of Southwestern forensic pathology, Dr. Mercy Westmoreland. (1-933110-25-2)

Honor Reclaimed by Radclyffe. In the aftermath of 9/11, Secret Service Agent Cameron Roberts and Blair Powell close ranks with a trusted few to find the would-be assassins who nearly claimed Blair's life. (1-933110-18-X)

Honor Bound by Radclyffe. Secret Service Agent Cameron Roberts and Blair Powell face political intrigue, a clandestine threat to Blair's safety, and the seemingly irreconcilable personal differences that force them ever farther apart. (1-933110-20-1)

Innocent Hearts by Radclyffe. In a wild and unforgiving land, two women learn about love, passion, and the wonders of the heart. (1-933110-21-X)

The Temple at Landfall by Jane Fletcher. An imprinter, one of Celaeno's most revered servants of the Goddess, is also a prisoner to the faith—until a Ranger frees her by claiming her heart. The Celaeno series. (1-933110-27-9)

Protector of the Realm: Supreme Constellations Book One by Gun Brooke. A space adventure filled with suspense and a daring intergalactic romance featuring Commodore Rae Jacelon and the stunning, but decidedly lethal, Kellen O'Dal. (1-933110-26-0)

Force of Nature by Kim Baldwin. From tornados to forest fires, the forces of nature conspire to bring Gable McCoy and Erin Richards close to danger, and closer to each other. (1-933110-23-6)

In Too Deep by Ronica Black. Undercover homicide cop Erin McKenzie tracks a femme fatale who just might be a real killer...with love and danger hot on her heels. (1-933110-17-1)

Stolen Moments: Erotic Interludes 2 by Stacia Seaman and Radclyffe, eds. Love on the run, in the office, in the shadows...Fast, furious, and almost too hot to handle. (1-933110-16-3)

Course of Action by Gun Brooke. Actress Carolyn Black desperately wants the starring role in an upcoming film produced by Annelie Peterson. Just how far will she go for the dream part of a lifetime? (1-933110-22-8)

Rangers at Roadsend by Jane Fletcher. Sergeant Chip Coppelli has learned to spot trouble coming, and that is exactly what she sees in her new recruit, Katryn Nagata. The Celaeno series. (1-933110-28-7)

Justice Served by Radclyffe. Lieutenant Rebecca Frye and her lover, Dr. Catherine Rawlings, embark on a deadly game of hide-and-seek with an underworld kingpin who traffics in human souls. (1-933110-15-5)

Distant Shores, Silent Thunder by Radclyffe. Dr. Tory King—along with the women who love her—is forced to examine the boundaries of love, friendship, and the ties that transcend time. (1-933110-08-2)

Hunter's Pursuit by Kim Baldwin. A raging blizzard, a mountain hideaway, and a killer-for-hire set a scene for disaster—or desire—when Katarzyna Demetrious rescues a beautiful stranger. (1-933110-09-0)

The Walls of Westernfort by Jane Fletcher. All Temple Guard Natasha Ionadis wants is to serve the Goddess—until she falls in love with one of the rebels she is sworn to destroy. The Celaeno series. (1-933110-24-4)

Change Of Pace: *Erotic Interludes* by Radclyffe. Twenty-five hot-wired encounters guaranteed to spark more than just your imagination. Erotica as you've always dreamed of it. (1-933110-07-4)

Honor Guards by Radclyffe. In a wild flight for their lives, the president's daughter and those who are sworn to protect her wage a desperate struggle for survival. (1-933110-01-5)

Fated Love by Radclyffe. Amidst the chaos and drama of a busy emergency room, two women must contend not only with the fragile nature of life, but also with the irresistible forces of fate. (1-933110-05-8)

Justice in the Shadows by Radclyffe. In a shadow world of secrets and lies, Detective Sergeant Rebecca Frye and her lover, Dr. Catherine Rawlings, join forces in the elusive search for justice. (1-933110-03-1)

shadowland by Radclyffe. In a world on the far edge of desire, two women are drawn together by power, passion, and dark pleasures. An erotic romance. (1-933110-11-2)

Love's Masquerade by Radclyffe. Plunged into the indistinguishable realms of fiction, fantasy, and hidden desires, Auden Frost is forced to question all she believes about the nature of love. (1-933110-14-7)

Love & Honor by Radclyffe. The president's daughter and her lover are faced with difficult choices as they battle a tangled web of Washington intrigue for...love and honor. (1-933110-10-4)

Beyond the Breakwater by Radclyffe. One Provincetown summer, three women learn the true meaning of love, friendship, and family. (1-933110-06-6)

Tomorrow's Promise by Radclyffe. One timeless summer, two very different women discover the power of passion to heal and the promise of hope that only love can bestow. (1-933110-12-0)

Love's Tender Warriors by Radclyffe. Two women who have accepted loneliness as a way of life learn that love is worth fighting for and a battle they cannot afford to lose. (1-933110-02-3)

Love's Melody Lost by Radclyffe. A secretive artist with a haunted past and a young woman escaping a life that has proved to be a lie find their destinies entwined. (1-933110-00-7)

Safe Harbor by Radclyffe. A mysterious newcomer, a reclusive doctor, and a troubled gay teenager learn about love, friendship, and trust during one tumultuous summer in Provincetown. (1-933110-13-9)

Above All, Honor by Radclyffe. Secret Service Agent Cameron Roberts fights her desire for the one woman she can't have—Blair Powell, the daughter of the president of the United States. (1-933110-04-X)